Reckless

Hate

Victoria Bailey

"For those who choose chaos over control, defiance over silence, and fire over fear. For anyone who's ever been told to sit still, be quiet, or do as they're told — and promptly ignored all of the above. May you always burn bright and never get caught."

Prologue

Sneaking out with her in the dead of night has become my favorite part of the day. It started out with one or two nights, now it's our little secret.

We stay silent on our feet as we slip past half-asleep guards. Successfully making it out of the palace gates and to the edge of the endless rows of roses undetected. It was the closest thing we had to an escape.

I guide her slowly down the path that I cut through the flowers, all the way to the stone fountain resting in the center. Careful not to let her stray too close to the hazardous thorns, for fear she may cut herself.

Making it to the fountain, I guide her to the lip so she can rest. We sit, side by side, letting water lick our backs.

"Grayson..." She murmurs, fear lacing her voice.

"Elena, I'm here." I take hold of her tiny face, turning it so she can face me. Just in time for me to see her eyes glass over. The hazel in them succumbing to the darkness within her.

"I'm scared, I-I can't see," she whispers.

"I know, I know, we'll find a way to fix this, I promise." I gently sweep my hand down her eyes. Pressing a light kiss to each one, before she flutters them open. Watching the shadows retreat from her eyes, we simply wait. Content to sit with the sounds of the Hollows and the scent of roses, just listening to the voices of the night until the moon dips behind Blackthorn Palace. Signaling our departure.

We go back the way we came, everything exactly the way it was. Elena clings to me for support.

"Almost there, Little Princess," I whisper into her wavy black hair.

"Grayson...something's wrong." She clutches my arm tighter just as we reach the palace gates.

"Everything is—" I'm cut off when the shadows around us start twitching. A cool chill runs down the length of my spine. He steps out from the shadows, casting one of his own over us.

"Out for a midnight stroll?" His voice was quiet. Mocking. That was always worse than yelling.

My breath hitched. I moved in front of Elena without thinking. "We didn't mean—"

"Didn't mean to defy me?" His smile didn't reach his eyes. "Didn't mean to sneak past guards, past curfew, past *me*?" He took a step forward, shadows curling around his boots.

Elena made a muffled sound behind me, and I held my arms out, blocking her completely.

He studied me. "You think you can protect *her*?" His tone was almost curious, like he found the idea amusing.

I didn't answer. I just stood there, shaking, but refusing to move.

And then he raised his hand.

The shadows curled upward, thickening into a jagged blade that shimmered with darkness, not metal. It pulsed in the air, hungry.

"She's making you weak," he said. "And I won't have weakness in my blood."

The blade swung toward me.

I never felt the impact.

… because Elena moved first.

She threw herself in front of me with a strangled "No!" and the blade drove into her tiny body like it was nothing at all. *A blade intended for me.*

The world fell still.

For a second, I couldn't wrap my mind around what had happened. She was just standing there, upright, her hands still reaching for me. Until she crumpled.

"Elena!" I caught her before she hit the ground, her bloodless lips parted in shock. My hands pressed against her side, but the wound was too deep, too dark. Shadows don't bleed like people do. They consume.

Her lashes fluttered. "Grayson?" she whispered. "It's c-cold, and I-I c-can't see." Her words are choked.

"*No, no, no*—you're okay." My voice broke as I kissed her eyes again, as if it could undo it, as if my strength could still save her. "Please, stay with me. Elena, please."

She smiled, so faint I almost missed it. "It's okay," she breathed. "Nothing hurts anymore."

Then she went still.

I held her tighter, as if I could hold her soul in too.

Behind me, our father turned. The blade vanished into smoke.

"Pathetic," he muttered, walking away. "She was never meant to survive anyway."

I didn't scream.

I didn't cry. No matter how much I wished to.

I simply sat in the dirt, now mixed with her blood, my sister in my arms, and let the shadows swallow us whole.

Chapter 1

Keira

It's my wedding day. Said to be the happiest day in a woman's life. But the words feel foreign in my mouth, bitter even.

I stared at my reflection in the tall, gilded mirror, the intricate folds of my wedding gown swallowing my frame like the night swallowing the day. The shimmering sapphire embroidery on the fabric glinted in the morning light streaming through the arched windows of my chamber. Aetheris' crest—an intricately woven blue phoenix—gleamed on my left hip, a reminder of the duty I was born into. It's a huge gown with flowing layers in every direction. With beautiful white heels adorned with a sapphire stone on the toe.

Sia, my maid who's been with me since I was small, bustled about with a comb in one hand and a string of pearls in the other. Her ginger curls bobbed as she worked, her nimble fingers weaving the pearls into the layers of my braided hair. "You look beautiful, Keira," she said, her voice steady but her eyes betraying a flicker of worry. She was trying to soothe me, but even her unshakable cheer couldn't hide the tension in the air.

"Do I?" I asked, forcing a smile. My fingers twisted the edge of my lace sleeve. "I feel like a lamb dressed for slaughter."

Sia paused, meeting my gaze in the mirror. "You're stronger than that," she said quietly. "You're not a lamb, Keira. You're a phoenix." As if she said something she wasn't supposed to, she averted her gaze.

The corner of my mouth twitched upward, but the smile didn't reach my eyes.

A sharp knock interrupted us. Sia straightened, smoothing her skirts as a Watcher entered. He bowed stiffly. "The ceremony is ready, Your Highness."

My stomach twisted into a knot. *It's time.*

Sia gave my hand a reassuring squeeze before slipping the delicate veil over my head.

As I walked through the halls of Aetheris, my heels make the perfect sound on the marble floors. I passed by the portraits of past Queens until I stop in front of the current Queen. She sits ever so regal on her sapphire throne. I never understood why our crest was a phoenix, but the Kingdom color is sapphire.

Another thing I will never understand about the Queen.

I stopped directly in front of the doors, my legs feeling like jelly. As the doors to the grand hall opened, a rush of whispers filled the air. The aisle stretched before me like a path to my fate, lined with noble guests and adorned with flowers in Aetheris' royal colors.

My footsteps echoed against the polished marble floor as I walked, each step heavier than the last. I kept my chin high, my expression unreadable, as my etiquette teacher had taught me. A princess does not falter, even under the weight of expectation.

When I reached the altar, I paused, praying to the Stars that I, at least, look the part of a happy bride-to-be.

The whispers turned into murmurs, then looks of confusion. I didn't realize until I was red with embarrassment.

The groom is gone.

Chapter 2

Keira

Everything after the ceremony passed in a blur. I think the Queen locked me in my room. I haven't seen Sia once, which is unusual.

I was really hoping to train tonight, just to clear my head. The training yard is rarely in use unless we are training new Watchers. The Queen despises the fact that I train with weapons; she says it's unbecoming of a princess.

However, she has never once tried to stop me. Mainly because my magic hasn't developed the way she wanted. Then again, nothing compares to her at my age even though she taught me herself. Not one spell works for me.

Hence, the reason I started training with a weapon that wasn't magic.

Not that I'm much good at that either.

I turn to my window, now noticing how dark it got outside. I stare at the stars glittering in the dark sky. Thanking the Stars my no-longer future husband ran from the altar-

I feel a burn in my heart, like it's burning through my chest. I grasp my dress, desperately trying to rip it off my body. I manage to loosen it, giving me room to take in more air. Unzipping the rest of the dress, I let it drop to the floor, leaving me in my shift. I notice a black burn mark, lifting the shift to get a better look. A small burn sits just at the top of my heart; it's as if someone lit a match and brought it to my skin. I glide a finger over the outline of the burn. Surprisingly, it doesn't hurt. *Strange.*

I grab my cotton shirt with the crest of Aetheris on it, throw it on, and pull on my leggings I wear for training. Deciding to keep my hair in the braid from the wedding, I head for the door. The knob of my door is cool to the touch, I desperately try not to make any noise as I twist it. The door swings open, causing me to jump back in surprise. A Watcher is standing before me, not looking me in my eyes as he states, "Princess Keira, I was ordered to keep you in your room until the Queen says otherwise." His expression is neutral, almost bored.

"Tell the Queen it's going to take a lot more to keep me in my room than well—*you.* I have been locked in here since my almost wedding. I am itching to train. Whether that be on the training fields outside or right here with you."

Still not making eye contact with me, he says. "I understand, Princess. I will make the Queen aware of your words and will be back momentarily." He shoves me hard, my back slamming against one of my bed posts. I reach for the dagger strapped to my thigh, but the Watcher is gone. The door makes no noise as he shuts it in my face.

"Ahhhhh!" I release the dagger at the closest wall in my room. The one already covered in dagger cuts. I yank it out of the wall, spinning it in my hands.

My whisper is so small I barely hear it myself.

"If she won't let me out of this cage, I might as well make it comfortable." With that, I throw the dagger as hard as I can.

Over and Over

and Over again.

Chapter 3

Keira

Seven days.

Seven days until I finally see a real face. I was locked away in my room, only receiving meal trays from a different servant each time. The only reason I assume my jail time is over is because Sia delivers my lunch. She nearly faints at the sight of my room.

Many marks from my dagger litter my wall, not to mention the mess of clothing, papers, and candles spread carelessly around my room. I probably don't look much better. I bathed but couldn't be bothered to tame my long, white, blonde waves. Sia sets the meal tray at the edge of my bed so she can hastily run around my room trying to tidy up.

"No need." I wave her off

"Princess, you can not live in such a state." My eyes widen as she continues to busy herself with my room. *Princess, she called me Princess.* Sia hasn't used my title in years, to the point it sounds scratchy on her lips.

"Oh, and the Queen sent for you," she adds.

When she says nothing more, I slide out from my soft silk sheets to the washroom. I throw cold water on my face, drying it with a cloth.

I go back into my room to find my outfit laid out on my now-made bed. Sia made quick work; my entire room is almost spotless. She excuses herself while I change into the outfit the Queen no doubt picked. It's all blue, snug around my waist, and flowy from my hips down. The sleeves are the same, off the shoulder and hanging loosely around my wrist, adding to the ethereal look of this afternoon's dress.

I open my door to find the Watcher standing directly in my path, with Sia right next to him. They both drop to a bow, and the Watcher barely glances at me when he turns to walk stiffly away. I follow behind at a good distance, as we fall into an uncomfortable silence. I get a flash of memories from when I walked down this hall a week ago. I was getting *married*—not anymore.

I nearly crash into the Watcher as he halts in front of the throne room. The intricately carved light brown doors tower over me. They open painfully slow, revealing the long blue velvet rug. The sapphire stone walls seem to glow with the huge chandelier hanging down from the heightless ceiling.

There, the Queen sits at the end of the rug, elevated by exactly eighteen stairs. Her throne is the exact same one from her portrait; her sapphire bejeweled gown gleams just like the crown that sits atop her head. I reach the edge of the rug, now realizing a boy about my age is bowing towards the Queen.

The boy's head remains lowered, dark hair falling over his face. He's dressed in black with gold accents, his outfit formal but not extravagant. His posture is stiff, like he's been holding the bow longer than necessary, waiting for the Queen's permission to rise.

My eyes dart between him and the Queen, trying to assess the situation. The Queen studies him with the same cold expression she uses on everyone, except when she wants something.

The burn above my heart starts to sting, and I lightly brush the tips of my fingers over the mark through my dress. Fortunately, even off the shoulder, the neckline manages to cover the burn.

"Keira," the Queen's voice snaps me out of my thoughts. She doesn't call me "daughter." She hasn't since I was five when we found out I was *different*.

"This is a messenger sent from Eclipsar. King Lucian has invited us to his annual Midnight Masquerade." The messenger finally stands, and I get my first proper look at him. He's taller than I expected, with sharp cheekbones and onyx eyes. His expression is neutral, though there's something about the tension in his jaw that betrays unease. He doesn't make eye contact with me—typical for a messenger.

"Your Highness," he says, his voice steady but clipped, as if he's forcing each word. "It would be an honor to have both Kingdoms united."

The Queen smiles, but it doesn't reach her eyes. "Indeed. I trust your journey to Aetheris was comfortable?"

The messenger inclines his head slightly, "Yes, Your Majesty. The northern winds are harsh, but we are accustomed to all kinds of weather."

My attention drifts as they continue exchanging pleasantries. My mind spins with questions. Why is the King of Eclipsar inviting us to a ball after decades of peaceful hate? Has the Queen already agreed? Why has she locked me in my chambers, only to parade me out now? And why, of all things, does my heart burn every time I think about what *could* happen? The Queen's gaze snaps to me.

"Keira, you will show this messenger out through the gardens. We have discussed everything he was sent to inform me." Her voice is sincere enough for show.

She only wants me to take him through the gardens so the flowers can catch his scent. Stars know what she will do with it. But it's not a request, of course. It never is with her.

I nod mechanically, and the messenger steps aside to let me lead. We exit the throne room in silence, the Watcher trailing behind us like a ghost. I can feel his presence, cold and vigilant, reminding me that I'm never truly alone, not even in my own quarters. The moment we step into the open air of the gardens, I finally speak.

"So, do you have a name, or should I call you Mr. Messenger?" He hesitates, his eyes scanning the path ahead before he responds.

"You can call me Gray." He responds with a half smile. In the afternoon sun, his black curls seem to shine.

"Well, I assume you already know who I am." He chuckles, a deep sound that comes from the throat.

"Yes, I was half paying attention to the Queen." Now it's my turn to laugh. Not exactly what one would want to admit to the Princess, especially as a messenger.

"Try doing that your whole life." He goes quiet, his smile disappearing. We reach the edge of the gardens, and I can't help the question that slips past my lips.

"Why is the King doing this?" He paused, brows meeting each other in confusion.

"My guess is as good as yours. However, from what I've gathered, your mother seeks power; maybe she believes the King can give it to her. That or she believes he can secure your position in the royal world." He locks eyes with me, almost urging me to believe him.

I flinch at his bluntness, and my hands clench at my sides. "I'm a Princess, aren't I? What better position could there be?" Gray's eyes narrow slightly.

"You'd be surprised. Magic runs deep in your bloodline. Your mother will stop at nothing to ensure Aetheris remains unchallenged." *Quite a bold messenger.*

His words hang in the air between us. It's the truth, of course, but hearing it out loud feels like a blow to the gut. I've always known the Queen is ruthless, but to hear a stranger speak so outright about her intentions brings it into sharper focus.

"The Queen," I say coldly.

"Excuse me?" He doesn't realize he called her my *mother.*

"You called her my mother. She hasn't been a mother to me for a very long time." I start picking at the skin around my nail bed.

"Sounds like my father. I'm here because of him, simply a chip to be used." His expression hardens at the mention of his father. Nice to know I have something in common with a messenger, though that confession is oddly meaningful.

I want to say something, anything, to reassure him that I understand. But how could I? I'm a prisoner too, locked in a cage of expectations and duty. His situation is no doubt completely different. We're still both pawns in a game neither of us chose to play.

As I watch him stalk off with surprising grace and ease for a messenger, a strange sensation washes over me. A whisper in the corner of my mind begins to sound. One hand flies to my head, and the other to the burn above my heart. I glance around the gardens, just my Watcher and I. And then I hear it—a voice, faint but unmistakable, whispering in my mind.

"Keira... it's time."

My Watcher comes scrambling over, steadying me on my feet. I can't move, can't think, can't speak. My Watcher is screaming at me, but all I feel is peace. My eyes are just about to drift shut when I catch the smallest glimpse of the Queen walking gracefully down the steps of the gardens.

Chapter 4

Keira

I blink, as the world rushes back to me in a swirl of sounds and colors. The Watcher at my side tightens his grip on my arm, snapping me out of my daze. I sway, trying to steady myself as I catch a glimpse of sapphire—*her.*

Walking gracefully yet powerfully down the steps, her crown shines in the warm sun, her stare lethal as she makes her way to me. My Watcher stands a little straighter with the Queen directly in front of us. He drops low into a bow, while I square my shoulders.

"Keira," her voice is calm, but there's a command woven into it. It feels like an invisible force pulling me towards her, a feeling I've come to know well. *Her magic.*

"I trust you saw our guest out with minimal issue." She pins me with a glare.

"Yes, your Majesty." I stare right back into her cold blue eyes.

"Good," she pauses, eyeing me, "I expect to see you in my salon after dinner."

Not giving me a chance to respond, she spins around without another word, not bothering to look back as she heads back the way she came, her sapphire skirts sweeping behind her. The air feels thinner in her absence. My Watcher stays rigid, but I exhale, letting my shoulders sag without the Queen present, urging my now aching body back to my chambers.

My Watcher walked me back to my chambers, and all I've managed to do is sit around waiting for the dinner bell. I can't stop thinking about that voice.

"*Keira, it's time.*" What does that even mean? Time for what?

The dinner bell rings.

Sia escorts me to dinner instead of my Watcher. When I get to the dining hall, the Queen is nowhere to be seen. I take my seat across from her empty one. The servants only bring cutlery for my side of the table, meaning the Queen will not be making an appearance.

I eat in silence as I contemplate what she might need to discuss that requires her to miss dinner but requests me to meet her after. I slam my fork down, startling the nearby servants. Rising with a half-finished plate, I storm out of the dining hall, heading for the Queen's salon.

Arriving at the door, Watcher in tow, I knock hard on the finely made door. Her first maid answers with a curtsy. Opening the door just wide enough for me to slip in while not letting my Watcher get a glimpse inside.

The scent of burning candle wax lingers in the Queen's salon. Rich tapestries soften the stone walls, and the flickering hearth casts long shadows over the polished floors. The Queen sits poised, sipping from a crystal goblet as if she's been waiting for me. Her room is littered with spell books, crystals, and an assortment of colorful candles.

I stop just inside the threshold. The door clicking shut behind me.

"Come in, Keira." Her tone is smooth, each syllable carrying the weight of a command.

I hesitate, then step forward. The silence between us is thick, expectant.

She studies me over the rim of her glass. "Sit."

I make no move. "I prefer to stand."

A single, slow blink. Then she places her goblet down with a delicate clink. "It seems defiance runs in our blood."

"I wasn't aware my posture counted as defiance," I snap.

"You seem uneasy, dear." Her voice is smooth, inviting, but laced with something formidable.

I stop a few paces away, keeping my posture straight. "Should I not be?"

She lifts her gaze, studying me with quiet amusement. "I suppose that depends on what you fear."

I don't answer.

She gestures toward the chair across from her. "Sit, Keira. We should talk."

I hesitate before lowering myself onto the cushioned seat, smoothing my hands over my skirts to keep them steady. The Queen watches me, her expression tense.

"Eclipsar is different from Aetheris. You must know that."

"I do." My voice is measured.

She smiles faintly. "Then you must also know that resisting change will only make things harder for you."

I meet her gaze, searching for meaning behind her words. "I wasn't aware I was resisting, or that much has changed."

"I see," The Queen leans back, fingers tracing the rim of her goblet. "Nonetheless, you've had a comfortable life. One where I have let you roam as you please, have as much freedom as you wish. It is time you step up and become the Princess you were born to be."

"Right," I say, the word sharp as glass. "Because being locked in a palace with guards at every turn is the epitome of freedom."

The Queen's fingers still against the rim of her goblet, but I don't stop.

"Forgive me if I mistook suffocation for luxury. I suppose I should've been more grateful for the privilege of gilded chains."

Her gaze hardens, but I meet it head-on. Let her be angry. I'm already drowning. A silence settles between us, stretching long enough to feel deliberate.

"You remind me of myself when I was your age," she says at last.

The statement catches me off guard. I school my expression, but something in my chest tightens. "Is that so?"

"Of course," she huffs with a laugh. "I was rebellious, sharp, beautiful, and strong-willed. Much like you." The Queen tilts her head. "Albeit not as defiant. However, I had spark." A wicked grin peeled up her face.

I swallow, forcing my voice to remain even. "Like mother, like daughter." I fight back the dizziness that comes with those words.

She studies me for a moment longer before standing. Her movements are fluid, deliberate as she circles toward the window. Beyond the glass, the night stretches endlessly, the moon hanging low in the sky.

"About that messenger that was here, have you written back? About the masquerade?" She turns back to face me, surprise playing at her features. I've caught her off guard, and I do my best to fend off the satisfaction blooming in my chest.

"As a matter of fact, I have. I told the King of Eclipsar we would be in attendance at his masquerade." Her voice is even, bordering disinterest. Our Kingdoms haven't been in contact for years.

"When is the masquerade?" I keep a steady voice.

"The masquerade is to be on the first full moon of the season. We leave for Eclipsar in the coming days." Once again, I'm at a loss for words. She wasn't even going to tell me.

"What made you accept the invitation?" I can't help the curiosity creeping into my voice.

"Eclipsar has extended an olive branch, and it would be foolish to refuse." The corner of her mouth tugs up as I give her a skeptical look in return.

I have no chance to respond before her head maid walks in. She whispers something into the Queen's ear. Causing her to shoot up from her chair.

"Keira, this was a delightful chat. However, I think it's time you head back to your chambers for the night." She faces me as she speaks, but her mind is somewhere else; I can see it in her eyes.

"Goodnight, your Majesty." I do no more than bow my head. I turn, with my back to the Queen and relax.

The cool air of the castle hall hits my face, which I didn't even realize was flushed. My Watcher escorts me back to my chamber. Flopping onto my comforters, I let my eyes drift closed. Just as sleep was about to claim me, Sia entered my room with a tray of tea. She places it at the edge of my bed with a curtsy.

"Your evening tea." Her eyes gaze over my tired expression.

"I see you had quite the day. I'll leave you to your rest." She backs away to the door.

"Thanks, Sia, I'll see you in the morning" I say as I reach for the teacup in time for her to see before she leaves the room. Then, as soon as she leaves, I drop my hand, whirling out of bed.

Fumbling through the dim candlelight, I manage to find clean, black training leathers, deciding to switch my uncomfortable day shoes with ones custom-made for my feet. I grab my dagger from its home in the wall, strapping it securely to my thigh. Heading straight for my window, I push it out, letting the cool night air rush over me. I hesitate only a moment before swinging a leg over the ledge. The stone beneath my fingertips is rough, cold, but I welcome the sting—it keeps me focused. The rest of my body follows, and I sit up fully on the small roof outside my window.

Taking a deep breath, I scale down the small wall. My drop was swift but controlled. My boots meet the garden path soundlessly. The palace is quiet, with only a few Watchers stationed near the entrance. Easy to avoid. The real risk begins as I slip into the Hollows. Few dare to venture into the enchanted woods, Aetherian and Eclipsarian alike.

But I do.

I find my spot by the Ironwood tree. The bark is battered from years of my fists meeting it. Tonight will be no different. I plant my feet, inhale sharply, and strike. Again. And again. Until my breath comes in white puffs and my knuckles bloom with fresh bruises. Until my mind quiets.

Then—

"Keira... it's time."

I freeze. The voice is barely more than a whisper, yet it cuts through my mind like a blade. My eyes dart everywhere, searching, scanning, trying to see something, anything.

There.

A glint of silver disappearing between the trees.

My feet move before my mind can catch up—dodging rocks, low branches, pushing past the undergrowth, not knowing what I'm chasing.

The trees break, revealing a glassy lake. I halt, scanning the shadows.

Nothing.

Suddenly—

I feel a cold pressure at my throat.

"Why are you following me?" The voice is hushed, rough—close. *Too close.*

I should have sensed him. I curse myself for being careless.

"I want nothing from you." My voice is steady. "I just want to know what you're doing out here."

A pause. His grip on the blade loosens, just slightly.

Mistake.

I move fast, twisting out of his hold, grabbing his wrist, and forcing his arm behind his back. He yelps as the knife clatters to the ground. A quick kick to the back of his knee, and he's down. I swing my leg over him, plopping myself on his chest.

"What was that for?!" he demands.

"You put a knife to my throat!" My hands tremble—adrenaline, not fear. At least, that's what I tell myself.

He doesn't answer. I'm caught off guard when his free arm connects with my stomach. He moves quickly, getting up as soon as I stumble from the impact of the hit. A flash of movement—then he's gone. Vanished into the shadows like he was never there.

I curse myself for being so stupid, and curse him for being a coward.

As I turn to leave, something glimmers near the ground. A ring, made from glittering onyx. I pick it up, rolling it between my fingers.

Strange. The stone almost seems to absorb the moonlight.

I slip it onto my thumb. Perfect fit.

With one last glance at the empty woods, I make my way back to the palace before sunrise.

I hide the ring in my bedside table and crawl into bed. Just as I'm about to drift off to rest, there's a knock at my door.

Chapter 5

Keira

Why did I stay out so late? It was that boy; he kept me out later than I had originally intended.

So far, no one has noticed the onyx ring on my thumb, not that anyone would say anything if they did. Sia knocked on my door this morning to tell me that we are heading to Eclipsar earlier than planned. She has already managed to pack most of my belongings. We are set to head north just after breakfast tomorrow.

I leave my room quietly. For some reason, my Watcher is nowhere to be seen. I'm in a different version of what I was wearing last night; however, this one is sapphire instead of black.

I roam through the halls of the palace with nothing to do but stare. I wander towards the Queen's study, deciding to slow down just outside the door. She is speaking with her first lady, Vale.

"We can't delay any longer," the Queen whispers. "Keira's magic hasn't manifested the way I'd hoped. The prophecy isn't holding true, we must enhance the ancient magic of the Stars."

Vale responds cautiously, "But, Your Majesty, the ritual hasn't been used in centuries. It's dangerous, and if she finds out what you plan, it could drive her away. Permanently."

My breath catches in my throat as I lean in closer. The Queen's voice is sharp now.

"She won't have a choice. If we ever wish to reign over the Kingdoms, we must do what is necessary to acquire what is beneath the skin of the future Princess. I-" There's a small pause. "*We* need her magic," she finishes.

Vale's tone is hesitant. "And if she resists?"

The Queen's voice turns cold and calculating. "Then we do what we must. Even if it means taking matters into my own hands... *again.*"

My heart is pounding in my chest. I back away silently, realizing I really am nothing more than a pawn to her. A piece in a game to be easily used and discarded. The room starts spinning as my body struggles to stay balanced.

I pivot on my heels, heading straight for the garden doors. The Watchers guarding the door see my storm of rage and scramble to open the doors. Once the scent of roses hits my nose, the world seems to right itself.

I look around searching for someone to talk to or perhaps someone to hit. Unfortunately, I found neither. That's when I catch sight of the Hollows, and all of last night's memories hit me like that elbow to my stomach.

The Queen's conversation is long forgotten as I set foot into the Hollows. It looks much different in the sun, I almost can't tell which way leads to the lake. Wandering the Hollows isn't a wise decision without some sort of defense magic.

Unfortunately for me, I don't have that. I imagine what it would be like, imagine what it would *feel* like to be gifted in such a way. It's never bothered me much that the Stars didn't grant me magic. It has, however, irked the Queen to her core.

I rip myself from my damning thoughts as I look around noticing every tree, bush, and branch look the same. I whip my head around trying to discern the way I came. Finally, I accept I'm lost.

"Curse my sense of direction." I kick a rock off the non-existent path but never hear it hit the ground. I kick another one. Same thing. They all seem to disappear past a boulder about three times my size.

Hesitant, I stick a hand out in front of me and slowly move towards the center of the boulders. Suddenly my hand disappears. An involuntary shriek escapes my lips. I immediately pull my hand back, and there it is, flesh and bone.

An illusion.

I take in a shaky breath. With a small step of courage, I go headfirst into the portal. I'm stunned to see a stone path, lined in greenery leading to a small cottage-like home. It's covered in moss and leaves with beautiful arched windows. I head down the path, making it to the emerald green door with a sign that reads:

"Truth is the Price of Entry: Fortunes Told, Futures Unraveled."

Stars, what have I gotten myself into? I reach for the knob when the door creaks open.

"Hello?" I say to the dim candle.

"Keira...It's time." My eyes go wide as I feel color drain from my face. I never realized it was a *woman's* voice.

I enter the small cottage. Scanning the room, it's so similar to the Queen's salon—candles lining the walls, glowing in various colors. There's an entire wall covered in spell books.

"Keira, I've been waiting." I whip around to see the outline of a woman who stands covered in shadows.

"Who are you?" I squint, trying to get a better look, until she steps into the candlelight. Whatever color was left on my face is definitely gone. The person in front of me hardly looks like a normal woman. Her hair is midnight black, her eyes the shade of firelight. The dress she wears seems to move with her, as if it's a part of her. There's a crescent moon between her eyebrows, the same glowy red as her eyes.

"Who are you?" I ask, trying to keep my voice steady and my face neutral, even though I'm itching to know.

"It matters not who I am but what I can do." Her lips tug into a bone-shivering smile as she takes small steps, coming closer and closer to me.

Then it dawns on me, the reason no one enters the Hollows is the Enchantress who's lived here for centuries. *It's every child's favorite bedtime story. Maybe I would have been better versed in the matter had I been gifted with a mother who cared for me.*

I pull myself from my thoughts and back to the matter at hand.

"Then what can you do?" I feel out of place, but not in an uncomfortable way.

"Truth is the cost of entry, dear one." I think she might be staring into my soul.

Her fingertips glow the same shade of fire as her eyes. The tips of her fingers brush my inner wrist. Her eyes close. The moon between her brows glows impossibly brighter.

"The closer you come to the flame, the further you walk from the shadow. Run for the flame or run for the shadow, for in that space, your power awakens."

"When fire and frost converge as one,

The lost heir's fate will be undone.

A choice of ruin or a Kingdom's frostbite—

The Daughter of Flame & Frost must choose the fight."

Her eyes fly open, scanning my hands. I look down in horror as I see my veins turn black. The tips of my fingers are completely black, but I feel no pain.

No, not pain but *power.*

I was so fascinated with my hands, I hadn't realized the Enchantress had vanished. The small cottage is now replaced by ruins with magical markings on them. The darkness on my hands is gone, and my face falls.

What the hell was that?

I drag my eyes over the ruins, as I reach to place a hand on one of the ruins. I now notice the sun has already slipped from the sky, casting beautiful shades of oranges and pinks.

I practically sprint all the way back to the palace, fueled partly by adrenaline and partly by fear. Something is very, very wrong with me *and* my magic.

Chapter 6

Keira

Sleep did not claim me in the night; all I managed to do was toss and turn. I couldn't help but gaze at my hands, *urging* them to change.

What had the Enchantress done to me? Did she do it, or did I? The more I think of it, the more I wonder if it wasn't just the Enchantress.

I'm pulled from my thoughts when Sia tosses something furry at me. I pull the fur-lined cloak over my shoulder. Seeing that we're heading north, it's going to be a terribly cold journey. I was more than happy to bundle up like a small kitten.

Sia set out a day dress for me, the color of fresh tears—the blue, so pale it's almost white, with matching heeled boots. It feels good to be informal. Once more, I'm grateful for Sia. I would've been miserable had she laid out a jeweled gown.

The Queen isn't entirely dressed up either. The only jewels she wears are the ones on her glittering crown. Thankfully, the ride to Eclipsar requires me to ride in my own carriage. The road there is less than a day away, making me wonder why she would request a separate carriage. Sia packed my luggage so all that's left is for me to meet the carriage in the courtyard roadway.

The Queen's carriage is in far better condition than mine, from the outside anyway. Hers practically glows bright blue; mine, though still pristine, seems dull. Nevertheless, the cushions on the inside are nothing to complain about.

I could practically sleep away my days on these cushions. My fingers twitch as I pull the velvet curtains closed, shutting out the palace. My hands are still my own, yet they don't feel like mine anymore.

The Enchantress's spell gnaws at my thoughts like an itch I can't scratch.

What did she do to me? Why won't it go away?

I'm still exhausted from thinking those exact thoughts all night. I slump onto the closest cushion, urging my eyes to close as my body relaxes into a comfortable position. I shift around until finally I drift off into shaky sleep.

Cracking my eyes open, it's grown significantly colder but not unbearably so. If anything, I feel a thin line of sweat under my cloak. I peel it off, tossing it on the seat opposite mine.

Pulling back the curtain just enough to get a glimpse outside, I choke on a gasp when I see a bush with black roses. Practically all the plants are colorless.

We ride through Shadowmere, the center town of Eclipsar. Everything is varying shades of blacks, grays, and off-whites; however, the town's people seem to be very vibrant.

I spotted many shops, Moonlit Brews, which looks like a pub, and The Gloomsmith, which seems to be an armory. I make a mental note of Tales of the Dark Moon and Starlight Trinkets.

I feel the carriage start gliding on a smoother road, marking our arrival. Glancing back out the window, Blackthorn Palace comes into view.

It was beautiful in a way that stole my breath, but not in the way a flower or a sunrise was beautiful. The palace was like a dark gem, cold, perfect, and dangerous. Every detail, from the sharp arches to the glowing windows, promised mystery and mischief.

My stomach twisted, a knot of awe and fear tightening as I stared. The palace seems to tower over everything, including the night sky. The fountain before the palace was a masterpiece of shadows and flowing darkness. Instead of clear, crystal water, inky black liquid cascaded from the intricately carved stone.

A shiver runs down my spine. How could such a cold place host such a ball, let alone one like the Midnight Masquerade? My heart beats out of my chest as my carriage halts and the Coachman opens my door. I hadn't realized my Watcher had not traveled to Eclipsar with me, or the fact that the horses have their own wool coats.

The Queen doesn't spare me a glance as we enter the halls of Blackthorn. It's a breathtaking mass of soft lights and swaying shadows. Small orb-like lights float around the top of the ceiling. The floors are deep black marble with gold veins throughout. A servant dressed in all black greets us to take our cloaks, and the Queen all but throws it at the poor girl. I drape it politely in her arms.

"Thank you." I incline my head towards her. She doesn't speak, just nods and wanders off.

I nearly run into the Queen as she halts directly in front of me. I notice we have just been roaming around mindlessly. No one other than that maid has tended to us. Suddenly, King Lucian seems to appear from the shadows. My surprise shouldn't have come so easily; it kind of comes with the territory.

"Queen Isolde, Princess Keira, I was delighted to hear you accepted the invite to my masquerade." His voice sounds like oil. Still ever so gentlemanly, he inclines his head toward the Queen and spares me a glance.

He wasn't what I expected; normally, a King doesn't meet company personally. He is striking, with gray hair and a light stubble lining his sharp jaw. His eyes, however, are *onyx.*

That messenger had onyx eyes.

Feeling silly for having remembered the eyes of a messenger, I wrap my arms around myself.

Completely missing whatever the Queen's response was, I realize King Lucian is nowhere to be seen. I stop and look around at this beautifully dangerous place. My favorite has to be the massive arch windows high up on the walls. "Th–"

"Please try to keep up, Keira, you're embarrassing me." I hadn't noticed she started walking, without a guide, I might add.

"Apologies, your Majesty." I don't bother trying to hide the sarcasm in my voice. My body is next to her, but my eyes are everywhere else; all the paintings, dark lights, and empty hallways.

The Queen turns down, probably one of the only halls that happen to have people. Three ladies stand patiently in the middle of the hall. As we approach, they drop their gaze, eyes finding the floor as they all curtsy in unison.

"Your Majesty, the two of us will be your maids throughout your stay." The tallest out of the three still doesn't make eye contact with either of us. The Queen pays no attention and brushes past them into what is most likely her chambers. Two of the maids follow immediately after her, swiftly closing the door.

"Princess Keira, I am to be your maid for the duration of your stay." She sways back and forth and swipes her palms on her dress.

"What's your name?" My voice is encouraging, urging her to peel her eyes off the floor.

"Maeve, your Highness." Something like surprise creeps into her voice.

"You can just call me Keira." Now her eyes dart to mine.

"I couldn't–" I don't give her the chance to finish her plea.

"Yes, you can, I am giving you permission. Now I would love to see my room. The ride over was extremely long." All I did was sleep, which seems like irrelevant information now. If I can get away from everyone, it will give me a chance to look around the palace.

"Of course." She pins her eyes back on the floor. We head quietly down the other hall, stopping outside a black door with a gold knob.

Maeve opens the door and steps aside to let me in first. The room is breathtaking, with a balcony overlooking the courtyard. It's like a void here, and everything is either black or gold.

The bed is twice the size of the one in my room back in Aetheris, with thousands of pillows, and a headboard made of gold. There's a half-empty bookshelf next to a small vanity with a fluffy stool chair. I think I might be able to like this place.

Chapter 7

Keira

My plan for exploring the palace went up in smoke the moment I sank into this surprisingly comfortable bathtub. It's black with small gold feet and a gold spout. Not to mention the softest silk robe with wool slippers on the nearby chair—everything in a deep shade of midnight.

I think the color black might suit me.

It's deep into the night before I even remember I wanted to roam around Blackthorn. I bring myself to slide out from under my warm sheets into the chilly air of my room. I grab my fur cloak and silently slip out the door.

Searching the halls, I notice huge double doors across from my room. Everyone seems to be in their rooms, so I take the chance and head for the doors.

Stepping as quietly as possible, I make my way to the doors. I stop to admire the huge arched door in front of me—black of course, dusted with gold, adorning star shaped knobs. I reach for one, gently turning it to the side. Shockingly, the door makes absolutely no noise as I crack it open.

Feeling my heart flutter in my chest, I step fully into the room.

It's a library.

Even in the dark, I can see the endless rows of all kinds of books. We don't have any books that aren't spell books in Aetheris.

Slowly making my way to the closest shelf, taking in just how high they go, I grab the first book I see and plop down on one of the black cushions strewn about the floor.

"The Secrets of the Missing Moon" is the title with a sky full of stars on the cover. It's a fairly thick book, bound in leather. Flipping through the worn pages, it's all words, no pictures. Our spell books have words, but normally reference images too. This is amazing, I finish flipping through this book and grab a different one. *I could do this forever.*

My eyes feel heavy as I gaze at the books stacked next to me. I'm about to shut my eyes and possibly drift off to sleep when someone pokes my shoulder. I all but jump to my feet, startled out of my almost sleep.

"You know sneaking into the library at this hour is highly suspicious," a sarcastic voice says.

"And what exactly are you doing here, lurking in the shadows? Trying to scare people to death, I presume?" I have fully recovered from my sleepiness, eying the boy responsible.

"Oh, I'm not lurking, I *live* here. But you, on the other hand, seem to be having a private affair with... books?" He glances past me to the stack of books.

"You live here?" I hadn't been paying attention to his face, but looking a little closer, I can make out his hair color. *A greyish blonde.*

Either gray is a popular hair color here, or I am standing in front of the future King of Eclipsar. Choosing the latter, I take a step back now realizing how close he was to me, dropping into a curtsy.

"You're Highness, please forgive me." I slip behind a mask of practiced precision.

It feels unnatural being so mannered in front of someone I am supposed to hate.

An annoying sound pulls me from my thoughts.

He's laughing at me. *Alright, niceties over.*

I shoot up, crossing my arms over my chest. "What's so funny?" I accuse. He catches his breath before answering.

"First of all, I am not the King yet, so you can call me Tristan. Secondly, why are you up so late in a *library*?" He glances at me, curiosity lining his eyes. I could be nice and answer his question, but that's not my style.

"I could ask you the same thing."

"You sure put up a fight, don't you?" Now *he* crosses his arms, matching my body language. I take that as my cue.

"You don't know the half of it." With that, I turn away from him and head straight for the doors, leaving him to pick up the mess I made.

Most likely not the best first impression on the future King of a Kingdom who's at war with mine. I hadn't noticed how flushed I had gotten until I stepped out of the library into the cool air of the hallway.

Heading for my hallway, I see a girl creep out of the room next to mine. I guess we had the same idea. I didn't want to scare her, so I waited until she noticed me. Her eyes widen when she sees me. *Weird.* Forming a friendship in this place wouldn't be so bad.

"Are you sneaking out late too?" I headed in her direction so she could hear me better.

"Something like that." She doesn't so much as look at me.

"I'm Keira." I blurt out, not knowing what else to say.

"I'm Princess Celestia from the Kingdom of Solara." Now she looks at me, her deep brown hair falling to one side of her face.

"Oh yes, I'm Princess Keira from the Kingdom of Aetheris." I completely blanked and forgot the most important part about me.

"Okay, well, it was lovely to meet you. I'm going to make my way back to my room. Maybe I'll see you at breakfast." She starts walking off, so I whisper-scream. "Looking forward to it!" She said she was going back to her room, yet she's walking in the opposite direction of the room she just came out of.

Whose room is that?

I hesitate in front of my door now, really wanting to know whose room that is. As I weigh my options, suddenly a blinding light shines in my eyes.

Stars, the sun is rising.

The mystery room can wait for another night. Sleep is a good idea for tonight. I swing open my door, about to change into a nightdress—until I look down to see I'm wearing my robe.

I wore my robe in front of the future King.

Not wanting to think about why that bothers me so much, I untie the robe, letting it fall to the floor. My thin slip is doing little to keep me warm, but wearing anything else will cause me death by overheating.

The blankets here are about as thick as the books. I get comfortable, settling into this huge bed when images of the Enchantress come back to me.

I need to see her again. Figure out what she did to me.

I try to remind myself that it's tomorrow's problem, but I've never been one to follow my logical side.

Chapter 8

Keira

My feet move as fast as they can. Trees, rocks, animals, everything is a blur.

Who knew I could run so fast?

I find the familiar way to the Enchantress's cottage. Within no time, I find the illusion that conceals her small living quarters. Without hesitation, I step through. *There it is, in all its glory.* I rush up to the door, knocking frantically.

Nothing.

"Hello!?" My lips move, but I hear no words. *Forget being a Princess.*

I burst through the door, calling out with no words. *Darkness.* No candles, no spell books, no magic. She's gone.

"Enchantress–"

I shoot out of bed, shaking off the dream, cold sweat covering my body.

"I'm so sorry, Princess Keira. I did not mean to wake you." Maeve carries fresh towels and new day clothes.

"It's okay, Maeve, you didn't wake me, and you can just call me Keira." I rub the rest of my sleep from my eyes. Watching Maeve's eyebrows fly up when I address her by her name.

"Y-Yes, of course." She sets the towels down in the wash room, then stands by my vanity, wiping her palms on her dress.

"Would you like something else?" Trying to sound pleasant, she stands there expectantly.

"I need you to either dismiss me, or I am to get you ready for breakfast in the dining hall." She doesn't meet my eyes. I'm not used to anyone but Sia tending to me.

"Yes, forgive me, I didn't get much sleep. I can dress myself if you pick out my outfit and do my hair; that would be perfect." I throw back my covers, cool air brushing my legs.

"Of course, I will do that now." She practically runs to my wardrobes. Thankfully, she's picking my dress, as I have no clue what's appropriate to wear here.

I catch a glimpse of myself in the mirror as I stand next to my bed. *What a sight for sore eyes.* I patiently wait for Maeve to come back with my outfit, admiring this breathtaking room. Maeve walks back in with a midnight blue dress. It's a thin material, so clearly she wants me to freeze to death.

"Um, based on what you brought, this is the best choice. Perhaps I could take a trip into town to pick up some appropriate clothes." She seems hesitant as she drapes the dress on the edge of my bed.

"Really? My maid back in Aetheris was the one who packed my gowns, but I guess new clothes wouldn't hurt. I, however, would like to do the shopping myself. Will there be time in my schedule to do that today?" I say as I pull the dress off the bed.

"Yes, you are only required to go to breakfast and dinner," she says as she grabs a pair of small heeled shoes.

"Perfect, then I'll head to town right after breakfast." Apparently, Maeve heard that as a dismissal because she walked her small frame to the door.

"I'll wait outside until you need me." She's out the door before I can respond.

I slip out of my sleepwear into the dress she picked. It's long, with a babydoll bodice, and flowy sleeves. Simple enough for breakfast. I stride over to the door and see Maeve talking to a gentleman. Maeve hears the door and turns around to face me while the mystery boy stalks off.

"Sorry, Pri- uh, Keira. I didn't mean to keep you waiting." She sounds skeptical, that maybe I changed my mind about her calling me Keira.

"Don't worry, I just finished. I am curious though; who were you talking to just now?" I try to sound uninterested.

"Prince Grayson." Her gaze falls to the floor as her face turns a deep blush.

Prince Grayson, the future Blade—Tristan's enforcer.

"Mm," I hummed, a little disappointed. Possibly hoping for the future King, not the future Blade. "If you are ready, I would like you to get started on my hair." That might have come off a little more harsh than I intended because she followed me to my vanity without a word.

I sit silently in my chair, as Maeve gathers all my colorless hair into a bun at the nape of my neck.

"Forgive me for asking, but have you ever thought of coloring your hair? Perhaps using some of our fruit stains we use on clothes?" She keeps her eyes glued on my hair, almost fascinated by it.

"Honestly, I haven't, I didn't grow up with many girls my age. I never thought it was *different* until I started attending galas, let alone think coloring it was an option." My eyes drift to the small pieces of hair that have fallen in my face.

"Well, you should be off to breakfast, but maybe when you go into town you could get a beautiful frosty color!" She seems extremely delighted at the idea.

"It wouldn't hurt to look." I rise to look at Maeve.

"I'm going to wander my way to the dining hall. Will you please lay out an outfit I can go to the shops in?"

"Of course, but are you sure you don't want me to escort you to breakfast?"

"Yes, I'll survive. I need to learn my way around anyway." She simply nods her head and wanders back to my closet.

I slip out my door and basically collide with a brick wall.

"I'm so sor-" I look up to find a boy with black curls and *onyx eyes* in my way. The onyx ring on my thumb feels heavier than usual.

"Apologies, I wasn't watching where I was walking." His eyes meet mine, and suddenly, I'm aware of his hand on my waist. I look down to see his hand is, in fact, on my waist. I look back at him. *He looks so familiar.*

"Gray?" His eyebrows fly up in shock.

"Uh—yea, how did you remember?" His hand leaves my waist only to tangle through his hair, causing his curls to fall into his eyes.

"Well, I don't know many people with onyx eyes." I arch a brow.

"Right, well, you should be at breakfast, and I take it you don't know where the dining hall is." *Who does this messenger think he is?*

"So, what if I don't know where the dining hall is?" That didn't have the same effect as I thought it was going to.

"Perfect, then I'll be your escort." He's awfully sarcastic but confusedly attractive, for a messenger.

"Fine, just this once. Think of the rumors that will go around if I'm caught arm and arm with a messenger." I tease. Gray, however, goes rigid.

"Right then, I suppose we can keep our arms to ourselves." He starts striding away.

Jogging to catch up with him, I keep his pace at a distance. Stars know what the Queen will say if she sees me with a messenger. Then again, the thought of provoking her is a little too thrilling.

Passing the library I found last night, we are now standing in front of an archway. Beautiful black swirls, and what looks like thorns? are carved out of the marble arch. I completely forgot Gray was here until he bumped my shoulder.

"I'm afraid this is where our scandal ends." I followed his line of sight to see a long table with many people already seated.

"Oh, right. I guess I'll see you around." I look back at him to meet his eyes.

"Something like that." The edge of his lips tugs into a smirk, showing off a small dimple.

As I start walking through the archway and down the steps, something in me wants to get one last glance at Gray. But when I turn around to try and catch him, he's gone.

Turning back to the table, I spot only one familiar face. *Celestia. How perfect, there's even an empty chair next to her.* I square my shoulders and tilt my chin up, just because I don't like my title doesn't mean I don't know how to act.

That is, until I realize I'm the only girl who is dressed plainly. All the other ladies at the table are draped in jewels, sparkly gowns, and have enough face coloring for the entire Kingdom. *The sun has barely been up for a couple of hours.*

Another odd thing—there are only ladies at this table. Shoving that thought aside, I slide into the chair next to Celestia. She barely spares me a glance. *I don't know what I expected. She didn't seem fond of me last night either.*

No food has been served yet. Everyone is just having polite conversation. The doors behind the King's chair fly open, all the chatter halting immediately.

"Good morning, Ladies, I trust you found comfort spending your first night in my palace. As you know, I have invited all of you here for my Midnight Masquerade in four days. What you ladies were not privy to is that I am looking to find a wife for my eldest son—meaning the masquerade will look a little different this year. Nonetheless, all of you, please eat."

So this is the real reason I'm here! My last wedding didn't work out so she hopes to pawn me off to a new family. We'll see about that.

As soon as the word "food" leaves his mouth, servants swarm around us with hot plates of breakfast food. None of the ladies move; they all watch the King sit gracefully in his seat at the head of the table. The majority of them look like all color has drained from their faces, though that could just be the effects of this Star's forsaken palace.

Breakfast was decent; none of the ladies ate until the King took his first bite. Even then, they barely chewed on a strawberry. *Absurd.* I probably looked like an animal the way I started to pile pastries and eggs on my plate. I noticed the ladies gawking at me, leading me to just push my food around my plate.

Now, dealing with an emptyish stomach, I remember Maeve saying something about going into town earlier. Deciding I'll find something to eat there, I head back to my chambers to start getting ready.

As promised, Maeve set out an evening dress on my bed. It's nicer than the one I wore this morning—a light purple color with long off-the-shoulder sleeves, beautiful cascading layers, and embroidered gold vines that dance up from the waist. It's a beautiful dress.

I can't help but wonder what it would be like if I could wear and do whatever I want with no one knowing who I am. I delight in this thought while I slip out of the dress from breakfast and into my training outfit.

I head for the door but stop as my hand settles on the knob.

Am I sneaking out?

The thought hadn't occurred until now; I wasn't doing anything wrong. *I'll be fine.* I twist the knob and head toward the grand doors. I manage to make it all the way to the doors when I am stopped by a voice.

"Princess Keira?" I whip around, secretly hoping for someone with onyx eyes, disappointed when I find brown ones.

"Yes?" The messenger is a little shorter than I am, which is rare, seeing how I barely reach the middle shelf.

"I have a word from His Majesty." This messenger isn't nearly as arrogant as Gray. *A little disappointing in my opinion.*

"Well, get on with it." I urge.

"Your mother..." He's hesitant.

"She's not dead, is she?" I probably could've sounded less hopeful.

"No, Princess, she has left town."

"Really?" Not what I expected. "Is that all?" My hand finds my hip as a million questions flare to light inside my head.

"Y-Yes?" His eyebrows knit together.

"Thank you." I offer a small nod that he returns with a stiff bow. I spin around and push open the doors. Realizing now, I have a lot to think about as I walk all the way to town.

Chapter 9

Keira

The gravel path beneath me crunches with every step I take away from the shadow that was the palace. The air feels lighter here, freer in a way, with a faint scent of smoke.

My—the Queen is gone.

The thought is so delightful, I feel a smile spread across my face. I quicken my pace, letting the cool breeze push me towards the distant hum of Shadowmere—named after the King's bloodline ability.

I pass through the arched gates, going unnoticed by the guards. I take comfort in my invisibility here; no one outside the palace calls me "Princess." No one bows. No one *pretends*. For the first time in my life, I really am just Keira.

Shadowmere unfolds before me like a painting coming to life. However, it's not as dark and blurry as the Queen described. Yes, the streets are uneven and winding in unexpected directions, but this town is full of *life*. Wooden stalls line the roads, colorful awnings shade merchants who shout about their goods. The smell of roasting meats mingles with the sweetness of candied nuts and the tang of sea salt.

It's a stark contrast to the orderly markets of Aetheris. Here, everything feels chaotic but alive, as though the town has a heartbeat of its own.

I find myself drawn to a stall selling fabrics: rich velvets, fine silks and rough, homespun cotton. The vendor, a plump woman with sharp eyes and calloused hands, smiles at me.

"Looking for something, dear?" she asks, holding up a deep crimson fabric.

"Just browsing," I say, running my fingers over the soft material. "It's beautiful."

She chuckles. "Beauty costs, but for you, maybe I can make an exception." Her eyes narrow slightly, studying me. I wonder if she senses something; my accent, my posture, something that marks me as an outsider.

Going with my gut, I politely decline and move on, weaving through the very populated streets. Children dart between stalls, laughing as they chase each other in circles. A musician plays a lively rhythm on a lute, his case open for coins. I toss in a sliver, earning a nod in gratitude from him.

Further down the road, the mood shifts. The houses grow smaller, their paint peeling. The laughter fades, replaced by murmurs and the occasional cry of a baby. My steps slow as I take it all in: the worn faces, the thin frames, the way people avert their eyes when I pass.

This is Eclipsar, too. Not the vibrant market or the elegant palace, but this—poverty and struggle.

A boy, no older than ten, sits on the edge of the road, clutching a loaf of bread as though it's the most precious thing in the world. His clothes are patched and too small, his face smeared with dirt. Our eyes meet for a brief moment, and he looks away, his shoulders hunching.

"Here," I say, pulling a few coins from my pocket and holding them out.

He stares at the coins, then at me, suspicion clouding his expression. Slowly, he reaches out and snatches them before darting off into an alley.

"Generous, aren't you?"

The voice, low and familiar, startles me. I turn to find Gray leaning casually against a wall, arms crossed, his dark eyes glinting with amusement. My onyx ring is heavy on my thumb.

"What are you doing here?" I demand, heat rising to my cheeks.

"I could ask you the same thing," he replies, pushing off the wall. "Does the Princess of Aetheris often wander into town alone?"

"I'm not here as a princess," I say, lifting my chin. "I'm here as me."

Gray raises an eyebrow, a small smirk playing at his lips, revealing dimples worth melting for. "And who are 'you,' exactly?"

Before I can answer, a commotion erupts further down the street—a shout, followed by the sound of breaking glass. Gray's expression hardens, the playful glint in his eyes replaced by something colder.

"Stay here," he says sharply, already moving toward the noise.

"Like hell I will," I mutter, following close behind.

The scene that unfolds is chaos. A man is being dragged out of a shop by two soldiers, his face bloodied. People gather around, some shouting, others standing silently, their expressions grim.

"What's happening?" I ask Gray, my voice low.

"Thief," he says shortly.

The man pleads with the soldiers, his voice desperate. "Please, I only took what I needed to feed my family. Please—"

"Enough," one of the soldiers snaps, raising his hand as though to strike.

Without thinking, I step forward. "Wait!"

The crowd turns to look at me, and for a moment, the world seems to hold its breath.

The soldier's hand freezes mid-air, his brow furrowing as he turns to face me.

"Who do you think you are to interfere?" he demands, his voice gruff and filled with authority.

Gray spins to face me with a warning in his eyes.

"Keira, don't—"

"I'm no one important," I cut him off, looking past him to address the soldier directly. "Just someone who believes a man shouldn't be punished for trying to keep his family alive." I summon all my years of etiquette classes and slip on a mask of unwavering confidence.

The soldier's eyes narrow. "Theft is theft. Laws exist for a reason."

"And mercy exists for another," I counter, my voice steady despite the rapid thudding of my heart.

The crowd murmurs, a few people nodding in agreement, emboldened by my words. The soldier glances at his companion, clearly debating whether it's worth making a scene.

"How much did he steal?" I ask.

"A loaf of bread," the second soldier replies begrudgingly.

I reach into my cloak pocket, pulling out the last handful of my coins. "Take this. It's more than enough to cover the bread." I shove my hand out, careful not to let them drop.

The first soldier hesitates before snatching the coins from my hand. "This doesn't mean he's off the hook. Next time, he won't be so lucky."

The man they'd been dragging collapses to his knees, clutching his side. His face is a mixture of relief and exhaustion. "Thank you," he whispers, his voice trembling.

I nod, helping him to his feet. I slip two slivers into his hand.

"Go home to your family."

He stumbles away, disappearing into the crowd. The soldiers exchange a final glare in my direction before retreating, their armor clanking as they leave.

The tension in the square dissipates, and the onlookers begin to disperse. Some offer me nods of gratitude, while others simply return to their business.

"You've made quite the impression," Gray says, his tone a mix of admiration and disbelief.

I turn to him, my cheeks still flushed with adrenaline. "Someone had to do something. Gray studies me for a moment, his dark eyes searching mine.

"You're brave, Little Flame. I'll give you that."

His nickname for me sends a feeling of warmth through my chest, but I quickly push it aside.

"I'm not looking for compliments. I'm just trying to do what's right," I counter.

"And that's what makes you dangerous," he says, a small smile peeling across his lips. "People will notice, and not all of them will approve."

I frown, unsure how to respond. Before I can say anything, Gray gestures toward the alleyway leading back to the main street.

"Come on," he says. "You've seen enough of Shadowmere for one day."

I hesitate, glancing back at the place where the man had been. The streets feel heavier now, the vibrancy of the market dimmed by the harsh reality I've just witnessed.

But as I follow Gray through the winding streets, I hear the grumble of my stomach, and apparently so does Gray, because on the way back, we stop at a stall selling turkey legs.

Chapter 10

Keira

The sun has already set by the time I make it back to the palace. Gray disappeared after we ate, saying something about messengers not being allowed to use the front gates while off duty.

My mind is still spinning from the events of the day: the market's vibrance, the man's desperation, Gray's cryptic warning. Everything feels heavier now, as if the weight of this place has finally settled on my shoulders.

Inside the palace walls, the air is cold and unwelcoming. Shadows cling to every corner, and the flickering torches along the walls seem to cast more darkness than light.

Maeve is waiting for me in my room, her hands folded neatly in front of her. "You were gone longer than I expected," she says, her tone gentle but curious.

"I got caught up," I reply, shrugging off whatever thoughts lingered. "The town is... different than I imagined."

Her brows knit together. "Different? How so?"

"Lively and surprisingly warm, but there's so much hardship. People are struggling just to survive. It's not what I expected from a Kingdom as powerful as Eclipsar."

Maeve hesitates, glancing toward the door as if checking for eavesdroppers. "The King doesn't see what happens outside these walls. Or maybe he does and pays it no mind. Either way, the people fend for themselves." Her timidness from our first encounters has vanished almost completely. Her words settle uncomfortably in my chest.

"That's not how it should be," I say softly, more to myself than to her.

"No," she agrees. "It's not." A sad smile plays on her face.

Before I can press further, there's a knock at the door. Maeve moves to answer it, revealing Celestia standing in the hallway.

"Keira," she says, her voice smooth and practiced. "The King has sent me to let you know it is your turn to meet with him in the library. He wishes to discuss the Midnight Masquerade."

My stomach tightens at the mention of the masquerade. I've been avoiding it, but there's no escaping it now. "Of course," I reply, forcing a smile of my own. Celestia nods, her eyes briefly flickering to Maeve before she turns and glides down the corridor.

"You should change into something more formal," Maeve suggests, already moving toward the wardrobe.

"If you think so." I begin to slip out of my purple day dress, noting the dirt along the hem.

"Also, I didn't find anything I liked in town. I think I'll take you up on your offer. You may get whatever you think is appropriate." Truthfully, I completely forgot I was supposed to buy dresses. She simply nods and picks a dress that resembles a night gown with sleeves.

"You think that's appropriate for meeting the King?" I raise an eyebrow.

"It will look excellent on you." Her face is a little flushed. I slip it on, a flush of my own creeping across my face. Although I have noticed she has reached for the simpler outfits in my wardrobe, making me extremely grateful.

As I head for the door, I smooth the front of my forest green dress, steeling myself as I leave the room and make my way toward the library.

The library is dimly lit, the towering shelves casting long shadows across the room. The King stands near a large table, his hands resting on a map spread out before him. He looks up as I enter, his expression neutral.

"Ah, Princess Keira," he says, his voice smooth but lacking warmth. "Thank you for joining me."

I nod, keeping my gaze steady. "Of course, Your Majesty, you wished to discuss the masquerade?" Once more, I slip on my mask of the *perfect Princess.*

"Yes," he replies, gesturing for me to approach. "It is a tradition here in Eclipsar, and this year it holds particular significance. As you may have heard, my eldest son is searching for a wife."

"I heard," I say carefully, my mind racing.

The King's eyes narrow slightly, as if gauging my reaction. "You will, of course, be expected to attend. It is a chance for you to… make an impression."

I bristle at his words, Gray's exact words while we were in town, ringing in my head. Somehow, I manage to keep my expression neutral. "Of course."

Before he can say more, the doors to the library swing open, and Gray strides in. His dark eyes fill with surprise when he notices me, but he quickly masks it with a polite bow.

"Father," he says, his tone formal. "You summoned me?"

Father?

"Yes," the King replies, turning his attention to Gray. "I was just discussing the masquerade with Princess Keira. I trust you'll ensure she, along with the other maidens, are properly acquainted with our customs."

Gray keeps his face and voice even, giving nothing away. "Of course, Father."

The King nods, satisfied. "Good. That will be all for now."

As the King exits the library, Gray turns to me, his expression softening. "Looks like you're stuck with me, Little Flame."

I stare blankly at him. *How could I have been so stupid?*

"Lucky me," I say, playing the part before everything explodes.

"So *Prince* Grayson, when were you planning on telling me you were royalty?" It's getting harder and harder to compose myself the way I was taught to.

"Seemed like irrelevant information in our little relationship we have." He shrugs.

"That's—" I inhale sharply. "That's something you tell someone, you don't just lead people on."

"You're making me sound like a bad guy—which that's fair—however, in this instance you have bigger things to worry about."

"Don't try and change the subject!" I want to scream.

"I'm not," He throws his hands up. "I'm simply pointing out you should be more concerned with the Midnight Masquerade than with what I did or didn't tell you."

When I don't say anything, he continues.

"Look, you have every right to be mad at me—I don't blame you, in fact I don't even care what you feel for me. But for now turn your attention to the masquerade and not me, no matter how hard that is for you." He smiles.

I fight the urge to hit him for how big his ego is.

"I think I'll survive some silly party your father is hosting to find your brother a wife."

Gray chuckles, moving closer. "The Midnight Masquerade isn't just a party, you know. It's a game. Everyone has their own agenda, and trust me, no one plays fair."

"Why are you telling me this?" I ask, crossing my arms.

"Because I'd hate to see you lose," he says, his tone light.

"And what exactly would losing look like?" I challenge, tilting my head slightly.

Gray's smirk deepens. "In Eclipsar? Losing could mean anything. A ruined reputation, a broken alliance, or worse... being trapped in a game you don't even know you're playing."

His words feel heavier than they should, laced with an unspoken warning. I open my mouth to respond, but Gray's voice cuts through.

"Keira, listen to me." He steps closer, his tone dropping into something more genuine. "Eclipsar isn't like Aetheris. Here, power isn't just inherited. It's taken, stolen, and manipulated. You can't trust anyone—not even *me*."

OF COURSE I CAN'T TRUST HIM, HE'S THE BLOODY FUTURE BLADE OF ECLIPSAR!

I raise an eyebrow. "You're really selling the charm of your Kingdom."

Gray laughs, though it sounds almost bitter. "I'm not here to charm you. I'm here to make sure you don't get eaten alive."

His words hang in the air, and for a moment, I see something raw in his eyes, a hint of something he's trying to hide. It disappears as quickly as it came, replaced by his usual aloof demeanor.

"Anyway," he says, stepping back and shoving his hands into his pockets, "you'll need a mask. Something that makes a statement. The masquerade might be a game, but it's also your stage. How you play it is up to you."

He turns to leave, but I call after him. "You're a lying bastard, Gray."

He pauses, glancing over his shoulder. "I never claimed to be anything else."

And with that, he's gone, leaving me alone in the dim library with nothing but the faint scent of smoke and the sound of my own thoughts.

Chapter 11

Keira

The palace halls feel both vast and suffocating. The polished stone floors echo with every step I take, but I keep my pace brisk, my head down, avoiding the occasional servant or guard. Gray's words from the library linger in my mind like a splinter I can't remove. *"I never claimed to be anything else."*

I trusted him. Well, as much as you can trust someone who calls you "Little Flame" with an insufferable smirk. But now? Now, I feel my insides twist with something ugly.

My thumb brushes against the smooth, cold surface of the onyx ring. A nervous habit, though I can't explain why. The ring feels heavier today, as if it's bearing the weight of my irritation with him.

I slip into the garden, needing air. The vines twist up the stone walls, their pale flowers glowing faintly under the overcast sky. The garden is one of the few places I've found where I can be alone—or so I thought.

"Princess Keira," a voice calls out, light and teasing.

I turn to see Tristan stepping out from the shadow of a nearby pillar. He's impeccably dressed as always, his black tunic tailored to perfection, his greyish hair catching the light. His smile is easy, disarming, as though he's just stumbled upon me by chance.

"Your Highness," I reply, keeping my tone even as I drop into a low curtsy.

"Please," he says, holding up a hand. "No titles. I've heard your people are much more formal than ours. Call me Tristan."

I nod, though I don't relax. Something about him feels too polished, too deliberate.

"What brings you to wander about the gardens at this time?" I ask, stepping to the side to give him space to pass.

"Ah, but the better question is, what brings *you* here?" he counters, his grin widening. "Are you avoiding something or perhaps *someone*?"

It's as if he's read my mind or heard something not intended for his ears. I fold my arms, deflecting. "Maybe I just enjoy the quiet."

"Hmm." He steps closer, mere inches from me. His movements are graceful, almost predatory, though his tone remains warm. "You're not like the others here. Most noblewomen cling to the palace halls, eager to catch my attention. Yet here you are, hiding in the shadows." He gestures to the dying sunlight.

"I'm not hiding," I counter, regretting the edge in my voice as soon as the words leave my mouth. After all, shadows are the Noctis bloodline's greatest power.

"Of course not," he says, raising his hands in mock surrender. "Forgive me. I just find you… intriguing." He corks a brow at me.

There's something in the way he says it, a spark in his green eyes that makes me flush. But before I can respond, he gestures to the ring on my thumb.

"That's an unusual piece of jewelry," he says, tilting his head. "Onyx, is it?"

I instinctively curl my hand into a fist. "A gift," I lied.

"From Grayson?" he guesses, his tone light but probing.

"No," I say quickly, too quickly. His smile widens.

"Interesting, he has a similar one," he murmurs, stepping back. "Well, I won't keep you. I'm sure you need your rest. I hope to see you around, Princess." He turns and strides off, his steps unhurried, leaving me alone with the faint scent of the garden flowers and the weight of his lingering gaze.

I let out a breath I hadn't realized I was holding. Something about Tristan feels… off. His charm is undeniable, but there's a sharpness beneath it, like a blade hidden in silk.

I glance down at the onyx ring again, twisting it around my thumb. For some reason, it feels warmer now. As I head back toward my chambers, I vow to stay clear of both Gray and Tristan for the rest of my stay.

I make my way back to my room, the uneasy feeling still clinging to me, fighting the temptation to glance over my shoulder. Tristan's words still linger in my mind, smooth and careful. It's as though he's trying to read me, to unravel me with a smile.

I shouldn't have snapped at him. Yet, I can't quite bring myself to stay angry at him. There's something so easy about him, something that rattles my instincts, as if I should trust him. But I shouldn't. Not yet.

The thought of Gray enters my mind, uninvited but not unwelcome. I still haven't figured him out—he's as unpredictable as the sea, calm one moment and churning with secrets the next. Secrets I'm not sure I want to know.

I brush my thumb across the onyx ring again, letting the cool smoothness steady me, as it becomes too familiar, like I've worn it my entire life. Funny how quickly I've come to rely on its weight as opposed to that of my dagger, which sits untouched on the night table in my room.

I push through my door and find Maeve smiling proudly next to Celetisa.

"What's going on?" I blurt out after a minute of uncomfortable silence.

"Celetisa helped me pick out some of your outfits for everyday wear and for the Masquerade!" She's grinning ear to ear. My eyes dart to my bed piled high with silks, cottons, and furs.

Celetisa makes her way to me. "I realize you and I may have gotten off on the wrong foot, and with the Masquerade competition so close, it would be nice for you to have someone on your side." She has the grace of an angel.

"I'm on my side." I peer at her.

To my surprise, she laughs. "Of course, I understand that. I understand you want His Highness to pick you, but we can't really control that." She hums.

"Wait, what? I know this Masquerade was to find Prince Tristan a wife, but I didn't know it was a competition?" I regret my words as soon as they're out, fearing I seem clueless now.

"I don't know much. All I heard was something about trials and seeing which one of us has the strongest ability." She shrugs it off.

"Anyway, we picked out some fabrics we thought you would like! You obviously still have to get them tailored into gowns." She smiles, proud of herself.

"Thank you, you didn't have to do that." I don't get why she did.

"It's no problem at all!" She makes a dramatic exit, her dress and hair swinging behind her as she leaves my room.

I glance at the heap of fabrics on the bed, my brow furrowing. Silks in hues of midnight blues and blacks, emerald greens, and deep golds spill across the covers, catching the faint light from the window. Maeve, standing beside the chaos, beams at me like she's just solved all my problems.

"Well?" she asks, clasping her hands in front of her. "What do you think?"

"I think…" I hesitate, running a hand through my hair. "I think this looks like it belongs in someone else's room."

Maeve's face falls for half a second before she recovers. "Oh, don't be like that, Keira. You'll look stunning in any of these! And with the Masquerade so close, it's important you make an impression." She beams.

Everyone here seems to be fascinated by first impressions.

"I wasn't aware making an impression was a priority here." I try to keep my tone light, but the truth is, her excitement grates against the knot of unease in my chest. "I thought it was just… a party."

Maeve's voice drops into a conspiratorial whisper. "It's never just a party when it comes to royals. Especially not one where they're parading you in front of Prince Tristan."

"I also wasn't aware I was being paraded." My words are sharper than I mean them to be, and Maeve flinches. I sigh, pinching the bridge of my nose. "Sorry. It's just… all of this feels so ridiculous. I don't need silks or fur to prove my worth."

Maeve steps closer, her expression softening. "No, you don't. But it doesn't hurt to remind people you're not someone they can overlook." She picks up a bolt of wine red silk, running her fingers over it. "This one would look beautiful with your eyes. Strong. Regal."

"I don't feel strong or regal right now," I mutter, sinking into the chair by the vanity. "I feel like a pawn in someone else's game."

Maeve kneels beside me, her voice low but firm. "Maybe you are, for now. But pawns can become Queens if they play their cards right," she says with a wink.

I glance down at her, surprised by the steel in her tone. "Since when did you become an expert on strategy?"

She grins, her lightheartedness returning. "I've had to outwit more than a few nosy maids in my days. And I've been watching this Court long enough to know one thing— no one wins by staying in the shadows. You don't have to play their game, but you do have to make them *see* you."

I don't respond, my gaze drifting back to the fabrics. My fingers brush over the onyx ring again, its cool surface grounding me. "Maeve... do you think Tristan would choose someone like me?"

She tilts her head, considering. "I think he'd be a fool not to. But if you ask me, I'm not so sure he's the one you should be worried about."

My stomach twists. "What do you mean?"

Maeve stands, smoothing her apron. "Just that sometimes, the person you're not looking at is the one who's already looking at you." She gives me a knowing smile before turning back to the bed.

"Now, are we going to pick something for you, or are you going to mope the rest of the night?"

I stare at her, unsure whether to laugh or throw a pillow at her head. "You're impossible, Maeve."

"And you're stubborn," she counters, holding up a different silk, the shade of glittering midnight. "But I think we can work with that."

Despite myself, I let out a small laugh. Maeve's determination is infectious, and for a moment, the weight in my chest feels a little lighter. But as I stand to sift through the fabrics with her, a small voice in the back of my mind whispers that she might be right.

About Tristan. About Gray. About all of it.

And that terrifies me more than I want to admit.

Chapter 12

Keira

The morning air buzzed with nervous energy as all fifteen of us were summoned to the Grand Hall. The high, arched ceiling stretched endlessly above us, casting an oppressive weight over the room. Sunlight streamed through black stained glass windows, splashing fragments of shadows across the polished marble floor.

I sat near the end of a long oak table, doing my best to avoid the other girls' gazes. Some whispered among themselves, their faces a mixture of excitement and fear. Others, like me, remained silent, their hands folded tightly in their laps.

Maeve had helped me dress in a simple cream gown with gold trim—a stark contrast to the vibrant silks and jewels worn by the others. It wasn't that I wanted to stand out less; I simply lacked the energy to care. My mind was elsewhere, replaying my conversation with Celetisa the night before.

Trials. Abilities. Strength. The words rattled in my mind like loose coins in a tin. What kind of trials would they expect from us? And what would happen when they realized I had no ability to show?

At the head of the table, a tall man in an ornate uniform cleared his throat. His voice boomed as he addressed us, silencing the scattered murmurs.

"Ladies, welcome," he began, his tone formal but laced with authority. "As you all know, the Midnight Masquerade is an honored tradition in Eclipsar. It is an opportunity for His Majesty, King Lucian, to find a future Queen for his Highness, Prince Tristan."

I glanced at the other girls, noting the straightened backs and practiced smiles. Most of them looked ready to leap at the chance to put on a show.

"However," the man continued, "this year, His Majesty has decided to add an additional… layer of festivities."

A murmur rippled through the room, but the man raised a hand, silencing it immediately.

"To ensure the strongest candidate is chosen," he said, his voice crisp, "each of you will participate in a series of trials leading up to the masquerade. These trials will test not only your grace and poise but also your strength, wit, and—most importantly—your abilities."

My heart sinks. *Abilities.* Of course. In Eclipsar, power is everything, and their obsession with magic runs deep. It's no wonder they want Prince Tristan's future Queen to embody that ideal.

The girl sitting directly across from me—Tessa, I think her name was—smirked as she leaned back in her chair. Her presence was hard to miss, with fiery red hair and sharp emerald eyes. She radiated confidence, as though the announcement had been made just for her.

"What kind of trials?" one of the other girls asked nervously, her voice trembling slightly.

"The specifics will be revealed in time," the man replied. "For now, you should prepare to demonstrate your strength and abilities in the coming days. This will be your chance to set yourselves apart from one another." The room erupted into whispers again, this time louder and more frantic. I gripped the edge of the table, my mind racing.

How was I supposed to display something I didn't have? And, unlike these other Ladies, I have no intention of marrying Tristan. But, at the same time, I'm all for a competition.

Tessa caught my eye from across the table, her smirk deepening as though she could sense my unease. She leaned toward the girl beside her, whispering something that made them both laugh quietly.

I forced myself to look away, focusing instead on the ornate pattern carved into the table. My fingers absently twisted the onyx ring on my thumb—a small, steadying motion distracting me from the chaos swirling in my mind.

"Silence!" the man barked, bringing the room to order once more. "You are dismissed. Use the time wisely."

The girls rose from their seats, some chatting animatedly as they filed out of the hall. I lingered behind, unsure where to go or what to do. Maeve approached me quickly, her expression a mixture of worry and determination.

"Keira," she said, her voice low. "Don't let them intimidate you. We'll figure this out." Her words were meant to comfort, but they only added to the weight pressing down on me.

As we left the hall, I couldn't help but glance back at Tessa. She stood near the doorway, her arms crossed and her gaze fixed on me. There was something calculating in her eyes, something that made my stomach churn.

The days before the masquerade were meant to be a time of preparation and excitement, but for me, it felt like a countdown to disaster.

Back in my chambers, Maeve hovered like an anxious bird, plucking at the hem of her apron as she paced.

"There must be something," she muttered. "Something you can do to… to make it seem like you have an ability." I had to tell her. She could sense something was wrong.

"I'm not going to lie," I said sharply, sinking into a chair by the window. "If they want me to prove I belong here, I'll have to do it without tricks."

Maeve stopped pacing and turned to face me, her eyes wide. "But you don't have an ability. How are you supposed to—"

"I don't know, Maeve!" I snapped, then immediately regretted it when I saw her flinch. I sighed, rubbing my temples. "I'm sorry. I just... I don't know what to do."

She hesitated before stepping closer, her voice soft. "Keira, you're stronger than you think. Abilities or not, you'll find a way."

Her faith in me was touching, but it felt misplaced. I didn't have the strength she believed in—not when I was up against girls like Tessa, who seemed born for this.

Later that afternoon, I wandered the palace gardens, seeking a moment of calm. The vines climbed the stone walls, their pale flowers lit with overcast light. It was one of the few places where I felt like I could breathe.

I wasn't alone for long.

"Keira," a voice called, smooth and unfamiliar. I turned to see Tessa stepping out from behind a pillar, her emerald eyes gleaming with mischief.

"You looked like you needed company," she said, her smile sharp as a blade.

"I was fine on my own," I replied, my tone colder than I intended.

Tessa only laughed, her confidence unshaken. "You're quite the mystery, you know. No one seems to know much about the Princess of Aetheris. You don't exactly... stand out."

I stiffened, but she continued before I could respond.

"Don't take it personally," she said with a shrug. "I'm just curious. After all, if we're competing for the same prize, it's only fair to get to know each other."

"Competing?" I echoed, narrowing my eyes.

"For Queen, of course," she said, her smirk widening. "Or did you think this was just a celebration?"

Her words sent a chill down my spine. There was something unnerving about her, something that felt too calculated, too deliberate.

"Well," she said, brushing past me, "may the best girl win."

As she disappeared into the shadows, I was left with the unsettling realization that I might not just be *competing* against her tomorrow.

I might be fighting to *survive*.

Chapter 13

Keira

Sleep didn't come easy last night. All I managed to do was toss and turn—not exactly ideal.

"Have you thought about what you would like to wear?" Maeve is lightly brushing on a powder, trying to hide the tired look on my face.

"Not really. I wasn't really worried about that part. Should I wear something formal?" I definitely didn't want to wear a sparkly gown.

"That depends. What are you planning to display?" She seemed genuinely curious as she glanced at me through the mirror.

"I was just trying to work that part out." I started spinning the onyx ring on my finger.

"What about me?"

I look up to see that Maeve has wandered over to my wardrobe to find me proper attire. I search around the room, noticing no one else is here.

"You always have me."

It's as if this voice was in my head, rattling around my brain. Suddenly, it came to me.

The Enchantress.

How was she able to reach me so far from the Hollows? More importantly, how do I communicate back?

Startled, I look back at the mirror and *she's there.* Covered in shadows, but still there.

"Keira, I only wish to help you." Her voice is as smooth as chocolate.

"How do you plan to do that?" I'm sure if Maeve were to walk back from the wardrobe, she would think I've gone mad.

"Don't fight it, lean into it, lean into me."

Before I could respond, she disappeared, leaving a pair of delicate black lace gloves, with a ruby on the wrist in her wake.

"I have the perfect outfit!" Maeve comes skipping back into the room, clothes in hand.

I wipe any remainder of confusion from my face.

"Will it pair well with gloves?" I pick up the lace gloves and dangle them in front of her.

"Anything will look amazing on you!" She was excited enough for both of us.

Maeve hands me what she thought would be suitable for today. Unfortunately, it is *not* nearly what I had in mind. It was a short thing, made of training leather but cinched at the waist and stopped mid-thigh. The sleeves are tight, leaving no space for any kind of accessory. Grateful for the belt Maeve strapped to my waist, seeing how it's the only thing that would be able to hold my knives.

I slip on the gloves, the only color in my whole outfit. And I swear to the Stars that I saw the rubies glow just a little brighter, once on my person.

"As I said, you look amazing." She beamed. She has been nothing but smiles lately.

"Thank you, Maeve, I'm almost ready. Would you mind waiting for me outside?" A little part of my heart twisted as she seemed to dim a little.

"Of course, I'll be right outside the door." She quietly excused herself. I crossed my room to my bedside table. I open the top drawer and stare at the dagger I had abandoned since I stepped foot in this place.

I secure the rest of my blades to the belt around my waist. My dagger, however, is strapped to my thigh just out of sight.

As Maeve had promised, she was waiting for me outside my door and led me to a place called the Shadowspire. It's a dome-like structure with a ceiling made of glass.

The fourteen other girls all sat elegantly in a row. There was a set of thrones at the head of the dome and a huge open area directly in front. Looking at it now, I realize it's our *stage*.

I take a seat next to Celestia. She greets me with a warm smile and sincere hazel eyes.

"Keira! Isn't this so exciting!" She is as radiant as her name.

"I can't wait!" I actually *could* wait many moons, but I couldn't ruin her light. She looked as if she was going to say more until the floor-to-ceiling doors swung open and three figures stood backlit in the threshold.

Chapter 14

Keira

The tallest of the shadows stepped forward first, the other two in tow. Gooseflesh snakes up my skin.

They stayed covered in shadows until a beam of sunlight flashed across the King's face.

I wasn't expecting the King to watch our performance, let alone run them. King Lucian took his seat in the middle of the three thrones. His throne was the largest, its arms carved from polished obsidian, while veins of smoky quartz webbed through the backrest like frozen lightning. The other two thrones, though smaller, gleamed with hematite and onyx, their sharp edges catching the rays of light.

The ring on my thumb started to warm, making me wish I had left it behind. For some strange reason, I can never bring myself to take it off. Unfortunately, I'll have to resort to a new form of fidgeting due to my gloves.

Clearly, I hadn't thought this through. *How am I supposed to fight with gloves on?* Granted, about half of the other girls had on gloves.

Glancing up, I realize we have a bit of an audience. The lords and ladies of the court sat to the left, their faces a sea of expectation and quiet judgment. Jewels and silks shimmered in the light, but their eyes—sharp and calculating—were fixed on us.

The room fell into a heavy silence as the King's deep voice echoed across the throne room.

"Ladies," he began, his tone calm but laced with authority, "you stand here today not just to perform, but to prove your worth. Your skill, your strength, your resolve— these are the qualities we demand in our future Queen. What you show us today may very well determine the course of your lives."

My heart thudded in my chest. *Queen.* The word hung in the air like a blade over our heads, threatening to fall with the slightest misstep.

"The trials ahead will not be kind," the King continued, his dark eyes scanning the line of girls before him. "They will not be easy. But if you succeed, you will not only win the favor of this court, but the honor of standing by the future King of Eclipsar."

The future King. *Tristan.*

I shifted uneasily, the warming of my ring growing more persistent, like it sensed my unease. My gaze flickered toward the two smaller thrones. It wasn't just the

King sitting before us. Two figures sat on either side of him, their faces obscured in shadow until now.

It hit me like lightning. Tristan. Gray.

Tristan lounged on the throne to the King's right, his posture deceptively relaxed, though the sharp set of his jaw betrayed his intensity. His greyish blonde hair gleamed in the slanting sunlight, his piercing gaze sweeping over us like a predator sizing up prey.

To the King's left, Gray sat in rigid silence, his black curls shadowing his onyx eyes. Unlike Tristan, he made no effort to mask his disinterest, or was it disdain? His presence felt colder, sharper, like the edge of a blade waiting to strike.

My breath caught in my throat. I hadn't expected them to be here. Tristan, maybe, seeing how he's the future King, but Gray—the future Blade?

The King continued speaking, but his words blurred as my thoughts raced. What was Gray doing here? Was he just a silent observer, or did he have some role in all this?

"First, you will showcase your physical abilities," the King said, pulling my attention back. "Strength, agility, and endurance. Then, you will demonstrate your knowledge of strategy because a Queen must be as sharp of mind as she is of body. Lastly, and most importantly, you will prove your loyalty to Eclipsar."

My stomach twisted at the weight of his words.

Prove your loyalty. What did that even mean?

The King leaned back in his throne. "You will begin immediately. Step forward when your name is called."

A court official stepped out from the shadows, a long scroll in hand. As he began reading off names, I forced myself to focus, though I couldn't shake the feeling of two pairs of eyes boring into me: one fiery and intent, and the other cold and calculating.

Tristan and Gray were watching.

And I wasn't sure which gaze unnerved me more.

The first girl stepped forward, her name—Amara—echoing through the chamber as the court official called it. She moved with confidence, her braided hair swaying behind her like a banner.

She curtsied deeply to the King before taking her place in the center of the arena. A servant rolled a wooden chest forward, opening it to reveal a set of weapons, swords, daggers, bow and arrows, and staffs gleaming in the light.

Amara selected a sword, its curved blade glinting in the few rays of sunlight. She flourished it with practiced ease, her movements sharp and precise. Her routine began—a flurry of strikes and spins, the sword slicing the air with a whistle.

The Lords and Ladies murmured approvingly, their whispers blending into a low hum. The King, however, remained stone-faced.

Tristan leaned forward slightly, his lips twitching into what might have been a smirk. Gray didn't move, though his fingers drummed once on the armrest of his throne.

Amara finished with a final, dramatic slash, the blade stopping just short of the ground. She bowed again, her chest heaving, and returned to the line, her face flushed with exertion and pride.

The next girl, a wiry brown haired girl named Liora, chose a pair of daggers. Her performance was less flashy, but it spoke of precision and control. She moved like a shadow, her strikes deliberate and her aim flawless as she hit every target set up around the arena.

Again, the court murmured. This time, Tristan's smirk faded into a contemplative frown, while Gray's fingers stilled.

Then, the official called Tessa's name.

I stiffened. Tessa glided forward, her head held high, her bright red hair gleaming like silk in the sunlight. Even the Lords and Ladies seemed to sit straighter as she approached the weapon chest.

She didn't hesitate. Tessa chose a staff, its dark wood polished to a sheen, and took her place in the center of the stage.

With a single, sharp motion, she began. The staff spun in her hands, a blur of motion as she launched into an intricate routine. She twisted and flipped, her movements fluid and precise, her strikes calculated to maximize power.

The court was entranced. Even the King leaned forward slightly, his lips pressed into a faint line of approval. Tristan's gaze followed her every movement, his expression intense.

Tessa finished with a flourish, slamming the staff into the ground with a loud crack that echoed through the dome. The audience broke into whispers, and even I couldn't deny her skill. She didn't look at the Lords or the Ladies—or even the King. She looked at *me*. Her eyes gleamed with confidence, as if daring me to outshine her.

The performances continued, each girl stepping forward, showcasing their skills in combat or agility. Some excelled, while others faltered under the weight of the King's piercing gaze.

I stood still, my breath steady but shallow, watching each display with a mixture of awe and unease. The ring on my thumb was practically burning now, though I couldn't tell if it was from nerves or something else entirely.

When the court official called my name, the air seemed to shift. The murmurs ceased, replaced by a heavy silence that pressed down on me as I stepped forward.

I could feel their eyes—Lords, Ladies, the King, Tristan, Gray—all watching, waiting.

I curtsied, my movements deliberate, and approached the chest. My gloves itched against my palms as I studied the weapons.

A sword? No, already used too much.

Daggers? Too small.

My fingers hovered over a staff before settling on a bow.

It was sleek and well-worn, its polished wood fitting perfectly in my hands. I glanced up at the targets set up at the far end of the room. They were smaller than I'd expected, the distance between us making them appear even smaller.

I nocked an arrow, drawing the bowstring back until it trembled against my cheek. The room was silent, the only sound the faint creak of the bow as I steadied my aim.

Then, I released.

The arrow flew, a whisper cutting through the still air, before sinking into the target dead center.

A collective murmur rippled through the guests. I didn't wait for it to settle. I nocked another arrow, adjusting my aim slightly, and let it fly. This time, the arrow struck the edge of the first, splitting it in two.

The gasps were louder now, but I didn't look at the court. I didn't look at the King, or Tristan, or even Gray. My focus remained on the bow in my hands, the tension of the string, and the rhythm of my breathing.

One final arrow. I turned slightly, aiming for a target farther to the side—a trick shot. The arrow curved mid-air, striking the target squarely.

Only then did I lower the bow, my chest rising and falling with the effort. The room was quiet again, the kind of silence that felt like the calm before a storm.

I turned and curtsied, bowing my head as I returned to the line. My hands trembled slightly as I adjusted the gloves, and for the first time, I dared a glance at the thrones.

Tristan was leaning forward, his elbows on his knees, his eyes locked on me with an intensity that made my stomach twist and cheeks flush. Gray, however, remained still, but his gaze followed me as I took my place.

The King's voice cut through the silence. "Impressive."

My breath caught, but I kept my head bowed, my heart racing in my chest.

This was only the beginning.

The court official called the next name. "Celestia."

I turned my head, watching my friend step forward. Celestia was a head shorter than most of the other girls, her petite frame almost swallowed by the vastness of the arena. She smoothed her skirts nervously, her movements jerky and uncertain as she approached the chest of weapons.

Celestia hesitated, her gaze flitting across the gleaming options. Her hand hovered over the daggers before settling on a staff. She picked it up cautiously, her fingers tightening around the wood as though trying to draw courage from it.

The court's murmurs grew louder, the whispers sharp and cutting. I could feel their judgment before Celestia even began. *They are going to compare her to Tessa.*

She stepped into position, her grip on the staff trembling ever so slightly. She swung it once, a basic strike, and then another. Her movements were slow, unpolished, like someone who had been forced to practice but never believed she'd need to perform.

The Lords and Ladies didn't bother hiding their snickers. One woman leaned toward her companion, whispering behind a feathered fan. I clenched my fists, nails biting into my palms.

Then, it happened.

As Celestia attempted a spin, the staff slipped from her grip and clattered to the ground. The sound rang through the dome, louder than it had any right to be. Celestia froze, her cheeks burning red, her hands fluttering helplessly at her sides.

The murmurs turned into stifled laughs. One of the lords chuckled outright, and even Tristan's lips twitched as if suppressing amusement. Gray didn't laugh, but his dark gaze shifted as he leaned back in his chair.

I can't stand this.

Celestia bent to retrieve the staff, her fingers fumbling as she tried to pick it up. Her shoulders trembled, and I could see the tears she was desperately trying to hold back.

Before I could think better of it, I stepped out of line. The court official sputtered in protest, but I didn't stop. My boots echoed loudly as I crossed the arena to her side.

"Keira!" she hissed under her breath, her eyes wide with panic. "What are you doing?"

"Helping," I whispered back. I crouched down, picking up the staff and handing it to her. "Take a deep breath. You can finish this."

She looked at me, her brown eyes swimming with unshed tears, and nodded shakily. Together, we straightened up, and I stepped back just enough to give her the space she needed.

The murmurs in the audience grew louder, and I could feel the weight of the King's glare. But I didn't care. Let them whisper. Let them judge. Celestia was my friend, and I wouldn't leave her to face this alone.

Celestia adjusted her grip on the staff, took a deep breath, and raised her chin. This time, when she moved, her strikes were stronger, her footing more stable. It wasn't perfect, but it was enough to finish without further mishap.

When she finally bowed and retreated to the line, I followed, ignoring the court official's disapproving glare. Celestia's hand brushed mine as we returned to our places, a silent thank-you passing between us.

The King's voice cut through the tension like a blade. "Do not expect such mercy in the future, Princess Keira."

I lowered my gaze, my heart pounding, but I didn't regret my choice.

Chapter 15

Keira

The air in the room was thick with tension after my interference. The King's warning still echoed in my ears, but I forced myself to straighten my spine, ignoring the whispers swirling around me like a storm.

I could feel the weight of Gray's and Tristan's gazes as I took my place in the line, though I refused to meet their eyes. My fingers itched under my gloves, the heat from the ring on my thumb now a steady pulse, a reminder of something I couldn't yet name.

The performances continued, but the mood had shifted. The girls ahead of me whispered nervously, their confidence shaken after Celestia's stumble and my defiance. I tried to focus on the trials, but my thoughts were scattered, darting between the King's dark expression and the glint in Gray's eyes.

When the last name was called, the court official rolled up his scroll and stepped back, his movements crisp and rehearsed. The King rose, his presence commanding even in silence.

"You have all demonstrated your skills, such as they are," he said, his voice cutting through the room like a blade. "But one performance is not enough to determine your worth. The next trial will begin tomorrow morning. Rest well—if you can." He states with a sly smirk.

The Lords and Ladies murmured among themselves as the King turned, his cloak sweeping behind him. Tristan and Gray followed, their expressions starkly different as day and night.

As they passed, Tristan's gaze lands on me. "Impressive show, Princess," he murmured, just loud enough for me to hear.

I stiffened. Before I could respond, he was gone, striding after the King with his usual air of confidence.

Gray, however, lingered for a fraction of a second longer. His onyx eyes locked onto mine, stirring something unnerving in my chest. Then, without a word, he turned and disappeared into the shadows.

That evening, Celestia and I retreated to my quarters. A fire crackled in the hearth, but the warmth did little to ease the chill in my bones.

"You shouldn't have helped me," Celestia said quietly as she sat on the edge of my bed, her hands twisting in her lap.

I look at her, startled by the tremor in her voice. "Of course I should have. What kind of friend would I be if I didn't?"

Her hazel eyes met mine, filled with a mixture of gratitude and fear. "You don't understand, Keira. The King—he doesn't forget. And Tristan..." She trailed off, biting her lip.

"What about Tristan?" I asked, my voice more breathless than I intended.

She hesitated, glancing toward the door as if expecting someone to burst in. "He's not as charming as he seems," she said finally, her voice barely above a whisper. "he'll follow anything and everything the King says..."

I frowned, the weight of her words settling over me like a shadow. "I'm not afraid of Tristan or the King."

"Maybe you should be." Her eyes searched my face. She must have known I was going to argue because she stood up and strolled out of my room before I could start.

The night was restless. I lay awake, staring at the ceiling, the events of the day replaying in my mind. The King's warning. Tristan's smirk. Gray's silence.

And the ring on my thumb, still warm against my skin.

When sleep finally claimed me, it was filled with fragmented dreams of obsidian thrones, shadowy figures, and a voice whispering my name.

Keira.

Chapter 16

Keira

The morning arrived too soon, the echo of the King's words still rattling around my brain. I could feel the weight of it, a silent pressure in the back of my head, almost as if the entire Kingdom was watching. The trials had only just begun, and already they felt like an endless storm.

Celestia and I made our way to the courtyard where the second trial would take place. The path ahead seemed even more daunting than the first, with every step feeling like a test in itself. I could hear the murmur of voices behind me, the weight of gazes following my every movement.

When we reached the trial grounds, I saw the familiar faces of the other girls, but none of them met my eyes—not after yesterday. Tessa stood near the front, her posture poised and confident as always. Her eyes darted to me for a brief moment, a small knowing smile split across her face. She knew she was ahead in whatever twisted game we're playing.

The King stood at the center, flanked by Tristan and Gray. Their presence was enough to silence the crowd, as everyone turned their attention to the three of them. The air felt thick with anticipation.

"This next trial will test your ability to lead," the King's voice rang out, his tone cold and commanding. "You will each be assigned a group of soldiers and given a mission to complete. You must use your wits, your strength, and your leadership to guide them. Fail, and you will be marked."

I couldn't stop my heart from racing at the thought of leading anyone. I wasn't ready for this.

I turned to Celestia, but she looked just as uncertain. She wasn't a leader by nature, and I knew she was only here because she was loyal; loyal to the Kingdom. Loyal to a crown that didn't care for her or any of us.

"Just follow my lead," I told her, though my own voice shook.

The trial began, and I was thrust into the role of a commander without so much as a moment to prepare. The soldiers, dressed in their ceremonial armor, stood at attention before me, waiting for my orders. My throat went dry as I tried to remember the strategies I'd learned in my lessons.

I can do this.

But as I began to speak, my thoughts kept drifting back to the trial yesterday—Tristan's smirk, Gray's piercing gaze, the weight of the ring on my thumb. The ring that seemed to burn hotter with each thought of Gray.

"Focus, Keira," I muttered to myself.

I gave my orders, trying to ignore the shaky feeling in my chest. Tessa, of course, moved with grace and confidence, her voice commanding as she directed her own soldiers. It wasn't just her skill that made her dangerous, it was the ease with which she navigated everything. Her confidence is her weapon.

Gray's voice broke through my concentration, a teasing comment drifting on the wind. "Careful, Little Flame," he said, loud enough for me to hear. "You don't want to lose focus now."

I clench my jaw but say nothing. He always pushes me to my limits.

I could feel Tristan's eyes on me, too. He didn't speak, but his presence was there—undeniable and steady. Surprisingly, it's Gray who taunts me this time. He seems to normally save that field for Tristan.

Suddenly, I snap back to reality, remembering the task at hand, the tension rising as I gave orders and maneuvered the soldiers across the field. Each move felt like a gamble, but somehow, I made it work. I wasn't sure how, but I did. I couldn't let myself fail. *Fight or flight had kicked in.*

As the final horn sounded, signaling the end of the trial, I stood there, heart racing. I couldn't tell if I had done well or not, but I had survived. That was the only thing that mattered right now.

The King stepped forward, stone-faced as ever. "You have all completed the trial," he said, his voice holding the weight of his judgment. "But remember, the Midnight Masquerade is only two days away. Prepare yourselves."

The words hung in the air, heavy and final.

Tristan and Gray both stepped forward, Tristan's eyes met mine, and nervously, I glanced away. Unfortunately for me, that glance happened to land on Gray. His expression is blank, but there was something else beneath that stone mask of his—a challenge, perhaps.

Tristan, however, was all smiles as he moved toward me. "Well done, Princess," he said softly, his voice like silk. "I'm impressed."

I didn't even have to force my smile as I said. "Thank you, Tristan." My voice, barely a whisper.

His green eyes softened before he turned away, striding past me with Gray close behind. As the two brothers walked away, I felt a warmth settle in my bones.

Celestia caught my eye and gave me a small smile. "You did well," she said softly.

"I'm not sure it was enough," I replied, my gaze still lingering on the future King and his future Blade.

Chapter 17

Keira

The promise of another trial continues hanging over me like a cloud. The tension in the air was tangible, a sharp contrast to the softer murmurs of last night. Today's challenge seemed simple on the surface—display your magic.

Except I didn't have any magic.

I glanced at my black lace gloves, the ruby embedded on the wrist pulsing faintly atop my skin. The Enchantress had told me not to fight it. But what did that even mean? As far as I'm aware, I wasn't fighting. Still, something in the gloves made me hesitate, as if they held a secret that I wasn't yet ready to know.

The girls ahead of me were already warming up. Celestia conjured a gust of wind that swept through the dome, making her hair flutter like a curtain. Tessa summoned a ball of light that danced in her hand, swirling through her fingers.

Then my name was called. The official's voice rang through the room, and I couldn't suppress the tension in my shoulders. I walked forward, my gloves feeling heavier with each step. My palms began to sweat beneath the lace, and I clenched my fingers at my sides.

"What will you show us, Princess Keira?" the official asked, his tone polite but probing. His gaze flickered to my hands, expecting something. Anything.

I swallowed hard and opened my mouth to say something that would excuse me from this trial, but no words came. The room was silent, the court's eyes on me, waiting.

I lifted my hands, unsure of what to do. I didn't want to disappoint anyone, but I also didn't want to pretend I had powers I didn't possess.

That's one quick way to get out of this place.

The ruby on my gloves began to warm, and I felt a sudden surge in the air around me—something strange, like a flash of heat.

The girls behind me whispered, and I could feel Gray's eyes burning into my side. He always had that smug confidence, the kind that made everything he did seem effortless. But today, I didn't want to feel his eyes on me. I didn't want to do anything that would draw attention.

But the warmth in my hands grew, and I had no choice but to react. I held them out in front of me, palm up, trying to remain calm. The ruby on my gloves flared, and a small flame flickered to life on the tips of my fingers. It was no bigger than a candle's flame, barely enough to be seen in the bright room, but it was there.

A gasp rippled through the room.

"Impossible," someone muttered.

I didn't know what to do. The flame sputtered for a moment, and I quickly clenched my fists, smothering it before it could grow.

But it was too late. The room had already seen it.

Gray chuckled from his spot in the back, his dark eyes glinting with that same cocky amusement I hated but—if I was being honest—kind of craved.

"Seems like Princess Keira has a little fire in her after all," he whispered next to me, his voice laced with teasing mockery.

I bit my lip, trying to keep my composure. "It's nothing," I said quickly, turning away from the crowd to avoid their eyes.

But Tristan's voice followed me, gentle and soothing, as if trying to lift the weight of the moment. "Impressive, Princess," he said, his smile soft and warm. "You have something rare."

It was then that I realized how different they were— Gray with his unshakable confidence and Tristan with his easy charm. Both of them were looking at me, but with such different expressions.

I glanced down at my hands. The warmth had faded, and the gloves now felt oddly heavy against my skin. I took a deep breath, heart racing as I wondered what had just happened. Was that really me? Or had the gloves done something to me?

Gray's voice interrupted my thoughts again. "Not bad, Little Flame. But don't get too comfortable. You might have something—" He paused with a mischievous smirk, "But you'll have to work harder to keep up."

The teasing tone in his voice made me go cold. I wanted to snap back at him, but the words died in my throat. Tristan's approving glance made me pause, the soft look in his eyes making my chest tighten.

I couldn't even explain what had just happened. It wasn't like the others' magic—it wasn't controlled or elegant. It was more like something deep inside of me had started to stir, something raw and untamed. Something *reckless.*

"Next!" the official called, and I quickly stepped back, away from the center of the room. The heat from my gloves still lingered on my skin, like a ghost.

Celestia was next. She summoned her wind once more, this time more powerful than before, swirling it into a neat vortex around her. But my mind was elsewhere. My thoughts were still on the flame that had flickered to life, on what I may have just unlocked, and whether I'm ready for it or not.

Chapter 18

Keira

All the sleepless nights seemed to have caught up to me because once I was back in my chambers, I flopped onto my bed, day clothes and all. Maeve knew something was off. I could see it on her face. But I was grateful for the fact that she didn't push.

It was almost sunset by the time I finished soaking in my black marble tub. Maeve set out a lovely night slip, pale blue with cream lacing. She has started to give me more colorful options lately.

After getting dressed and finding matching slippers, the tiredness left my eyes. I sent Maeve away for the night because she deserves some time to herself. With that though in mind, I don't have anyone to stop me from sneaking away to the gardens.

I barely made a sound as I crept my way through the castle. I was praying to the Stars that there weren't any guards on watch. Pausing in front of the double door, with only the faint torchlight to illuminate the silver swirls, I cracked open the door, enough to get a numbing breeze.

The air outside was crisp, the scent of roses and night-blooming jasmine wafting through the gardens. The moonlight cast a silvery glow over the neatly trimmed hedges, and the delicate petals of flowers swayed in the soft breeze. I let out a breath I hadn't realized I'd been holding.

This place was beautiful, a stark contrast to the suffocating tension of the trials and the whispers of court politics. Here, I could breathe.

I wandered aimlessly, letting my fingers trail over the cool stone edge of the fountain at the garden's center. The water shimmered under the moonlight, reflecting the stars above. It was peaceful, almost enough to make me forget the weight of everything waiting for me inside those castle walls.

"Couldn't sleep, Princess?"

The voice startled me, and I spun around, my heart leaping into my throat. Tristan stood at the edge of the clearing, his grey blonde hair glinting faintly under the moonlight. He was still dressed in his formal clothes, though his jacket was unbuttoned, giving him a relaxed, almost disheveled look.

"What are you doing out here, at this hour?" I asked, keeping my voice low.

He smiled, a soft, charming curve of his lips, and for some strange reason, I find myself looking for a pair of dimples. "I could ask you the same thing."

I crossed my arms, trying to steady my nerves. "The garden's big enough for both of us, I suppose."

He laughed quietly and stepped closer, his boots crunching softly against the gravel path. "Fair enough. But I didn't take you for someone who'd sneak out of her room."

"There's a lot you don't know about me," I replied, lifting my chin.

"Hmm," he mused, stopping a few steps away from me. "I'd like to change that."

His green eyes locked onto mine, and for a moment, I couldn't look away. There was something about the way he looked at me—curiosity, warmth, and a hint of something I couldn't quite place. Something about his gaze had my mind screaming *DANGER.*

I turned my gaze back to the fountain, my fingers brushing the cool stone edge. "It's quiet here. Peaceful. I needed a break from... everything."

"The trials," he said, his voice softening.

I nodded, though I didn't say anything. The trials were only *part* of it. The court, the whispers, the expectations— it all felt like too much.

Shows just how much being a Princess suits me.

Tristan moved to stand beside me, his arm brushing mine as he leaned against the fountain. "You did well today."

I gave him a sidelong glance. "I'm not even sure what I did."

"You don't have to," he said, his smile faint but genuine. "Sometimes it's not about what you show but the way you carry yourself. You surprised everyone."

I wasn't sure if that was meant to be a compliment or just another veiled reminder of how out of place I was in this competition. Either way, I didn't respond.

The silence stretched between us, not quite awkward but not entirely comfortable either. The sound of the water trickling in the fountain filled the space, a soft, soothing melody.

"You know," Tristan said after a moment, "the garden has always been my favorite part of the castle. It's the only place that doesn't feel... heavy."

I glanced at him, surprised by his candor. "Heavy?"

He shrugged, his gaze distant. "When you grow up with so many expectations, so many people waiting for you to make a mistake... it gets heavy."

For the first time, I saw a crack in his perfect, charming facade, a hint of vulnerability he usually kept hidden behind his easy smiles and clever words.

"I know the feeling," I mutter.

He turned to look at me, his green eyes studying my face. "Do you?"

I nodded. "Maybe not in the same way, but yes."

For a moment, the weight of everything seemed to lift. He reached out, his fingers brushing a stray strand of hair from my face. "You're different from the others, Keira. That's why you stand out."

His words sent a strange warmth through me, but before I could respond, the sound of footsteps echoed in the distance.

Tristan straightened, his charming smile returning like a mask slipping back into place. "It seems we've been discovered," he said, his tone light.

I turned, my heart racing, but the footsteps passed by without pause.

When I looked back, Tristan was already walking away, his figure disappearing into the shadows.

"Goodnight, Princess," his voice drifted back to me, soft and teasing.

I stood there for a moment longer, the warmth of his words lingering even after he was gone. Then, I turned back to the fountain, staring at the water and wondering why my chest felt so tight.

Chapter 19

Keira

Today is somewhat of a treat. A much-needed day of rest, leading to a slow morning.

"You have a guest at the door." Maeve is as polite as always; she would probably make a better princess than I.

"Who?" I finished tying on my silk robe as I looked toward the door.

"It's Princess Celestia. She seems rather excited." Maeve's smile beamed.

"I wasn't expecting her..." I look around my room, realizing now that the number of daggers might be concerning.

"I could tell her to come back later." Maeve had already made her way to the door.

"No, wait!" Maybe some company would be nice. "She can come in." Maeve gives a small nod before opening the door to a beaming Celestia.

"Keira! I'm going to spend the day with you! Back home, my ladies and I always had days just for us!" She wrapped me in a warm embrace.

"That sounds amazing!" *I don't have ladies back home, aside from Sia.* Deeming that information unnecessary, I plaster on a smile.

"I know this is our rest day, however, I was thinking we could start designing our gowns for the Midnight Masquerade!" My eyes drop to the handful of papers along with an ink pen in her hand.

"That—that seems fun." I haven't even thought about what I wanted to wear. Part of me hoped Maeve would take care of it.

Celestia clapped her hands in delight, the papers in her grasp rustling. "Oh, it'll be such fun! I brought some sketches from my favorite designer back home. We can use them for inspiration!"

She spreads the papers out across the small table by my window, her excitement infectious. The designs are intricate, each one a masterpiece of embroidery and lace.

Maeve lingers at the door, glancing over with curiosity. "Should I fetch tea?"

"Yes, please," I reply, grateful for the distraction. I'm not used to this— chatter with a friend. But something about Celestia's warmth makes it feel less foreign.

Celestia plops into the chair, tucking a loose strand of hair behind her ear.

"So, tell me, Keira—what's your favorite color? We have to make sure you shine brighter than anyone else at the ball."

The question catches me off guard. It's been so long since anyone asked me something so... normal. I glance at the papers, each dress more dazzling than the last. "I suppose... blue?" I say hesitantly, thinking of the icy hue of Aetheris winters. Before adding, "However, black seems to be a favorite here."

Her eyes light up. "True! But blue it is. Oh, we'll make you look like a goddess, especially with that hair!"

I let out a small laugh, shaking my head. "I think I'll settle for 'presentable.'"

"Nonsense!" she exclaims, waving her pen dramatically. "We're Princesses. Presentable doesn't cut it."

As she begins sketching with exaggerated flair, I lean back, letting myself enjoy the moment. For the first time in what feels like ages, the weight of my feelings and expectations seems to fade, replaced by laughter and the scratch of a pen on paper.

Chapter 20

Keira

Yesterday was a surprisingly fun 'girls day' as Celestia had called it. We both managed to design all of our possible gowns for the masquerade. I've actually started to like the idea of the masquerade.

As long as I don't run into Gray.

It's gotten a little easier to forget he lied, especially when Tristan has been so warm. Maybe a small part of me wouldn't mind being his Queen.

That part of me is stupid.

Today is the last day of trials before the masquerade. Maeve set out a modest gown, apparently, they are testing our etiquette. The dress she picked makes a perfect impression. A beautiful shade of midnight blue with a neckline that only exposes my collarbone and a full skirt, tiered with layers. I decided to leave behind the gloves since the dress has lace sleeves weaved with gold beads. Maeve pulled dazzling gold shoes to tie in with the beads on the gown.

"You look like a future Queen." Maeve is always nothing but smiles. Today is no different.

"All thanks to you, I would have never found such a beautiful dress." I give the skirt a little twirl.

"Do you have an idea as to what you would like me to do with your hair?" She gazes at the messy braid on my shoulder.

"I was thinking of wearing it down." I haven't worn my hair down in what feels like forever. I'm not sure why; it just hasn't felt right.

"Excellent idea!" Maeve guides me to the vanity to take out my braid and brush through my tangled hair. She takes her time with each strand of hair as she curls it around a hot wand.

When she's done, white blonde waves cascade down to my waist.

"I love it!" I catch Maeve in a hug, and she seems taken aback.

"I'm so glad." Her eyes are glassy, but her face is warm and smiley. "Now you might want to head to the dome before you run late." She waves a hand in the direction of the door. I give her my best smile before turning in a swirl of midnight blue and gold towards the door.

Once out of my room, I can feel the chill of the palace. My room was warm from the fire, always ablaze, but there was merely torchlight in the halls. I square my shoulders and sway towards the dome as I try to remember what my etiquette teacher taught me.

Too soon, I am standing in front of the dome, now filled with tables covered in cloth and fine dishware. *They plan to serve us lunch?* I immediately spot Celestia with her gleaming smile. I make my way to her and take the chair next to her. Her dress isn't as full as mine, but it is a bright shade of sunflower covered in glossy beads.

"I can't contain my nerves, even though I am excited, this is the last trial." Her eyes dart around the room, most likely looking for Tristan.

"I feel the same. At least we have breathtaking gowns for the masquerade." I genuinely am excited for the dresses. "How many days will the Midnight Masquerade last?" I wasn't too sure. The Queen brought me here and left the next day.

"I believe it's just one night, giving us the day to get fancy!" Finally, her eyes land on me.

"Your hair, it's different." She carefully takes a strand of my white hair into her fingers.

"Thank you—"

King Lusican walks in with Tristan in tow, cutting me off. I try not to let my gaze linger, but he makes it very difficult. He wears an ash grey tunic with black embroidery on the collar. As well as matching trousers and a gold-encrusted sword slung low on his right hip. Both of them take their seats on their thrones. I didn't even notice Gray until he took his spot next to the King. He was wearing all black, even his sword is bejeweled with onyx stones.

"Welcome, ladies, to your last trial. This final trial will determine whether or not the court deems you fit for my son. The Midnight Masquerade is simply Tristan getting his pick of the litter." The way he said *litter* causes my stomach to clench. His face is neutral but his tone suggests more, snapping me out of whatever illusions I thought this morning.

"With that being said, please enjoy this lunch, for it's just the beginning." His eyes sweep over all fifteen of us, no doubt landing on his favorites, *including me.* I avert my eyes as his cryptic words linger in my head. Don't we just get to go home if we aren't chosen? I don't get the chance to formulate anything before servants bring out monstrous amounts of food. Setting everything gently on the table where we sit. Celestia wiggles beside me as we all begin to dish out food.

Chapter 21

Keira

I mindfully portion out my serving, scooping braised boar with a honey spice glaze on my plate, along with black bread, charred root vegetables, and aged cheese. This food is the most colorful thing in the palace, other than us. I glance at Celestia's plate. She has far less food and no animal meat. My eyes dart to the others at our table. *Their plates have practically no food.* Either they aren't hungry, or I have apparently eaten with my eyes. I straighten my spine, raising my head ever so slightly. With all the grace I can muster I place a cloth on my lap and begin to pick at my plate with my fork and knife.

We engage in polite, quiet conversation as we finish our plates. I dare a glance at Tristan and catch him whispering to the King. Unintentionally, my gaze travels to Gray, and he's as uninterested as always, picking at an invisible fur on his doublet. I may have stared a bit too long because Celestia nudged my arm.

"Already daydreaming about what the wedding would look like?" She asks with a calculated smile, something I haven't seen on her before.

"Oh...well, I was just wondering which of us he favors." Not my finest cover-up, but Stars be damned before I admit I was gazing at the wrong brother. Celestia just nods.

The servants come to clear the dishware as a royal announcer steps forward.

"Ladies, we have provided eligible Lords for you to dance with as we finish the extravagance of today. Think of it as a sort of practice for tomorrow night's festivities." The room fills with delightful noises as we rise from our chairs and make our way to the gentlemen in a row on the floor. *Now I get why Maeve picked such a gown.*

We wait for the Lords to take their pick, each of them striding towards the first girl they see. My eyes happen to land on a golden-haired boy with a devious smile. He gently places a hand on my waist as he guides us into a waltz. Lord Adrian Hale, an important Lord in House Hale, he is taller than me and carried himself with easy confidence.

"You look breathtaking, Princess." His words are whispered against my ear, sending a warm shiver down my spine. I forced a polite smile. He was smooth, too smooth. The kind of charm and flattery that had other ladies wrapped around his finger. His steps were practiced and calculated, more political than intimate, lacking the depth of someone truly invested.

"A kind compliment, my Lord," I reply with a neutral tone.

"Only the truth," He says as he sweeps me into an unexpected twirl. "Tell me, do I have any chance of getting a second dance? Perhaps at the Masquerade?"

"That isn't up to me, I suppose." I force my eyes to widen in mock innocence. It is nice to be desired, even if it's not from the right person. Adrian chuckled.

"Then I shall savor every second." His eyes don't fully convince me of his words.

The rest of the dance was pleasant but impersonal, filled with well-rehearsed charm and shallow flirtation. He moved well, but he never felt close; his touch never lingered, his words never truly sinking in. A man used to winning attention, not holding it. And then, just as the final note of the song played, another figure stepped forward.

Gray.

The contrast was instant, like stepping from a performance into something real.

"Mind if I steal the Princess away?" Gray's voice was smooth, but there was an edge beneath it, a challenge unspoken.

Adrian released my hand with an exaggerated sigh. "A shame. But I suppose I can't compete with a prince or, in this case, the future Blade." He winked at me. "Perhaps another time, Princess."

In your dreams.

And just like that, I was in Gray's arms, his grip firm, his presence far more tangible than the empty charm of Lord Adrian.

"Enjoying the attention, Princess?" he murmured, his voice low.

I lift my chin, refusing to let him rattle me. "Should I not?"

His dark eyes flickered. "He seemed... eager."

I arched a brow. "Jealous, Your *Highness*?"

Gray let out a quiet chuckle, but there was no humor in it. "Hardly. Just amused."

We moved in perfect rhythm, each step precise and effortless. He was a skilled dancer, though something about the way he led felt different from Adrian's polished grace; less about performance, more about control. It was surprisingly natural as if we had done this a hundred times before.

My mind drifted back to the first time I had met him, not as Prince Grayson, future Blade of Eclipsar, but as a mere messenger.

"You lied to me," I hiss, keeping my voice quiet enough that only he could hear.

His fingers tensed slightly against my waist, but his expression didn't falter. "Did I?"

"You did," I insist, eyes locked onto his. "You let me believe you were nothing more than a messenger. That day in the gardens—"

"I never said I wasn't more," he interrupted smoothly.

I exhaled sharply. "You didn't correct me, either."

A slow smirk formed at the corner of his lips. "Would it have changed anything?"

My next step was sharper than necessary, the pointed tip of my shoe barely missing his. Gray only tightened his hold on me, ensuring I couldn't pull away.

"It would have," I start. "I wouldn't have—." I trail off.

Wouldn't have what? Trusted him, even for a moment? Let myself be drawn into a conversation with him under the warm sun, where he had been nothing but sharp wit and quiet intrigue?

He tilted his head slightly, watching me struggle for words. "You wouldn't have what, Little Flame?"

"I wouldn't have wasted my time on you."

Something flashed across his face, but it was gone in an instant. He exhaled softly, the smirk returning. "And yet, here we are."

I hate that he is right.

Before I could respond, a shadow loomed over me *again*.

"Mind if I steal her away?"

Great, the other brother.

The air shifted, thick with something unspoken.

Gray's hand tightened ever so slightly at my waist before he stepped back, his stone facade cracking just a little.

I barely had a moment to react before Tristan's hand replaced his, and the waltz continued—though the game had entirely changed.

Chapter 22

Keira

Tristan's hand found mine.

His grip was firm, almost possessive. He pulled me into the next movement without hesitation, his steps sharp. Where Gray's presence had almost felt as effortless as breathing, Tristan's was entirely different. Calculated. Commanding.

"You looked rather... cozy with my dear brother," he says, his green eyes gleaming as he spun me.

I forced a neutral expression. "We were dancing. Is that not what I was instructed to do?"

His fingers pressed slightly against my waist as he spun me into another turn. "Dancing, yes. But you were also arguing." He guesses with a slow curve of his lips.

I nearly missed a step. *Was he paying that much attention to us?*

Tristan noticed.

His smirk widened. "Ah. So you *were* arguing." I hate how good he is at reading me—I can't possibly be that much of an open book.

I swallowed back the irritation clawing at my throat. "And what? You were just content to watch us like some stalker?"

He chuckled. "I know everything that happens in this castle, Princess."

There was something unsettling about the way he said it, like he wasn't just talking about that day, but about me in general, as if I were a piece on his board, a game he was already winning. Gone was his charm, and in its place was a much more calculated Prince.

I lifted my chin, refusing to give him the satisfaction of me second-guessing myself. "Then I suppose you also know that your brother is a liar."

Tristan hummed thoughtfully. "A liar? Perhaps. Or maybe just someone who plays his cards close." He pauses, eying me. "Much like you." I stiffened, but Tristan only smiled, pulling me closer as the music swelled.

The room around us blurred, the golden candlelight reflecting off polished floors and swirling silk. I was hyper-aware of how close he was, the way his grip never faltered. Unlike Adrian's empty flirtation or Gray's effortlessness, Tristan's touch felt like something else entirely. *A claim.*

He leaned in, his breath brushing against my ear. "Tell me, Keira… do you trust him?"

My stomach knots.

I knew what he was doing. Twisting words, planting doubt. And yet, the question burrowed beneath my skin, sinking deep.

Did I?

Before I could answer, the final notes of the waltz rang out, and Tristan slowed, his hold lingering for just a second too long before he released me.

His smirk never wavered. "Something to think about."

And just like that, he was gone, disappearing into the crowd, leaving me standing there, flushed, furious, and far more uncertain than I cared to admit.

I managed to find Celestia after the dancing had finished. She, too, had danced with Lord Adrian, and apparently, I was the only one 'graced' by dancing with both princes. Tessa danced with Gray, which sent a pang of something I don't want to think about through me. Celestia also would not stop talking about how she danced with Prince Tristan. I danced with him, too, but I was not head over heels for him. *At least, I don't think so.* Celestia and I parted ways after she finished telling me about Tristan's flirtatious emerald eyes.

"How was it?" Maeve is more than excited to hear about the pre-ball as she sets out my sleep clothes.

"It wasn't so bad at first; I danced with Lord Adrian then-" Her eyes lit up with pure excitement. Or perhaps it was concern?

"Gray *and* Tristan." I finished.

"Both? In that order?" Maeve seems over the moon.

"Not by choice, but yes, both in that order." I pull on the silk ruby red night slip Maeve laid out.

"Well, I am not surprised Prince Grayson danced with you, but I am surprised about Prince Tristan." Her gaze seems to wander.

"Ouch." I threw a pillow in her direction.

"I didn't mean it like that—" Her face goes red. "All I am saying is the maids talk," Her eyes fall back on me with color from her face going to her neck. "We see the way he looks at you."

"I think you better start praying to the Stars for better eyes." Against my better judgment, warmth settles in my chest.

"If you say so," She pushes up from her stool. "It's getting pretty late, and I wouldn't want to have to cover up dark patches under your eyes tomorrow." She flashes a warm smile and strolls out.

I sink into my bed made of black silk sheets. I finally let my limbs relax. As my eyes drift shut, everything from the ball plays over and over in my mind as I sink further into sleep.

Chapter 23

Keira

Drifting in and out of sleep, somewhere between the haze of a restless night and the soft whispers of the wind outside my window, the memories of the ball still lingered in my mind: Gray's hands, Tristan's words. They were pieces of a night I couldn't fully forget, no matter how hard I tried.

A knock pulled me from the daze, soft but persistent.

I froze, eyes wide in the darkness. The sound was at the balcony door, faint but definitely there. My breath caught in my chest, the quiet of the night suddenly deafening. Seeing the moonlight casting streaks of light around my room, etiquette would say it's too late for visitors. However, I've always been one for scandal. Another knock, this time a little louder, more deliberate.

My pulse quickened. For a moment, I stayed still, debating whether I had imagined it. But I knew I hadn't. My heart pounded harder now, curiosity blooming with it. Was it Tristan? It had to be. Who else would risk being caught at this hour? He also wouldn't get much punishment if he were caught.

I slipped out of bed, my bare feet making no sound as I crossed the room. The air was cold against my skin, but it wasn't the chill of the night that sent a shiver down my spine. It was the anticipation crackling in the space between my racing heartbeats.

I reached the door, my hand trembling ever so slightly as I slid it open.

My mind and body temporarily froze at the sight before me.

Gray stood there as if he hadn't just woke me in the dead of night. His black curls were tousled, and his dark eyes locked onto mine with an intensity that made my breath catch.

"Little Flame," he murmured, his voice low and unmistakable in the quiet of the night. "Still awake?"

I swallowed hard; my thoughts scrambled. "What are you doing here?" I couldn't mask the bite in my voice, but something inside me—something I couldn't quite name—kept me from slamming the door in his face.

"Come with me," he said simply, his gaze steady. "No questions. Just trust me."

I wasn't sure why I didn't tell him to leave. Maybe it was the way he asked or the rawness in his eyes, but I found myself stepping closer to him, my heartbeat pounding in my ears.

His fingers brushed mine, sending an unexpected jolt through me. It was a light touch, but it felt like fire, like an unspoken promise wrapped in a question I wasn't ready to answer.

"I don't have time for questions," he continued, his voice dropping even lower, the tension between us tangible. "We have to leave now. I can't explain, not here. But I need you to trust me."

My chest tightened as I glanced back at my room. The safety of the walls, the vulnerability of my situation—it all hit me at that moment. I could tell him no. I could lock the door and walk away. But something told me I wouldn't— that I couldn't.

And before I could second-guess myself, I nodded.

"Okay," I whispered, the word barely escaping my lips.

Without another word, Gray stepped into my room. His hand still holding mine as he led me out of my room into the shadowy halls of the palace. The soft click of the door behind us was like the sound of a cage closing.

Chapter 24

Keira

He didn't say another word as he led me through the castle, past dark hallways and quiet corners, until we reached the outer grounds. The night air was cold against my skin, the moonlight covered by tall tree tops.

Where was he taking me?

We walked in silence, the only sound being the soft crunch of leaves under our feet. My heart was pounding in my chest. I wanted to ask him a thousand questions, but I didn't dare disrupt the silence.

Finally, after what felt like forever, Gray stopped. We were in front of a small, forgotten stone ruin, barely visible under the overgrown vines and trees. The place looked ancient as if it had been here long before either of us had been born. I felt a strange pull in my chest, a sense that I'd seen this place before, even though I knew I hadn't.

The Hollows, the Enchantress's ruins.

"This is where I wanted to bring you," Gray said quietly, his voice low, almost like he was afraid of being heard. "It's important."

I stared at the crumbling stone walls, the weight of his words settling in my chest. Something about the place felt wrong, like a secret that had been buried for centuries. I could feel it in the air, the tension, the ancient power that seemed to hum beneath the surface.

"Why here?" I asked, my voice barely a whisper.

Gray took a deep breath and glanced around as if making sure no one else was around. He stepped closer, his gaze locked on mine, and for a moment, I saw something in his eyes that I hadn't expected—hesitation.

"This place… it's tied to you, Little Flame," he said, his words slow and deliberate. "And the prophecy."

I froze. *The prophecy.* The one I had heard whispers about, the one my mother had told her First Lady about. "What do you mean?"

He looked away, his jaw clenched, and I could see the struggle on his face. "When the moons align, and shadows bind the sun… the Daughter of Flame and Frost is the one who can either fix or destroy it all." His voice was soft, almost like he was afraid to say the words aloud. "Suspicion has been going around that *you're* the Daughter of Flame and Frost."

I feel as if I can't breathe. The prophecy? It can't be real. Could it?

No.

It's just a bedtime story parents tell their children. A story engraved in stones simply to entertain.

"I don't have magic." My voice was far more breathless than I hoped.

Gray turned back to me, his gaze intense. "This is why I brought you here. You need to know what's coming."

I was at a loss for words. The weight of his words pressed down on me, heavy and suffocating. I wasn't ready for this. I didn't want to be the one they talked about in whispers. But I was here in this place, and it felt like the first step in something I couldn't undo.

The silence between us stretched on as I tried to wrap my head around everything Gray had just told me. Then I remember who I'm talking to.

"All you've done since we've met is lie to me. Why should I believe you? Perhaps you're jealous that Tristan has shown interest in me?" That last question got his attention, and I swear I saw his jaw tighten.

"I'm simply following orders." His voice comes out sharp, like a knife slicing my skin. He steps back, putting some space between us.

Of course, how could I have been so stupid? Gray doesn't care about me, let alone be jealous of his brother.

"Right, my mistake. Now that I'm here, you can leave." I turn away from him to face the ruins. I feel his gaze on the back of my head, forgetting I am only in a night slip. The embarrassment chasing away the cold of the night.

"As you wish, Little Flame." I whip around to scream at him and his stupid nickname, but I'm met with emptiness. *He vanished. Typical.*

Turning back to the ruins, I take in their full beauty. The odd shapes of the stones, the strange symbols that marked them. One with a flame, one with a star, one with a crescent moon, and one with a gust of wind—or maybe it was a shadow? I enter the circle of ruins and eye the stone bowl in the middle. I run my fingers over the closest ruin—with the fire symbol. It's warm to the touch until...it starts glowing.

A fire comes to life in the bowl at the center. I take a glance around, checking for anyone, realizing I'm completely alone. I look to the beautiful full moon without a single glittering star in sight for any sort of comfort. It casts harsh light, making frightening shadows through the forest. I stare at the fire, running my hands around the bowl. Noticing words carved into the side.

"Flame and frost, the line is thin; blood must spill to crown the kin."

As soon as I said it the flames in the bowl started flashing all different colors. Emerald green, sapphire blue, amethyst purple, ruby red, bone white-

"Stick your hand in the flames." The voice is so silky I could have imagined it until I turn to my left and see the Enchantress perched atop the ruin with the flame.

I think she sees the hesitation on my face and feels the need to add more encouragement.

"It doesn't hurt, I swear on the Stars." She holds a hand up to the starless sky.

"Why should I? I want nothing to do with any of this." I wave my hand in the direction of the bowl, and to my surprise, the flames move with it.

"Because Keira, it's meant for you. And I know deep down that little girl in you wants to be special." She practically floats down from the rock in a swirl of glowing red and sheer fabric, dancing and twirling when her feet hit the ground.

"You're wrong." I raise my chin and urge her and myself to believe it, even though the beautiful flashing colors of the flames say otherwise.

"If you insist, but believe me when I say both paths end in blood. *You* choose whose blood it is." She gives another show of her lanky fingers as she sways out of the circle, the fire dimming ever so slightly.

"Just know, if you give in, you won't be disappointed." She tosses the words over her shoulder before disappearing into the Hollows.

Shaking off her words, I turn back to the dancing flames. *They look so pretty; maybe one touch wouldn't do anything.* I reach out a hand, hovering it over. Just enough to feel the heat of the flames. I glanced around to make sure I'm completely alone this time. Then, before I could think better of it, I plunge my right hand into the mesmerizing flames.

Chapter 25

Keira

As soon as my hand made contact, the colors stopped flashing, almost as if the flames decided ruby red was the perfect color. With my hand swirling in the flames, nothing hurt; a numb feeling washed over me. I mix around the flames a moment longer before bringing my hand out. When the tips of my fingers leave the flame, searing pain shoots up my arm and throughout my body. My knees buckle as I clutch my right arm to my chest. With an ungraceful thud, I tumble to the floor. My eyes feel heavy as they roam over the burn all up my forearm. My heart slows, and my mind stirs. Finally, with the rising sun, I let my eyes fully close, deciding I can get ready for the Masquerade later.

When I open my eyes again everything is awful shades of dull. I'm in a room I've never seen before, still in my night slip. Taking in my surroundings, I notice everything is shades of black and gold like the rest of this Star's forsaken palace, from the huge curtains to the lush bed and the desk covered with books and stationary.

Slipping out of the sheets, almost convinced everything that happened was a dream until I saw the now painless burn, faintly reminding me of the one I got on my chest not too long ago. Except, this one is far more permanent. Quietly making my way to the desk, I notice every single book has to do with the history of Eclipsar *and* Aetheris. I pluck one from the pile and skim through it.

"You're a nosy little Princess, aren't you?" I freeze, embarrassment forming in my stomach. Slowly, I turn to see him standing fresh out of the washroom. With a black towel slung low around his waist and his curls, a darker shade of gray sticking to his forehead.

"What do you want, Tristan?" I try to sound neutral as I keep my eyes firmly on his face and not on—well, anywhere else.

"Excuse me, *you're* the one in *my* room." He gestures around us, clearly amused. My face turns impossibly more pink.

"I woke up here. It's not like I stumbled in here to see you." He finally makes a move to his wardrobe, which is far less royal than I had imagined. This whole room is. *Not that I've been imagining his room.*

"Hey, I wouldn't be mad if you did." He throws a smirk over his shoulder before pulling on a light gray doublet.

I roll my eyes and turn back to the desk as he reaches for a pair of black trousers, trying—*desperately*—to focus on the book in my hand instead of the Prince getting dressed behind me.

"I'll take that." Before I can react, he plucks the book from my hands.

"I wasn't done with th-" I reach for it, but he smoothly moves it behind his back. Instead of giving it up, he catches my wrist.

"What happened here?" He makes a show of examining my wrist.

"As if I would tell you." I tried to pull my wrist free, but he yanks me closer. Close enough for me to smell the cedarwood and leather soap he used, momentarily forgetting he is the future *King* of Eclipsar.

"Oh, we have all day." His smirk returns, slow and knowing. "Though you *do* seem like you need some time to get ready for the Masquerade." His gaze drifts from my wild hair to the dirt clinging to my ankles.

"I *do*, which is why I should get back to my room." This time, he lets me twist out of his hold. The heat of his touch still lingering on my wrist as I head for the door. Still, one question begs to be asked.

I pause. "Tristan?"

He tilts his head. "Yes, Princess."

"How did I end up in your room?"

His lips curl like he's savoring a private joke. "Who do you think found you half-dead at the edge of the Hollows?"

Before I can process that, there's a knock at the door. I open the door, and a tall boy in all-black training gear stands in front of me.

Gray. Perfect timing.

His sharp eyes dart from me to Tristan, taking in the scene. I don't even have to look to *know* the smirk Tristan's wearing right now.

"I thought you'd want to have a little fun before the Masquerade," Gray says, words light, but his stance isn't. "But I see you're *busy.*"

"Don't worry, little brother." Tristan leans lazily against the desk, utterly at ease. "She was just leaving."

I shot Tristan a glare, and his only response was a wink. I roll my eyes—and *of course*, Gray catches it before I step out and he steps in.

I take in the now-familiar halls of the palace. It's mid-afternoon, but something about the empty corridors makes it obvious everyone is getting ready for tonight.

I reach my room and slip in quietly. As soon as the door shuts, I'm met with a very nervous Maeve. Or was it irritation?

"Where have you been? I was so worried. Were you with someone? Did you leave the palace grounds? Are you alright?" Without a breath, her words tumble out, leaving no room for me to answer.

"Maeve," I pull her into a hug. "I'm fine. I managed to wake up early enough to explore the palace before everyone woke." Lying to her felt wrong but I knew for certain the truth wasn't something I could tell her.

"You could've left a note. I was scared half to death." She looks at me fully, her gaze a softness I fully welcome. Definitely worry.

"You're right. I'm sorry."

"Well, now that you're here, I'll draw you a bath, and you can start getting ready for the Masquerade!" Her cheery voice returns at the mention of the ball.

"A hot bath sounds amazing. Have my dresses arrived?" I glance around the room, still exactly as I left it.

"Yes! I tucked them in your wardrobe. We can pick the perfect one after you wash up. Would you like something to eat while you get ready? I can have a lunch tray prepared."

"I could eat," I missed breakfast so the thought of a hot lunch is enough to make my stomach grumble. "Bring enough for you too; this getting fancy thing seems like a whole lot of work for the both of us."

"Of course, I'll draw your bath and then head to the kitchens!" She quickly heads to the washroom.

"Thank you!" I call after her. She comes out moments later.

"The water is extremely hot, so maybe wait before getting in, and I set your towel on the stool. I'll go grab lunch now!" She practically skips off, humming to herself. I *could* pretend to share her excitement; she seems so happy about it. But I would also be lying to myself if I said I hated the getting ready part.

I make my way to the tub, taking off my night slip and letting it fall to the floor. Maeve was right. The water was hot, but not uncomfortable. I sink into it, allowing the crown of my head to dip under. Reaching for the vanilla-scented soap, I notice for the first time that the burn on my arm has practically faded. *Strange.* All the better, because now I don't have to worry about covering it up tonight.

I soak in the tub until the water cools to room temperature and my hands and feet become creased with wrinkles. I only get out when Maeve comes back with our lunch tray.

"Now, let's get you dressed. Hopefully, you'll spark Prince Tristan's fancy!" She says it so excitedly, so happy to be able to help, even if I do hear tremor when she says the future King's name.

"If he needs a gown and jewels to notice me, he's more blind than I thought."

Chapter 26

Keira

A box nearly as tall as I arrived. It's black velvet with a gold glittery bow. Maeve and I decided to open it after we finished my hair and painted my face. After many different styles, we decided on a loose braid with gold accents woven into it.

"We actually need to pick a dress before I can do anything to your pretty face. I wouldn't want to use blue if you're wearing a green dress." She heads for the wardrobe to retrieve the dresses. Deciding to take that as my opportunity to get up from my vanity seat and examine the box, I slid off the lid to see the most beautiful crimson red dress I have ever seen, with a note.

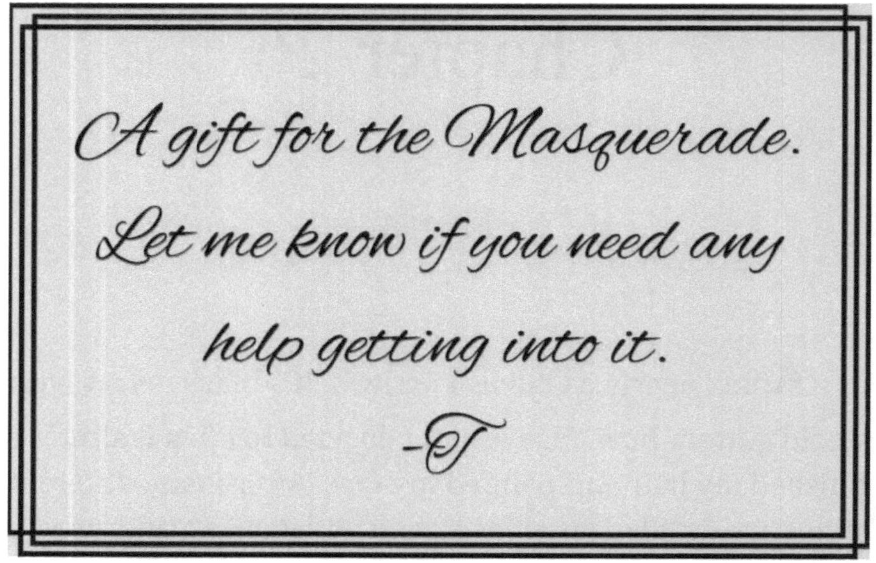

He probably sent dresses to all the girls.

"I grabbed my favorite of the dresses you designed." Maeve comes back with four dresses and drops them all to the floor at the sight of the dress in the box. She lets out a gasp as she reaches for the dress.

"I'm sorry, Keira, but all the dresses you designed are nothing compared to this," That's when she saw the note. "And it's from the future King?! You *have* to wear this dress. Even if it weren't from him, I would make you wear it. I mean, look at it." She held up the top half with a very daring neckline. She was right, it was better than the ones I designed.

"Well, I hope this dress comes with a warning; it may cause excessive amounts of attention and possibly some scandal." Maeve just giggles and guides me back to my stool at the vanity.

"Looks like we're doing red; it will go beautifully with those blue eyes of yours."

It took nearly the rest of the afternoon to finish, between the breaks for eating and mixing colors to get the perfect shade of lip tint. I might actually be late for something that starts at midnight. Maeve finishes with deep red paint for my lips and dusted glitter on my eyes.

"Wow, Maeve...you've outdone yourself." I admire her work in my mirror.

"It's really nothing. Most of the girls I work with are already pretty." She says as she wipes off her hands. "Including you." She smiles.

"Have you ever done any on yourself?" I'm not sure what brought the question up but I saw the way her eyes sparkled as she eyed all of the paints.

"The maids aren't given any supplies for it, so I rarely do." Feeling sympathetic I say, "you are more than welcome to use anything from mine that you would like. I don't favor doing all this every day." I gesture to my face.

"That's very nice of you." She says, some of her giddiness returning hesitantly.

"Now, we have just enough time to get you into that dress and find all the extra pieces to make you really stand out!" Maeve starts doing circles around me, going from the vanity to the wardrobe, then to the dress laid out on my bed. She comes back and dumps hand fulls of jewels and golds next to me.

"Maeve," I catch her by the wrist when the top of the pile reaches about the height of a candle. "I think that's plenty to choose from, and I don't want to be late."

She seems to snap out of her haze.

"Right!" She claps her hands and motions for me to grab the dress.

As soon as the dress is on, it molds completely to my figure. The neckline plunges just enough to be daring with thin off-the-shoulder straps, leaving my collarbones exposed. With a laced-up corset in the back, the fabric around my waist is tight. The bottom starts hanging loosely from the hips down with a slit that starts mid-thigh. There's gold embroidery along the hem resembling swirling flames, which matches the design along the neckline. The silk of the dress exaggerates my moves as I pick my jewels from the pile.

I settled for two gold armcuffs with the same detailing as my dress and a thin gold necklace with a ruby pendant. Maeve convinces me to trade the dagger showing through the slit of the dress with a dainty gold chain. She also brings over gold heels that glitter beautifully. I slide them on and give Maeve a twirl.

"You will *definitely* get Prince Tristan's attention in that, and if not him, then perhaps another prince." She exclaims as if she is dazzled by the dress too. "Wait, it's almost perfect." She starts going around in circles again, looking for something. While she does that, I put the onyx ring on my finger just before she comes back.

"Here—it goes with the dress." She hands me an eye mask on a wooden stick. It looks as if it's on fire, a fire made from rubies.

"Thank you, Maeve, it's perfect, all of it is." I gesture up and down with my mask.

"Well, make sure to thank Prince Tristan for the dress; not all of this was me." She gives me an amused wink as I head for the door.

"Have fun, Keira, and don't forget," She paused to give me a smile. "Be a little bold." And for some reason, I can almost make out a little sadness in her eyes.

Chapter 27

Keira

I'll admit I did get a little lost on my way to the ballroom, but once I reached the doors, I suddenly wanted to be lost all over again. The guards at the doors push them open, revealing a breath-taking ballroom. Black sparkling crystals everywhere with black wax candles in the chandelier. My feet move before my mind.

The sound of the grand staircase beneath my feet echoes through the ballroom as I descend slowly, the weight of everyone's gaze on me like a physical pressure. It feels as if the whole ballroom paused to watch me enter. The dress clings to me like a second skin, the crimson red silk shifting with every step, catching the light just enough to make me feel exposed, scandalous, even. The slit runs dangerously high, the plunging neckline almost too daring.

Curse the Stars, I shouldn't have worn this dress.

I can feel the eyes of the nobles boring into me as I move lower. Their whispers mingle with the haunting music that fills the air, and I can't tell if it's admiration or judgment they're speaking. Either way, it doesn't matter. I didn't come here to please them. Looking around now, I see minimal color. Even the ladies are in shades that range from pale to dull.

Nearly at the bottom of the stairs, the noise in the room seems to die down, leaving only the hum of my heartbeat and the steady clack of my heels.

And then I see him.

Tristan.

He stands there, leaning casually against the balcony, grinning like he knows exactly what I'm about to do as if this whole thing was planned.

His eyes lock on mine the moment I reach the last step, and I see a flash of amusement cross his face, quickly masked by something darker.

"Well, well, Princess," he calls out, his voice smooth and dangerous. The way he says it almost feels like a challenge, the way his eyes roam over me with obvious interest. "I see you decided to wear it after all."

I don't respond at first, my feet moving on their own, drawing closer to him. I feel the dress shift with every movement, the fabric practically whispering against my skin, taunting me.

"Are you trying to start a war tonight?" he adds, his voice dripping with smug satisfaction, the smirk never leaving his lips. "Because you're definitely on your way."

I want to say something cutting, something that will wipe that smirk off his face, but instead, I just raise an eyebrow and take another step forward.

"Or maybe you want to be the one to start it, huh?" His voice lowers, teasing, daring.

His words linger in the air as if he's trying to force me into playing his game. But I'm no fool. I know exactly what he's doing. The dress, the note, the looks, this is all part of his plan.

I push back the flare of heat that rises in my chest, trying to keep my cool, but the tension in the room is suffocating. I turn to walk away from him, a decision that should have been easy. Until I hear it—

"Reckless," Gray's voice cuts through the guests who have turned their conversations elsewhere. I feel a jolt in my stomach. My whole body froze momentarily.

It's like everything slows down as I turn to face him. He's standing in the doorway, his gaze locking onto mine. The way his jaw tightens, the way his fists clench by his sides, tells me how deeply the sight of me in this dress affects him.

I open my mouth to speak, but the words get stuck in my throat. Gray doesn't move at first; he simply watches me with an intensity that sends a shiver through me.

His eyes flick to Tristan, then back to me. There's something about the way he looks at me, protective, possessive, but still guarded, that makes me feel like a piece of porcelain on display.

"I'm not letting you out of my sight tonight," he mutters, the words coming out more like a command than a suggestion.

I want to retort, but there's something about the way Gray holds himself, the way he watches Tristan with barely restrained tension, that silences me.

It seems I'm the one in control, at least for now.

"I'm not a child who needs watching." My mind finally manages to catch up with everything that just happened.

"Listen, Little Flame," He takes a step closer, pulling at my arm. "You-"

"Would you mind letting go of the most beautiful girl in the room? I would like to have a dance with her." A familiar voice says from behind.

"Actually, I-" Gray starts to say something, probably foolish, before I cut him off.

"That would be wonderful." I muster a fake smile before setting my mask down and offering my hand to *Lord Adrian.*

Perhaps I was better off staying with Gray.

Chapter 28

Keira

Gray's grip on my arm tightens for a moment, but then his fingers loosen as I step away, a flash of jealousy crossing his face. He doesn't say anything, but I can feel the weight of his gaze burning into my back as I turn to face Lord Adrian, who stands there with a grin that's both charming and calculating.

Without missing a beat, I place my hand in his, trying to keep the unease at bay. The moment my fingers brush against his, a cold sweat lines my body. He holds my hand with confident ease, his thumb brushing the back of my knuckles.

"You've made the right choice, Princess," Lord Adrian says, his voice smooth and almost teasing. "I don't think you'll regret it."

I bite back a sarcastic remark, not wanting to give him the satisfaction of seeing my discomfort. The last thing I need tonight is more drama and more complications. The tension between Gray and Tristan is enough to send me spiraling, and Adrian, for all his polished charm, isn't much better.

As we glide into the center of the ballroom, I feel the weight of the hundreds of eyes on me, the pressure building in my chest. The soft rhythm of the music pulls us into motion, and for a moment, I allow myself to relax, to forget the chaos.

But then I hear the faintest rustle of footsteps from behind us. No doubt in my mind, it's Gray. I can practically feel his eyes boring into me as he watches us, a mix of protectiveness and frustration hanging in the air. And then there's Tristan, who seems to be watching both of us with a smoldering intensity that makes my skin prickle.

"You seem to be enjoying yourself, Princess," Adrian murmurs, his breath hot against my ear.

I try to ignore it and focus on the movement of my feet, but I can feel the weight of his stare, the way his fingers slide a little too low on my back. I can't help but shift uncomfortably.

"Stop calling me that," I snap, my irritation bubbling to the surface.

Adrian's lips curl into that infuriating, all-knowing smile. *One I normally see on Gray.* "Ah, but it suits you. A princess of fire, still chasing her frost, balancing on the edge of two worlds. It's a dangerous place to be, don't you think?"

I swallow, trying to ignore the unsettling feeling his words bring. I have no idea what he knows or what he thinks he knows; I don't even know what I know. All I can think about is Gray's tension, Tristan's burning gaze, and Adrian's smirk. All of it threatens to drown me in this ballroom of glittering eyes.

I try to meet the pair across from mine, forcing my expression into something neutral. "I'm not interested in your games, Lord Adrian. You can drop the façade."

He raises an eyebrow, his smirk never wavering. "But this isn't a game, Princess. This is simply...the beginning."

Before I can respond, the music shifts, the tempo slowing. Adrian pulls me in closer, his chest brushing against mine as we sway in time. My breath hitches at the closeness, the sheer intensity of his presence.

I glance over his shoulder, only to meet Gray's gaze once more, and this time, it's different. He gives away nothing as he watches me. Nothing except the clench in his jaw, his rigid posture, and the barely contained tension in every line of his body.

Something in me wants to pull away from Adrian and walk back to Gray, but that very same something also holds me in place. Adrian doesn't let go of me, doesn't loosen his hold.

The dance continues, and with it, the quiet war between Tristan, Gray, and Adrian simmers beneath the surface.

Chapter 29

Keira

The music seems to stretch, becoming almost too long and too drawn out as I try to keep my focus. Adrian's hand is still low on my back, and I can feel every inch of his chest pressing against me with each slow step we take. I wish I could pull away, but I can't bring myself to break the dance.

Every once in a while, I catch Gray's eyes, still burning with that untamed intensity. I don't know if it's jealousy or something darker, but whatever it is, it makes my pulse quicken.

Then, as always, there's Tristan, standing just beyond the crowd, his green eyes locked on me with a fierce expression. It's almost as though the two of them are competing without saying a word, making everything worse. The way Gray's jaw tightens and the way Tristan's smile doesn't reach his eyes tells me neither of them are thrilled by the fact I'm currently in the arms of Lord Adrian.

And honestly? Neither am I.

Adrian tilts his head slightly, sensing the tension, no doubt. "What is it, Princess? Don't like the competition?"

I could barely stop myself from rolling my eyes, fighting the urge to snap back at him. Instead, I force a smile—the kind that I've used time and time again. "There's no competition, at least not for me."

His eyes gleam with amusement, though I can see a spark of disappointment behind them. "Such a shame. You'd make a fine player, Princess. But I suppose I'll have to settle for this dance."

Before I can retort, the music swells to a crescendo, signaling the end of the song. My hand is still resting on Adrian's shoulder, but it's Gray's eyes I'm locked onto. He's watching us, the air between us thick with unspoken words. The tension is unbearable, almost suffocating. The voice in the back of my head trying desperately to remember *who* he is and what he has done.

Adrian steps back as he bows his head in a mockingly formal gesture. "A pleasure, Princess. I'll let you go for now. I should like to keep my hands." His eyes find Gray, and I see that familiar challenge pass between them, like an invisible flare that neither is willing to let die. I don't even get a chance to breathe before *Tristan* is right at my side.

His green eyes are locked onto mine, steady and unyielding, as he reaches for my hand. His touch is just as commanding as his gaze, fingers warm and firm around mine. My heart stutters in my chest, the world around us fading into nothing as his other hand comes to rest on my lower back, pulling me toward him with a gentle yet firm grip.

"I didn't think I'd get this dance," I murmur, forcing the words out despite the way my pulse spikes under his touch. He doesn't answer right away, his lips curving into that half-smile that makes everything inside me twist in ways I can't explain.

"And I didn't think Lord Adrian would be your *first* dance." Tristan's voice is low, just above a whisper, as he guides us into a slow waltz. His steps are graceful and confident, but there's an intensity to the way he moves that makes my every instinct scream to stay on guard.

I stiffen slightly, still aware of how many eyes are on us, but when Tristan's hand presses lightly against my spine, I'm forced to relax, allowing myself to be drawn deeper into the dance. The room around us continues to blur, everyone else fading into the background until it's just us, spinning and twirling in the spotlight.

His eyes are still locked onto mine; the weight of his stare is electric. I can feel coolness radiating from him, a silent command, as though he's trying to draw out every emotion I've worked so hard to keep buried.

"You don't get to control me," I say, the words slipping out before I can stop them. I force my expression to remain neutral, but my heart beats faster under the pressure of his gaze. "I won't just follow you around like a puppet."

The arrogance in his smile is evident. "Of course not, Princess. But that's exactly what will make you a suitable future Queen." His voice drops lower. "You seem to forget that you're already tangled in this web with me."

I fight to steady my breath, shaking my head slightly as if the movement can shake the feeling of being trapped. The music swirls around us, heavy with the weight of a too tight room. I can't tell if it's the proximity or the force of his presence, but my chest tightens, my mind spinning with conflicting thoughts.

"Let me go, Tristan," I say more forcefully now, the demand rising in my throat. "This dance is done."

He chuckles, low and dangerous, and I can feel the vibration of it through my chest. "I don't think you quite understand, Keira," he says, his hand tightening just a fraction on my back. "You and I... we're bound by more than just this dance."

My eyes flare with irritation, but before I can argue, the tempo of the music shifts, and Tristan spins me out, his grip still steady on my wrist. My heart races as the movement flows fluidly, spinning me back into his arms with a snap of his fingers, and we're back in sync as though we've never stopped.

"Stop acting like you don't feel it, too," he murmurs, his lips just a breath away from my ear. The words should have irritated me, should have made me pull away, but there's something about his voice, the way it wraps around me as it invades my very soul, that makes me sink into him more.

I force my thoughts to break free from him, trying to clear my mind, but it's like wading through fog. His scent, the cool of his body against mine, the power in every step he takes—it's all too much.

"I don't know what you want from me," I whisper, my voice betraying me as it wavers. I want to push him away, but my body reacts to him in ways I can't control. He leans in closer, his lips almost touching my skin, and for a moment, everything goes still, save for the pounding of my heart.

His lips brushing against my ear, he answers softly, "I want you to see, Princess. I want you to understand that we're both trapped in this together. Whether you like it or not."

The music comes to a sudden halt, the final note hanging in the air like a breath held too long, and I'm left standing in the center of it all, breathless, my thoughts scattered and chaotic.

Tristan's gaze is unwavering, his smile a mixture of victory and something far darker. "We're not done yet, Princess. Not by a long shot."

I try to step away, my heart still racing in the aftermath of the dance. But I'm held in place by the way his eyes hold mine, the tension lingering between us—

Something explodes to my left, and I feel someone's arms wrap around me, pulling me away. The chandelier comes crashing down in the same spot I had just been moments ago. Everything is ringing; my head, my eyes, and my body, all feel heavy. And for a split second, I relax into the arms wrapped around me as everything around me goes quiet.

Chapter 30

Keira

I don't know where I am or what day it is. Everything is aching, and I'm still in my dress from the ball. My limbs feel heavy, my throat dry, and for a moment, I can't remember what happened—just the scent of smoke, the deafening roar of an explosion, and the sharp sting of panic before everything went dark.

The ground beneath me is cold and uneven, the faint scent of damp stone filling my nose. I blink against the dim torchlight flickering across jagged walls, my vision still swimming. Wherever I am, it isn't the palace. The air is thick and the weight of unseen eyes prickles against my skin.

I'm underground.

I shift, muscles protesting, and push myself up onto my elbows. That's when I realize, I'm not alone.

"Well, well. Look who's finally awake."

The voice is smooth, amused. *Familiar.*

I force my head to turn and find Lord Adrian watching me from across the room, arms lazily folded. Beside him, *Maeve* stands stiffly, hands clasped in front of her, eyes filled with something between concern and wariness.

"Adrian." My voice is hoarse, but my sarcasm is still intact. "I'd say it's a pleasure, but I try not to lie within the first five minutes of waking up."

He chuckles, stepping closer. "Charming as ever, Princess."

I ignore him and shift my gaze to around the room. It's a *hideout* with rough stone walls, wooden beams supporting the ceiling, and a handful of makeshift cots pushed against the edges. A few other figures linger in the shadows, watching silently. Definitely not palace guards. Definitely not where I'm *supposed* to be.

Fight or flight kicks in, my pulse quickening. I curse the Stars that I didn't bring my dagger. Maeve-

No wonder Maeve told me not to bring my dagger. She had other plans, clearly. "You should take it easy," Maeve finally speaks, her tone softer. "You hit your head when—"

"When you kidnapped me?" I cut in, swinging my legs over the edge of the cot, my bare feet touch the icy stone. "Yeah, I kind of figured that part out on my own."

Adrian grins, but there's something calculating in his gaze. "You should be thanking us. If we hadn't taken you,

you'd be buried under the rubble of that charming little ball of yours."

My stomach jumps at the memory, but I school myself to appear indifferent. "How thoughtful of you," I say dryly. "I assume this is the part where you explain why I'm here instead of letting me walk out the door?"

His smile sharpens. "Something like that."

Maeve shifts uncomfortably, but she says nothing. My mind races, trying to piece together what's happening, what they want, and how the hell I'm going to get out of here.

One thing is certain, I'm not waiting around to find out.

Chapter 31

Keira

Adrian watches me like a cat toying with a mouse, waiting for me to ask the obvious question. But I refuse to give him the satisfaction.

Instead, I lean back against the cot, tilting my head. "Go on then," I say, voice as casual as if we were discussing the weather. "Tell me why I'm here before I get bored and leave."

"You really think you can walk out of here?"

"I know I can." I smile wide.

A chuckle, low and dark. "I do love that fire of yours, Princess. But let me make one thing clear—you're not leaving until we get what I need."

I cross my arms. "Which is?"

His expression shifts, amusement fading just enough to make my adrenaline spike. He takes a slow step forward, closing the distance between us. "You."

I stiffen. "Vague. Creepy. Try again."

"You have no idea what you are, do you?" His voice is almost pitying. "What you could be."

I hate that his questions trigger me. My mother's secrecy, the prophecy, the way whatever magic I have feels like a stranger under my skin.

But I refuse to let him see that.

I roll my eyes. "Is this the part where you tell me I'm special and you need me for your grand rebellion?"

Adrian sighs as if I'm exhausting him. "I don't need you, Princess, but there are people who do. People who are tired of being crushed under the weight of King Lucian's rule. And your dear mother isn't as innocent in all this as you might think."

A cold tendril of doubt slithers down my spine. "What do you mean?"

He steps even closer, so close I have to tilt my chin up to meet his gaze. "I mean, your mother and King Lucian have been playing their own game for years. And you? You're their greatest piece."

My breath catches, but I mask it quickly. *Lies.* They have to be.

Still, a seed of doubt takes root.

"I don't believe you," I say, but my voice lacks conviction.

Adrian studies me, then sighs as if he's grown bored. "Believe what you want. It doesn't change the fact that you're not leaving."

I shrug. "We'll see about that."

Before he can react, I jump up from the cot and bolt.

Not thinking, just moving, adrenaline flooding my veins as I dart toward the nearest exit, a narrow tunnel at the far end of the chamber. My bare feet slap against the cold stone, and I hear Adrian curse behind me, but I don't stop.

Torchlights line the walls as I race down the passage, the air thick with the scent of damp, moldy earth. The tunnel curves, leading to another darkened corridor, and for a brief moment, hope flares in my chest.

Then, a figure steps into my path.

I skid to a stop, heart hammering.

Maeve.

Her stance is firm, blocking the only way forward.

"Move," I snap.

She doesn't.

"Keira," she says softly. "You don't understand what's at stake."

"I understand that I was kidnapped," I counter. "I understand that you're helping them."

Her jaw tightens. "It's not that simple."

"It never is." I bite back.

I take a step back, ready to pivot, but I don't get the chance.

A strong arm hooks around my waist from behind, yanking me back against a solid chest. My breath rushes out in a startled gasp as Adrian's voice murmurs against my ear.

"You really thought I'd let you slip away that easily?"

I thrash, but his grip tightens. "You're making this harder than it needs to be, Princess."

I snarl, elbowing him hard in the ribs. He grunts but doesn't let go, dragging me back toward the chamber. Maeve follows.

My heart pounds in frustration, in fear, in barely contained rage.

I don't know what Adrian's endgame is. I don't know if what he said about the Queen and Lucian is true.

But I do know one thing.

I *will* get out of here.

And when I do, I'll make them regret taking me.

Chapter 32

Grayson

The smell of smoke still clings to the air. It seeps into my clothes, my skin, and my lungs, no matter how many breaths I take to clear it. The grand ballroom, once blinding black and gold, and filled with laughter and music, now lies in ruins.

Bodies have been dragged away, the injured tended to, but the echoes of screams haven't faded. Neither has the knot in my chest.

Keira's gone.

I roll my shoulders, forcing my hands to stop clenching and unclenching at my sides. My knuckles are already bruised from taking out my anger on one of the surviving rebels, a mistake since we needed him alive long enough to talk.

But I got what I needed.

And now, I know exactly where to find her.

The heavy doors to the war room creak open behind me. I don't need to turn to know it's Tristan. His presence is something I can feel, an oppressive weight pressing between my shoulder blades.

"You're going after her," he says.

It's not a question.

I lean over the table, scanning the rough map one last time. "Obviously."

He moves closer, stopping just at my side. "Alone?"

I grit my teeth. "I work better that way."

A long silence stretches between us. I know Tristan better than anyone, which means I know exactly what he's about to say before the words even leave his mouth.

"Bring her back." His voice is quieter than I expected. No teasing, no arrogance, just something raw underneath.

I look at him then meet his gaze. There's tension in the hard set of his jaw, in the way his fingers curl slightly at his sides.

The Prince who once smirked and pulled Keira into the gardens has been replaced by a man who knows just how much has been taken from him.

I nod once. "I will."

I don't wait for a dismissal—I don't need one.

I turn on my heel, cloak billowing behind me as I stride out of the room. There's no time for hesitation, no time for anything but the mission. Ignoring the pit of emotions in my chest, I steel myself for the task at hand. Little Flame is out there, trapped in some rebel hideout, and I refuse to let them keep her.

Not them.

Not anyone.

I'm getting my spark back.

And Stars help whoever stands in my way.

Chapter 33

Tristan

The scent of ash fills my nose, no matter how many doors and windows have been thrown open. It clings to the stone walls, the silk tapestries, and the polished marble floors and to me.

I crack my knuckles as I stride down the familiar halls, forcing my mind to sharpen and my focus to return. I don't have the luxury of losing control, not here, not now.

The guards posted outside my father's study step aside at my approach, and I push open the heavy doors without hesitation.

My father stands near the towering bookshelves, fingers tracing the worn spines as if lost in thought. A decanter of dark liquor sits untouched on the polished desk beside him, the candlelight casting flickering shadows across his face. He looks as he always does, composed, collected. But I know him well enough to recognize the sharp edge of his focus, the calculation in his thoughts.

"You sent for me," I say, my voice even.

He lifts his gaze to mine. "Yes, my son, close the door."

I do. The click of the latch echoes through the room before silence settles between us.

Then—

"They took her," he says.

I don't flinch. I don't react at all.

Because I already knew.

I've spent the last hour prying information from guards, from witnesses, from anyone who saw what happened after the explosion. The chaos, the smoke, the screams; Keira vanishing in the midst of it all.

"What do we know?" I ask, stepping forward.

My father watches me closely. "A rebel faction. One that has managed to evade us for longer than I care to admit."

His gaze sharpens.

"They've been growing bolder," he continues. "And this, this was a message."

A message.

My fingers twitch at my side. "Then let's send one back."

He lets out a low hum, something almost like approval. I revel in it. "I've already sent Grayson after her."

Of course. My father values efficiency, and when it comes to retrievals, Grayson is his best option. But that doesn't stop the slow burn rising in my chest.

"She belongs here," I say, voice steady. "With me."

My father tilts his head slightly, studying me.

"With you?"

It's a test. One I won't fail.

"With Eclipsar," I correct smoothly.

A pause. Then, the faintest nod.

"She's more than just a pawn, Tristan."

"I know."

"Excellent." He turns back to the bookshelf, fingers trailing absently over the titles. "Make sure she remembers that, too. For a Princess, she has a hard head on her shoulders."

The weight of his words settles over me like a blade pressed against my skin.

I don't intend to let her forget, once she is back with *me*.

Safe with me.

Chapter 34

Keira

I wake to the sound of hushed voices. The stone ceiling above me is rough and uneven. My body aches from my failed escape attempt, but I push past it, forcing myself upright on the cot. I haven't eaten since the lavish lunch with *Maeve*. Even thinking her name causes my chest to ache. *She betrayed me.*

The air is still damp, thick with the scent of earth and burning torches. I listen closely.

"She won't cooperate," a man murmurs from beyond the iron-barred door. "She tried to run once. She'll do it again."

A pause. Then Maeve's voice, quieter. "She won't get far."

We'll see about that.

The heavy door creaks open, and Maeve steps inside alone. She carries a tray with bread, cheese, and a small pitcher of water, but I make no move to take it.

"I don't suppose you poisoned it?" I ask dryly.

She sighs, setting the tray down on a nearby wooden stool. "You need to eat."

"What I need is for you to let me go." I snap.

Maeve leans against the cold stone wall, crossing her arms. "You could make this easier on yourself."

"And miss out on all the fun?" I scoff. "Not a chance."

I search her face and sense something—hesitation? No. *Uncertainty.*

"Why are you helping them?" I press. "You work at Blackthorn Palace for Star's sake."

Maeve exhales, looking away. "I *used to.*"

Past tense.

"Do you even know why you're here, Keira?" she asks, voice softer now.

I lift my chin. "Because Adrian's a self-righteous bastard who thinks he can use me for whatever rebellion he's plotting?"

She doesn't smile at my sarcasm. "Because you're the key to something much bigger than you realize."

There it is again, that same cryptic nonsense Adrian fed me before. I want to roll my eyes, to throw back another sharp remark, but a sliver of doubt blooms in me.

"What are you talking about?" I ask, keeping my voice measured.

Maeve hesitates. "Ask your mother, if you ever get the chance."

Before I can push for more, footsteps echo from the hall. The iron door swings open again, and Adrian steps inside. He looks effortlessly composed, dressed in deep shades of red, his dark hair neatly swept back. He looks at me the way a fox might look at a rabbit caught in its den.

"Enjoying your stay?" he asks.

"Oh, it's been delightful. I was just about to request a tour of the dungeons next. Perhaps a new outfit."

He chuckles. "Still full of fire, I see. *Good.*"

I don't like the way he says that.

He paces toward me, slow and deliberate. "You think I'm your enemy, Keira. But you should be thanking me."

"For what, exactly?" I ask. "The lovely hospitality? The kidnapping? The complete lack of personal space?"

"For showing you the truth."

His words settle like a stone in my chest, but I don't react.

He leans in slightly, his voice lowering. "Your mother and Lucian have been working together for years. Long before they knew the extent of your magic. Long before you ever became a pawn in their little game."

I want to call him a liar. But I can't. Because deep down, a part of me wonders if it's true.

He watches me carefully, gauging my reaction. "You're more important than you know, Princess. And when the time comes, you'll have to decide which side you're truly on."

I shake my head. "I don't play sides."

He weighs this, then responds. "Then I hope, for your sake, you choose wisely."

A silence stretches between us before Adrian finally straightens, nodding at Maeve. "Watch her."

Then, with a lingering glance in my direction, he strides out of the room, leaving me alone with a tray of untouched food and far too many questions.

One thing is certain: I need to get out of here. And I need answers.

And more importantly, I need to find some new clothes.

Chapter 35

Keira

The sounds from my stomach are the only things that fill the silence between Maeve and me.

"You should probably eat. You'll regret it later if you don't." She now sits with her back against the stone wall a few feet away from me.

"This is most likely the part where I'm supposed to pry for more answers, but I want nothing to do with anything that comes out of your mouth." There's a little extra bite in my words.

"I'm on your side, Keira. How many times do I have to tell you that?"

"Oh really—were you on my side all those days we spent getting ready? Or how about when you fed me all those lies about Tristan and Gray? Or maybe when you told me to leave my dagger behind in my room!" My words came out harsh, all of my rage bubbling over.

"Keira...Adrian said I could help. I'm *helping* you." She toys with a strand of her deep brown hair.

"If you really wanted to help, you could at least get me fresh clothes." There's no need to fake the hurt in my voice.

Maeve quietly gets up, eyeing the room for a moment before slipping out of the iron door. As soon as she leaves, I leap from my cot. Frantically, I search for any other way out. There isn't much in here: a cot, the iron door, a dresser, and the small wooden table with food. Again, my stomach rumbles.

No, you can eat after you escape.

I search the cot. *Nothing.* The iron door was out of the question. With time running out, I pull out every drawer in the dresser, feeling a cool breeze sweep across my legs.

I take a minute to glance around the room once, then twice. Another cool breeze brushes my legs from *behind* the dresser. I quickly pull the small dresser off the wall to reveal a carved hole in the wall. Just big enough for someone to fit. Without a second thought, I slip into the hole, not bothering to put the dresser back. For now, I'll focus on getting out of here. The rest I'll figure out later.

The tunnel is dark, and I can't even see my own hand in front of my face. The walls are slimy and the air is moist. I'm not sure how long I've been down here or how lost I am. Turning down every passing tunnel I see, none have proven to be the way out. Frantically, I try searching around the walls, feeling for something I may have missed. Nothing but slime and stone. Then I hear it, *footsteps. They've figured out I'm gone. I'm running out of time.* This time, my legs break out into a full-on sprint. Moving in the opposite direction as fast as my legs will go.

I don't turn back. I don't slow down.

I just keep running and running.

Chapter 36

Grayson

The night is a void of ink and shadows as I weave through the dense, twisted trees, my cloak barely grazing the ground. The moon is nothing but a sliver overhead, its dim glow doing little to light my path. Not that I need it. I know where I'm going.

I have to.

Little Flame is close.

I can feel it—a pull towards *my* onyx ring she always wears. Every second that passes is one more where she's trapped with those rebels, one more where something could go wrong.

I tighten my grip on the hilt of my blade.

I won't be late.

Not this time.

The hideout isn't much, just a crumbling underground structure hidden beneath the roots of the forest. I'd expected something more elaborate, more fortified, but this? This is *desperation*. A faction clinging to survival, too foolish to realize they've just painted a target on their backs.

Good.

The information I pried from that rebel back at the palace led me straight here, and after hours of tracking, I've confirmed it. Only two guards stand at the entrance, stationed near the heavy wooden door set into the hillside. *Pathetic.*

Slipping my dagger free, I move fast. Silent. The first guard barely has time to exhale before I drive my blade into his side, muffling his strangled gasp with a gloved hand. I let him drop and pivot, catching the second one by the throat. He struggles, reaching for his weapon, but I twist the dagger and he goes limp.

I lower him carefully. No need for unnecessary noise.

Breathing steadily, I press a hand to the door, feeling the weight of it. *Locked.*

A little force, a precise kick to the weak point near the hinges, and the wood splinters apart. I step inside, blade ready.

Inside I notice a spiraling staircase. Heading down silently, I sneak up on the guard waiting at the bottom, using the hilt of my blade to knock him out cold. Unfortunately, he hits the floor with a noticeable thud. There is an archway in the wall—nothing but black.

Tunnels. With a few quick strides I grab a torch from stone walls and enter. The tunnels are narrow, damp, the only light coming from my torch, casting just enough light for me to see a few feet in front of me. The scent of earth and stone lingers in the air but mingled with it is something faint, familiar. *Vanilla.*

Little Flame.

I move quickly, following instinct.

Then I hear it.

Footsteps.

Light but moving fast.

I stay at the edge of the tunnel. Waiting for whoever it is to round the corner—a thin cool forearm presses against my throat, pinning me against the wall. Whoever this is has skill, but I have strength. I grab her wrist and twist it behind her back sending her face straight into the grime covered wall.

"Don't you have any manners?" Her voice is strangled and harsh.

"You already know the answer to that." I fight the urge to laugh as I release her.

Her white hair is messier than I've ever seen it, her dress torn and dirt-streaked. There's something wild in her blue eyes, something fierce. She hasn't been broken. She had been *escaping*.

That's my girl. *No, not* your *girl.*

I take a step back, so she can fully see me.

"Gray?" Relief and disbelief flash in her voice, but I don't miss the way her shoulders relax.

She lets out a breath, "How did you—?"

"Tracked you." My gaze scans her quickly for injuries. "Are you hurt?"

"No," she says, shaking her head. "Just irritated."

"Nothing new, then."

She huffs. "Gray—"

A shout echoes from further down the tunnel. The rebels know. They're coming.

I shift immediately, reaching for the dagger I nicked from her room.

"We need to move."

Keira hesitates for half a second before stepping fully into my space, gripping my wrist.

"Let's go." I squeeze her hand once, brief but firm, before leading her into the darkness.

She's safe. With me. For now.

But this isn't over.

Not by a long shot.

And by the time I'm done, whoever took her will wish they hadn't.

Chapter 37

Keira

The damp air of the tunnels clings to me as I stumble forward, trying to keep my steps steady. My mind is a chaotic swirl of confusion, suspicion, and a tiny sliver of hope. I can't afford to be weak. I can't let him get to me, no matter how much my heart wants to.

"I didn't think you'd come for me," I mutter under my breath, though I know he'll hear.

I don't want to admit how relieved I am or process the feelings swirling in my chest. I refuse to give him that power over me; I'll die before I do that.

"Why would you think I wouldn't?" Gray's voice is low, the edges of it rough like he's fighting something; it pulls at that something in my chest. The something I can't explain. "I told you before. I'm looking out for you."

I roll my eyes, even though he can't see my face. "You really love the sound of your own voice, don't you? The great Grayson Noctis, hero of the day." I snort, my sarcastic edge returning. "I'm not some damsel in distress. I'm fine."

I'm definitely far from fine. But I can't let him see how much I'm struggling. Not yet.

His footsteps slow, but he doesn't stop moving forward. "You sure about that? Because you don't look fine."

"Looks can be deceiving," I reply quickly, spinning around to face him. "And I'm not the one who needs rescuing, *your Highness*. I'm perfectly capable of getting myself out of this mess."

Something crosses his face, amusement, maybe? But then it's gone, replaced by that familiar, guarded expression I've seen so many times before. He steps closer, but not enough to crowd me.

"You're stubborn," he observes, his voice almost affectionate, though it's hard to tell if he's being serious or just teasing. "It's one of the things I like about you."

I blink, caught off guard by the compliment. I feel the heat rise to my cheeks, but I refuse to let him see. I swallow it down, pushing back the warmth that threatens to betray my true feelings.

"I'm sure you like a lot of things about me, Prince Charming," I say, keeping my tone light. "But you'll have to wait for me to warm up to you before I start returning any of the sentiment."

Gray doesn't take the bait. Instead, he smiles, a small, knowing curve of his lips revealing two beautiful dimples, making my stomach flutter in ways I refuse to analyze. "I'm patient. I can wait. But I'm certainly no Prince Charming."

For a moment, I can't speak. I just stare at him, caught somewhere between annoyance and intrigue. Maybe it's his confidence. Maybe it's the way he makes everything feel... *easier* despite the chaos. But I push those thoughts aside. I'm not here to be charmed, and I'm certainly not here to lose myself in whatever this is between us.

"Well, if you ask me, this looks like a rescue mission so..." I drag out my last word. Earning me another breathtaking smile.

"Who said I was saving you? Maybe I just missed your company," he says, feigning indifference.

"You're either a terrible liar or dangerously charming. Not sure which is worse." I laugh.

"Maybe I'm both... and maybe you don't mind it nearly as much as you pretend to." His gaze lingers on my face a beat too long, and suddenly, I'm grateful for the lack of light.

Ignoring the storm in my chest, I force myself behind a mask made of stone.

"I'm not going anywhere unless you start explaining exactly what's going on," I say, folding my arms across my chest. "I may not need rescuing, but I do need answers." And I'm not about to follow him into the unknown without knowing what the hell I'm walking into.

Gray gives a long, measured sigh as if he knew this conversation was coming. "I don't have all the answers yet, but I know you're not safe here. Trust me, Little Flame. That's all I'm asking for right now. We'll figure it out later."

It's tempting. It's more tempting than I want to admit. But I don't let myself soften. Instead, I narrow my eyes at him as if to remind him that I'm not some fragile Princess to be coddled.

"I'll come with you," I say slowly, "but only because I'm not dumb enough to stay here and wait for whatever mess you've left behind to catch up to us."

"Fair enough," Gray replies, a flash of amusement in his eyes. "Stay close."

And as we turn through the winding tunnels, I can't help the strange feeling in my chest. It's not love or affection, that's for sure. I will *never* let him or anyone bring those feelings out of me. It's just... a *pull*. And no matter how much I fight it, no matter how much I try to convince myself that I don't care, it's there, always lurking beneath the surface.

I hate it. And I hate how much he affects me.

But I'll never admit it. Not to him. Not to anyone. Not even to myself.

Chapter 38

Keira

Once we exit the hideout, I'm met with a shadowy sky and such a beautiful sliver of moon. *I should tell Gray that it was Adrian who took me—that's the smart thing to do.* I just can't shake what Adrian told me, maybe I can keep his secret a little longer—just until I get answers.

"We have a long way back, and we have to find somewhere to rest for the night." I let Gray lead the way; the cloak he wears whipping behind him. The cool breeze I felt earlier is even more chill-inducing now that I'm outside. He seems to hear the chattering of my teeth because, in one swift movement, he turns to face me, lightly draping his cloak over my shoulders.

"Fine," I kick a pebble in his direction. "And don't worry, I won't slow you down. But if you start getting too dramatic with your hero act, I might have to trip you on purpose."

Gray casts me a look, one brow arching in that infuriatingly smug way of his. "Oh? And here I thought you'd be grateful I saved you."

I scoff, pulling the borrowed cloak tighter around me. "Grateful? Please. You didn't save me. I had everything under control. "

He hums, clearly amused. "Right. That's why I found you sprinting through the tunnels like a sewer rat."

I gasp, placing a hand over my heart in mock offense. "I'll have you know, that was a very strategic escape. Not all of us have the luxury of storming in like some brooding knight with a hero complex."

"Brooding knight?" He smiles, stepping over a root as we move through the trees. "I prefer fearless rescuer."

"Well, fearless rescuer, unless you're planning to carry me the whole way back, you better find us a place to rest before I collapse from exhaustion."

He chuckles, shaking his head. "So dramatic."

"Says the one that had a billowing cloak," I shoot back. "You've got more flair than half the nobles at court."

That actually earns me a laugh, low and rich, like he forgot to keep his usual cool indifference up. I don't let myself linger on the sound, or the way the moonlight catches in his onyx eyes. Or the fact that, despite everything, I feel a little safer with him here.

Stars help me.

"Come on, Little Flame," he murmurs, nodding toward the trees ahead. "All my heroics will be for nothing if you collapse from exhaustion." He mocks. I roll my eyes and follow him, ignoring the way my pulse jumps at the nickname.

The cold is getting to me. I hate to admit it, but I'm shivering, the damp night air cutting through the fabric of my borrowed cloak. Gray doesn't seem bothered, but even he seems more focused than usual as he scans our surroundings.

After what feels like an eternity of walking, he finally stops. "There."

I follow his gaze to see a shallow cave, barely more than an indent in the hillside, but it's better than nothing.

I sigh, pushing past him. "It'll do."

I'm about to start gathering firewood when Gray catches my wrist. His grip is firm, his touch warm despite the cold. "I'll handle it."

I arch a brow. "Oh? And what am I supposed to do? Watch and offer moral support?"

"That'll do," he says, already turning away.

I let out an exasperated huff. "I do know how to build a fire, you know."

He crouches near the entrance, already stacking wood he somehow collected without me noticing. "And yet, here you are. Cold. Shaking. Complaining."

I narrow my eyes. "I am not complaining."

"You're always complaining."

I huff, wrapping his cloak tighter around me. "You act like you don't love the attention."

He doesn't answer, too focused on striking flint against steel. Sparks fly, and then a flicker of flame catches. He shields it with his hands, coaxing the fire to life with practiced ease. Within moments, the flames are crackling, casting a warm glow against the stone walls.

I hold my hands toward the heat, trying not to seem too eager. "I still could've done it."

Gray leans back against the rock wall, stretching out his legs. "Sure."

I scowl. "You're insufferable."

"And you're complaining," he says, with a smug tilt of his lips.

I have the sudden, irrational urge to throw something at him. Instead, I settle for rolling my eyes and sitting as far from him as the cave allows, which isn't far.

Silence settles between us, the fire crackling softly. Despite myself, I feel my muscles finally begin to relax. The exhaustion from everything: my escape, the cold, the confusing emotions…it all starts to weigh on me all at once.

I tug his cloak tighter around me, inhaling the lingering scent of smoke and something else, something undeniably him. I quickly shove that thought aside.

Gray watches me for a beat before shaking his head with a quiet chuckle.

"What?" I ask, instantly defensive.

"Nothing," he says. "Just wondering how long you'll keep pretending you're not freezing."

I glare at him, scooting an inch closer to the fire. "I hate you."

"Sure you do." A small smile spreads across his face, revealing those dimples.

Stars help me.

I *do* hate him.

I think?

Chapter 39

Keira

I wake to the dying fire and the sound of morning bird songs. The fire has burned down to glowing coals, casting the cave in a faint light. For a brief moment, I forget where I am. The cave walls are rough and uneven, the air still chilled from the night before, but at least I'm not shivering anymore.

Unfortunately, that has more to do with the warm body next to me and not the dying fire.

At some point in the night, Gray must have shifted closer, because his arm is now draped loosely over my waist, his breathing steady and slow. I don't move at first, my mind sluggish as I process the weight of it, the warmth of him.

Then I remember who exactly I'm being held by.

"Oh, you have got to be kidding me." I shift, pushing at his arm. "Get off."

Gray makes a sound that is half a grunt, half an annoyed sigh but doesn't move.

"Gray." I push harder, but he's practically a boulder.

His voice is still thick with sleep when he finally mutters, "Five more minutes."

I scoff. "Five more minutes, and I'll set you on fire."

That gets his attention. After blinking at me with groggy amusement, he lifts his arm and rolls onto his back. "You're a menace."

"And you're a bed hog." I sit up, stretching out the soreness in my limbs. My body still aches from my time in the underground prison, but at least I don't feel as weak anymore.

Gray watches me for a moment before sighing and running a hand through his mess of black curls. "We should get moving. We're still too close to the rebels' hideout."

He's right, but I don't like that he's the one saying it. So I just huff and stand, dusting myself off.

By the time we leave the cave, the morning sun is casting a golden hue over the density of the Hollows. We move quickly, following a hidden path that weaves through the trees.

Hours pass in near silence, save for the occasional quip from me that Gray mostly ignores. Then we step into a clearing, and I nearly stop in my tracks.

A field of red roses stretches before us, their petals so vivid they almost look like drops of blood scattered across the earth. The scent is intoxicating, sweet and for a moment, I just stare.

"Lovely." Gray's voice is dry as he eyes the thick, thorn-covered stems. "I'm sure this will be a painless walk."

"What, scared of a few thorns?"

He gives me a look. "I'd rather not spend the rest of this trip pulling them out of my skin." He says indifferently, but I don't miss the way his jaw tightened.

I step forward, reaching down to brush my fingers over a petal. It's soft, velvety, almost warm. A strange sensation hums beneath my skin, something stirring in my chest.

Then, the rose bursts into flames.

I let out a yelp, jerking my hand back as the fire flickers across the petals, burning bright before fizzling out, leaving behind nothing but a charred stem.

Gray is at my side in an instant. "Little Flame—"

"I didn't mean to," I say quickly, staring at the scorched remains. My heart is racing. I can still feel the heat in my fingertips, like embers smoldering just beneath my skin.

Gray exhales, running a hand down his face. "Alright. So that's a thing now."

"I do not brood."

"Tell that to the last five miles of silence."

I huff, eyeing some potentially good rocks to throw at him. He's irritatingly observant. I hate that he can read me so easily. But I refuse to let him see how much this is actually rattling me.

"It's not brooding," I say airily, "It's deep, intellectual thought. Something I wouldn't expect you to understand."

Gray snorts. "Right. Because setting roses on fire is a very scholarly pursuit."

I narrow my eyes. "You're just mad because once I figure this out," I wave my hands in his face. "I'm going to set *you* on fire."

He considers this. "Admit it, Little Flame. You'd miss me if I burned."

I look away before he can see my amusement.

We continue walking through the flowers, the tension between us shifting into something familiar, something that almost feels comfortable. But the closer we get to the palace, the heavier the air feels, the more the weight of reality settles onto my shoulders.

By the time the massive iron gates of Eclipsar come into view, my stomach is tight with dread.

And then the gates swing open.

Tristan is already waiting, the moonlight casting strange shadows around him. His eyes find me instantly, sharp and searching. There's something in his gaze that makes my pulse quicken: not quite relief, not quite anger.

Gray stiffens beside me.

I inhale deeply, steadying myself. He will not see me shaken, not by magic, not by my own thoughts, and certainly not by him. So, I play the role of the Princess I was raised to be.

The Princess I don't want to be.

Chapter 41

Keira

Tristan doesn't move at first. His sharp green eyes scan me from head to toe, taking in every detail. The dirt on my dress, the faint bruises dusting my arms, the weariness I'm trying so desperately to mask. Then he turns his gaze to Gray, lingering for just a second too long. A silent question passed between them.

I brace myself.

And then—

"You're late," Tristan says, his voice cool but quieter than I expected.

"Apologies, Your Highness. I got a little tied up."

Tristan stares but instead of biting back like he usually would, he just exhales, stepping closer. I can feel the resentment in Gray's gaze as he eyes his brother.

"Are you hurt?"

The question catches me off guard. I hesitate too long, and he tenses.

"I'm fine," I say, softer this time.

His gaze lingers on mine, like he doesn't quite believe me, like he's searching for something more. But then he extends his hand as every gentleman does.

"Come inside."

I place mine in his, letting him lead me through the palace gates. His grip is steady, cool, and anchoring. I remind myself it's just the exhaustion making me feel dizzy, just the aftershocks of everything that's happened. But it's the way he's holding my arm, as if he's afraid to let go, that makes my pulse stutter.

The castle halls are strangely silent as we walk. Servants cast me quick, assessing glances before averting their eyes, and guards shift their stances, hands tightening on their weapons.

They're *watching* me.

Or maybe they're waiting for something.

I glance up at Tristan, whose expression remains unreadable, though his grip on my hand has yet to loosen. It's only when we reach my chambers that he finally releases me.

"You should rest," he says.

I arch a brow. "Is that a suggestion or a command?"

His lips twitch slightly. "A request."

That surprises me. Tristan—the future King, simply making a request.

"I don't need rest," I counter, folding my arms.

Tristan exhales through his nose, shaking his head slightly. "Keira."

The way he says my name sends a strange warmth through me. I force myself to ignore it. His words mean little compared to someone else's.

"Well," I say instead. "I don't *want* rest. I want answers."

Tristan doesn't react right away. Instead, he studies me, eyes dark and calculating. "Answers about what?"

I shift uncomfortably, still feeling the remnants of magic beneath my skin, the warmth curling at my fingertips. "Everything."

His expression sharpens. "Did they hurt you?"

There's nothing dangerous in his tone, just concern.

I shake my head. "No. But..." I hesitate.

But *something* happened. I don't know if I can say it or if I even know how to say it.

Tristan steps closer, his voice quiet. "Keira, what is it?"

My heart skips a beat.

I could tell him. I *should* tell him.

Call it instinct, but something stops me. Instead, I shake my head, forcing a smile. "You really do worry too much."

Tristan pauses, but he doesn't argue. He exhales, running a hand through his hair.

 "Come with me."

I blink. "What?"

"Just trust me." I seem to be hearing those three words often. His hand finds mine again, fingers curling around my wrist. Before I can protest, he tugs me gently down the corridor. I should argue. I should demand to know where we're going. But the words never leave my lips. Because, for some reason, I'm more than curious.

Chapter 42

Keira

The garden is quiet this late at night, the air cool against my skin. The lanterns that usually illuminate the pathways are dimmed, casting shadows over the stone benches and hedges.

Tristan doesn't let go of my hand until we reach the center, where a fountain trickles softly, its inky black water reflecting the sliver of moonlight overhead.

"Why are we here?" I ask.

He exhales, turning to face me. "Because I thought you might need a moment to breathe."

I open my mouth to argue, but I stop myself.

Because Stars help me.

He's right.

After everything that's happened, after being *taken*, after *escaping*, after *discovering* something inside me that I don't understand. I need this. The quiet. The stillness.

Tristan watches me carefully, his expression softer than I've ever seen it.

I clear my throat. "So what now? Are you going to lecture me about how reckless I am?"

His lips twitch. "Would you listen if I did?"

"Absolutely not."

He huffs a quiet laugh, shaking his head. "Didn't think so."

I look up at him, *really* look at him. He looks… tired.

"Did you worry about me?" I ask, half-teasing.

Tristan meets my gaze. "Of course I did." He says softly.

I shift, glancing away. "Well, I survived. I was only gone two days."

His fingers brush against my wrist, just a light touch, barely there. "That doesn't mean I'll stop worrying."

I freeze.

He's too close. His warmth is too distracting. The weight of his words is too much.

So, I do what I do best. *I tease.* "Careful, Tristan. You almost sound fond of me."

His gaze darkens, and for a second, I think he might step dangerously closer. Instead, he exhales, shaking his head. "Come on, I have a surprise for you."

"What?" My voice is a mix of confusion and delight.

He tilts his head. "You'll see."

He starts walking, and I have no choice but to follow. *Again.*

Chapter 43

Keira

Tristan leads me down the dimly lit corridors of the palace, his pace steady but unhurried. I follow behind him, my steps light against the marble floors, my mind still tangled with the day's events.

At first, I assume he's walking me back to my room, but as we continue deeper into the palace, a strange sense of unease settles in. These halls feel different. Less and less familiar the further he takes me.

Then we stop.

He turns to a door, one that looks no different from the others, and pushes it open.

The room beyond is dimly lit, a fire crackling softly in the hearth. It's decorated with plush furnishings—a grand four-poster bed draped in rich fabrics, a vanity set against the far wall. It's luxurious, that's for sure.

I glance back at Tristan. "Whose room is this?"

He smiles broadly. "Yours."

I blink. "Mine? I already have a room."

Tristan steps inside, gesturing around as if presenting some grand gift. "You didn't think I'd let you go back to the far end of the palace, did you?"

I step inside, eyes sweeping over the details I hadn't noticed before: the placement of the furniture, the balcony overlooking the garden, and the warmth of the space. This is not just some random guest room.

It's closer. Much closer. *To the royal sleeping quarters.*

Realization dawns.

I turn to Tristan, my arms crossing. "Why is my new room here?"

He glances at me before speaking. "Like I said, it's a surprise."

I narrow my eyes. "You moved me *without* asking me?"

He leans lazily against the doorframe, completely unbothered by my irritation. "Would you have agreed if I had?"

"That depends," I retort. "What exactly is the surprise? Moving me without my permission or is there something else?"

Tristan exhales, his gaze settling on mine with an intensity that makes my pulse quicken. "Security. Privacy.

A place where *I* know you'll be safe." His voice dips slightly. "Where *I* can keep you safe."

I shift uncomfortably, trying to ignore the warmth seeping into my heart. "So this is about safety?"

"Would you rather I say it's because I enjoy having you around?"

I huff. "You enjoy irritating me."

"That too." He steps closer, just enough that I catch the faintest hint of something crisp and dark, laced with cedar wood. "But mostly, I don't want you tucked away in some distant wing where no one can reach you if something happens."

I swallow. The weight of his words settle over me, heavy and unshakable.

This isn't just about protection. It's about control. About keeping me within reach.

I should be annoyed. I *am* annoyed.

But a small part of me also feels... *cared for.*

I shake my head, stepping past him. "If this is some elaborate way to make sure I don't run away, I hate to break it to you, but I do know how to pick locks." I keep my voice light.

Tristan chuckles, his voice low and amused. "Not this one."

I turn, glaring at him. "You'd lock my door?"

"Of course not. But if you try sneaking out in the middle of the night, I will know." There's no mistaking the seriousness in his voice.

Tristan watches me for a beat longer before finally stepping back. "Get some rest, Keira."

And then, before I can think of another snarky response, he's gone, vanishing down the dimly lit corridor, leaving me standing in front of my new room with far too many thoughts racing through my head.

I exhale, pushing the door closed.

I look around the room again, not sure whether I should feel privileged or caged.

Either way, I know one thing for certain. Tristan is intent on keeping me close.

Chapter 44

Keira

The morning light trickles through the heavy drapes of my new chamber, casting a golden hue over the silk sheets tangled around my legs.

I should feel at ease. Instead, there's a restlessness in my soul, tight and unwanted.

Pushing off the covers, I make my way toward the washbasin, splashing cool water over my face. The girl in the mirror looks... different. Maybe it's the lack of sleep weighing down my features, or maybe it's something else entirely.

I shake off the thought and get dressed, slipping into a soft robe before stepping toward the sitting area, where a tray of breakfast awaits. The scent of warm bread and honey tea fills the space, making my stomach grumble.

Settling into a chair, I take a sip of the tea, letting its warmth seep through me. The moment is almost peaceful until a knock at the door pulls me from it.

I barely have time to set my cup down before the door opens, revealing *Tristan*.

He leans casually against the frame, dressed in his usual dark finery but there's something different about his expression today. It's softer, almost hesitant.

"You're up early," he notes, stepping inside without invitation. Not that he needs one.

I arch a brow. "So are you."

"I have my reasons."

I don't press. Instead, I motion toward the tray. "If you're here to steal my breakfast, I may stab you with a butter knife."

Tristan chuckles, shaking his head. "Tempting, but no. I came to escort you to court."

My stomach twists, but I keep my expression neutral. "Is that another request?"

"Does it matter?" His tone is teasing, but there's an undercurrent of something more.

I sigh, setting down my cup. "Give me a moment to change."

He makes no effort to move.

I narrow my eyes. "I meant alone."

He takes a step back. "Fine. But I'm not leaving. And before you go rummaging through whatever uninspired gowns were left for you, I have a suggestion."

I pause mid-step. "A suggestion?"

He nods toward the wardrobe. "Pick something royal."

I cross my arms. "Why?"

Tristan steps closer, his voice dropping to something almost kingly. "Because you're a Princess, and people need to be reminded of that."

There's an intensity in his gaze that unsettles me, but I roll my eyes all the same and open the wardrobe anyway.

Rows of dresses, all in rich fabrics and intricate embroidery, line the space. My fingers trail over them before settling on a deep wine-red gown. It's regal without being overwhelming, fitted at the waist with delicate gold threading.

Tristan nods approvingly. "Good choice."

I shake my head, cursing the Stars as I take the dress behind the changing screen.

By the time I step out, fully dressed, Tristan is already waiting by the door. His green eyes sweep over me, not with the usual teasing glint but with something quieter. Almost adoring.

I clear my throat. "Well?"

He offers his arm. "Shall we?" I hesitate before looping my arm through his.

As we walk through the corridors, the whispers follow.

"She's still here?"

"At least she looks the part."

"Out of all those girls, he picked her?"

I keep my head high, pretending not to hear.

Tristan, however, doesn't seem to mind the attention. If anything, he walks taller, his grip on my arm tightening ever so slightly.

When we reach the grand hall, the doors open before us, revealing the assembled court. Nobles and high-ranking officials murmur amongst themselves as they stare at us with poorly concealed curiosity.

I suck in a breath, steadying myself. Looking for a familiar face, *his face.* To my disappointment, I don't find him.

Tristan doesn't let go of my arm. Instead, he guides me forward without hesitation. When we reach the dais, he speaks.

"With everything that has happened in recent days, I feel it is time to put certain matters to rest." His voice is strong, unwavering. "Eclipsar stands at the precipice of change, and we must move forward with clarity and purpose."

The court falls silent.

My pulse pounds. *Does he really want that change?* I glance up at him, but he doesn't look at me. Instead, he looks out over the gathered nobles and states, "Princess Keira of Aetheris will be my bride."

The words slam into me like a physical blow. I knew everything: the gowns, the jewels, the masquerade, and the trials, was to find Tristan a wife but I would have thought the women chosen would have been given a choice.

Gasps ripple through the court.

I stand frozen, my mind struggling to process what just happened.

Tristan finally turns to me, his grip firm but not forceful. There's no uncertainty in his gaze, only quiet determination.

I should protest. I should demand an explanation.

But I don't.

I stand there a beat too long, merely staring at Tristan.

Then, I do the first thing that comes to mind.

Run.

Chapter 45

Keira

I run as fast as my body will carry me in this lousy dress. Dashing past blurry guards, one of the blurs looked familiar, but I didn't slow my pace. Making it past the gardens, courtyard, and even the gates with burning lungs and aching legs before I slow to walk.

Realizing I'm somewhere familiar.

The ruins.

I step into the circle, the fire lighting in the bowl immediately. A scream builds in my throat, clawing to get out. I press my hands against the cold stone, my fingers trembling, my breathing ragged.

How dare he?

How dare he take MY choice away?

I curl my hands into fists, nails biting into my palms. I cared for him, and he went behind my back. Red lines my vision until I notice...it's not anger clouding my sight. It's the fire in the bowl.

It now burns exceptionally bigger than before. I unclench my hands, taking note of how the fire relaxes ever so slightly. I sway my right hand, watching the flames respond, matching the movement. A whisper of something alive inside me stirs.

I feel it, then, the *power*. Not just the magic that flows in my veins but the *fire*. It's not a force I can simply control or ignore. It's part of me. A part of who I am now. A reflection of my rage, my sadness, my confusion.

I throw my hands up and let everything out, the scream that's waited so patiently. The frustration about Tristan, about being a Princess, the idea of being Queen, about Gray, about everything I've been thrust into without warning. Everything that's been decided for me, without my say.

The fire in the bowl nearly triples in size, a violent orange and gold spiraling upward, causing me to jump back as the heat presses against my face. The sleeves of my dress barely escape the flames, the fabric curling at the edges as if to remind me of my loss of control.

I don't care.

It's as if I've ignited everything inside me, burning away the doubts, the restrictions, and all the walls I've built to keep myself contained. The fire roars, and I roar with it.

But then, *silence*.

The flames simmer down slowly, quietly, as if acknowledging my surrender to the chaos. I blink back tears, my breath coming in shaky sobs. I sink to my knees, the weight of everything crashing down. My legs finally give out from the run, from the fury.

I dig my fingers into the cool dirt of the earth beneath me, grounding myself, finding the quiet after the storm.

I won't stay at the palace, either here or in Aetheris.

I let the tears fall, not just for the betrayal but for the loss of myself. The girl I was before everything turned upside down. The girl who had dreams and ideas. The girl who believed in love and choice. I allow myself a few more minutes for self pity, for anger, for everything I don't understand.

With the last tear hitting the fresh dirt, I rise. The sun is warm on my face, and it reminds me of what I've lost and what I could gain if I walk away from it all.

I look toward the horizon, my resolve firming. It's now or never. I turn my back to the ruins, to the palace, and to the Kingdom that is no longer mine to claim.

If this is my last day in Eclipsar, I'm going to make the most out of it. I don't know what tomorrow will bring, but today, I want control. I take a deep breath, feeling the weight of my decision settle over me.

And then my feet move, leaving behind everything that's been decided for me, stepping into the unknown, away from the life they want to choose for me.

I'll make my own fate, even if I have to run.

237

Chapter 46

Keira

The Hollows aren't nearly as frightening in the daylight. The dappled sunlight filters through the thick canopy, casting shifting patterns on the forest floor. The air is thick with the scent of dampness, mingled with the distant chirping of birds. It's almost peaceful.

Something I could lose myself to.

I've been tramping through these trees for what feels like hours. Every direction looks the same, gnarled roots breaking through the dirt, endless trunks stretching toward the sky. I lost the gravel path long ago, my aching feet sinking into the softer forest floor with each step. At some point, I abandoned my heels entirely, tying them together and slinging them over my shoulder. They were useless anyway.

The adrenaline from this morning has long since burned away, leaving my limbs heavy and my stomach aching with hunger. I didn't think this far ahead. I didn't pack food, didn't pack anything for that matter. I was too focused on getting *away* to think about what would come after.

My pace slows as I reach a small hillside, the sight stopping me in my tracks.

I know this place.

It's partially hidden by overgrown vines, the entrance barely visible unless you know what to look for. But I do.

Because I've been here before.

The memory crashes into me all at once: the cold stone beneath me as I huddled close for warmth, the sound of steady breathing beside me. The flickering glow of the fire casts shadows on the walls. *Gray.*

For a moment, I just stand there, holding my breath. Why did I come here? I should've kept walking, should've put as much distance between myself and Eclipsar as possible. But my body had led me here, to the only place in these cursed woods that felt familiar.

With a quiet sigh, I push past the vines and step inside. The cave is small, just deep enough to provide shelter without feeling like a tomb. The remnants of our old fire pit still linger in the center, nothing but cold ash now and fresh wood. I kneel beside it, running my fingers over the soot-stained stone.

I don't have flint. No way to start a fire.

But I shouldn't need it.

I exhale slowly, stretching a hand over the fresh wood, willing the magic inside me to awaken. My anger still simmers beneath the surface: the betrayal, the humiliation, the sheer audacity of Tristan taking *my* choice away.

He had no right.

A flicker of warmth rushes through me.

Then, a *spark*.

Flames curl to life, licking at the dry wood, bright and hungry. The glow reflects off my hands, the fire mirroring my own storm of emotions. My power is tied to my feelings. I understand that much now.

I wrap my arms around myself, staring into the flames. Tomorrow, I'll keep moving. I don't know where I'm going, but I won't stop.

I refuse to be trapped again. But tonight, I'll rest.

Chapter 47

Keira

It was an uncomfortable night, but I was able to stay warm, even if stone is not ideal to sleep on. Not to mention this dress and lack of food. I save a moment for myself before I stand and brush dirt off my face and out of my hair.

Not nearly looking like the Princess I'm supposed to be.

I close my eyes for a moment, listening to the sounds of the forest around me, the chirping of birds, the rustling of leaves. Then, something else, a faint rustle in the distance. My head snaps up, eyes scanning the mouth of the cave.

I'm not alone. Could it be Gray? Already?

I rise to my feet quietly, instinct kicking in. The sounds grow closer, and a figure steps into view. A boy no older than I am, his dark hair disheveled and his face partly obscured by the hood of his cloak. He doesn't seem to notice me at first, too focused on something in his hands.

I take a cautious step back. "Who are you?" I demand, wishing I had something to defend myself.

The boy raises his hands, a gesture of peace. "I'm not here to hurt you. I'm Cass," he says, his eyes scanning the cave before landing back on me. "You're Keira, aren't you?"

. I school my expression to something akin to disinterest. "And what do you want with me?"

He hesitates, shifting uncomfortably. "I was sent to help you" he says, his voice quiet but firm.

The words *bring you back* stir something in me. My mind races, but I keep my expression neutral. "Why?"

"Because you're important," he replies simply. "We need you."

I look at him, studying his face. There's something about the way he says it, something that feels more like an invitation than a demand. Still, I don't trust him. His words sound awfully familiar to Adrian's.

"I'm not going anywhere with you," I say, my voice stronger than I feel. "I don't owe you anything."

Cass steps closer, a bit tentative. "No one's asking for anything. You don't have to come with me. But you need food. Shelter. I'm just offering you a *safe* place for the night. And... a chance to figure out what to do next."

I look down at my hands, the dirt still clinging to my skin. I know I can't keep running forever. And as much as I hate it, Cass's offer makes sense.

This isn't just about food. It's about safety.

And maybe... it's about finding a way to fight back.

I glance at the ashes from the fire, then back at Cass. He doesn't seem dangerous. In fact, there's a certain calmness about him that makes me hesitate even more.

"Alright," I say, my voice quiet but steady. "I'll go with you."

Cass nods, offering a small smile. "Fantastic. You won't regret it."

Chapter 48

Keira

Cass and I fall into an uncomfortable silence as I follow a few steps behind him, just enough not to trip on the bottom of his cloak. It's hard to see the sun through the tall trees, but I'm pretty sure we've been walking all morning. At least, that's what it feels like.

Cass has made no effort to be polite. Then again, neither have I. My gaze stays mostly on the pebbles I kick off the path, my thoughts too tangled to speak. The Hollows are eerily quiet, only the occasional rustle of birds in the trees or the distant rush of water breaking the stillness.

Water.

My mouth dries at the thought. I haven't had anything to drink since before the court gathering.

Something glitters to my left—

A lake. As if the Stars heard my thoughts.

I slip away from Cass, careful with my steps, barely breathing as I move off the path. I don't really need him anymore. He got me far enough from the palace. The ache in my stomach is manageable. I can figure out the rest on my own.

The lake is breathtaking, nestled beneath low-hanging trees, their green leaves floating on the crystal clear water. Small creatures float along the banks, some slipping beneath the surface in quick, darting movements. The sight is mesmerizing.

I kneel on the flat stones lining the water, swirling my fingers through the water, sending ripples across its glassy surface. It's cool against my skin, soothing the heat I hadn't even realized was burning under my flesh.

I could bathe.

Probably not one of my finest ideas, especially without anything fresh to change into. I sink both hands into the lake, hoping for more relief—

I bite back a shriek as my fingers turn black.

It starts at my ring, spreading up my hands, creeping over my arms like ink seeping through fabric.

I rip them from the water, frantically rubbing them against my dress. My hands tremble as they return to their usual soft pink, but my heart pounds wildly against my ribs.

"Good thing you didn't drink it."

Everything in my body goes rigid.

That voice.

Slowly, I stand, my back still to him, as if delaying the inevitable will change what I already know.

With a shaky breath, I turn.

Gray.

He leans carelessly against a thick tree, arms crossed, looking as if he's been standing there for some time.

"Hey, Little Flame."

I take a step back, the rock cool beneath my bare feet.

"Easy." He pushes off the tree. "I'm not here to hurt you." He throws his hands up, partially in mock innocence, partially in readiness to catch me if I run.

"That might be true," I say carefully, "but you *are* here to take me back to Eclipsar." I steel my spine, summoning whatever dignity I can. "And I am *not* going back."

There's more bite to my tone than I intended, but I don't regret it.

Gray exhales sharply. "Listen, I'm only following orders. I *always* follow orders. So you either come with me the easy way or the hard way." He takes a step closer.

Then another.

"You should marry Tristan. It's what you're *supposed* to do." His voice tightens like the words hurt to say.

I hate that word.

Should, suppose to, what does that even mean?

I stiffen. "*No.* I shouldn't have to do anything. I'm not being a piece in someone else's game."

"It's not like you have anywhere else to go." His jaw sets. "You could go back to Aetheris, but once your mother hears about the proposal, you won't have a choice." He pauses, letting the weight of his words settle. "Or… you could come back with me, ask Tristan for forgiveness, and live happily ever after."

Who does he think he is?

"Those aren't my only options. I was just on my way—"

"Are you talking about that boy you were with?"

"How did you—" *Cass. He'll be long gone by now.*

Gray hums, like he's amused by my realization. "Yeah, I've been trailing you since he found you at *our cave.*"

Our cave. The words send unwanted memories flashing through my mind, but I shove them down and stand my ground.

"Regardless, he promised me a safe place to stay—"

"He's dead."

I laugh. A sharp, broken sound. "You're lying."

Gray doesn't flinch. His face remains blank.

I search for something, some flicker of dishonesty, a crack in his expression, anything.

There's nothing.

My breathing turns ragged, too sharp, too fast. My stomach twists like it's rejecting the very idea that he could have killed Cass. He was just here. Walking ahead of me, silent but solid. Now he's—no.

Then, I see him. Further down the path. Lying still.

My breath catches. He's fine. He has to be fine. If I just get to him—

I step forward. Then, another step.

Then, I'm running.

Two arms wrap around my chest, locking my arms in place.

"Grayson, let me go!" I scream, thrashing, kicking, fighting his grip with everything I have.

"There's nothing you can do for him now." His breath is warm against my ear, his voice infuriatingly calm.

I don't stop fighting.

"How could you! He wasn't a threat! He was helping me!" My voice cracks. Even if I didn't know Cass well, he was still a person. A person who did nothing wrong.

Gray exhales through his nose. "Like I said, Little Flame, I'm following orders."

The scent of belladonna wafts through the air as Gray brings a small cloth to my nose.

No!

I try to hold my breath, but the damage is already done. My limbs grow sluggish. My eyelids droop.

I shake my head, willing my body to keep fighting, to keep moving—

"You'll thank me for this later, Little Flame," Gray murmurs.

My vision tunnels. My body sags against his. I try to fight it, but sleep drags me under like deep water.

And just before my mind goes numb, only one thought remains—

Grayson killed Cass.

As the world blurs around me, I realize too late.

Maybe I was never meant to escape.

Chapter 49

Keira

The world sways beneath me.

At first, it feels like I'm drifting, floating somewhere between sleep and consciousness, but then I realize it isn't the ground shifting beneath me. It's a horse. *I'm on a horse.*

And I'm not alone.

My cheek is pressed against something solid, warm. The steady rise and fall of breathing. The scent of leather and something faintly smoky fills my nose. My pulse stirs sluggishly, my body too heavy, too slow.

Then, it all comes back.

Cass. The lake. Gray's arms locked around me as everything faded to black.

I jolt upright, or I try to. The moment I move, a leather band tightens around my waist, keeping me pressed firmly against a familiar chest.

"Easy," Gray murmurs.

My skin burns where his arm holds me in place, not warmth but fury.

"Let me go." My voice is hoarse, but the venom is still there.

He doesn't answer. The only sound is the rhythmic clopping of hooves and the rustling of wind through the trees.

"Grayson." I push against his arm, but it doesn't budge. "I'm serious. Just leave me. Let me go."

Still, nothing.

I hate this. I hate how weak my voice sounds, how my body still feels drained, how I have no control in this moment. I hate that I have to ask him for anything, let alone beg him.

"I don't belong in Eclipsar," I whisper, my throat raw.

He exhales sharply like he's annoyed. "You think I don't know that?" I didn't expect his words to sting.

"Then why are you doing this?"

He doesn't answer right away. I can feel the tension in his chest, the way his fingers twitch slightly against the reins.

"I don't have a choice," he says finally. His voice is low, laced with something I can't quite place.

I squeeze my eyes shut. "Please."

That word tastes like poison on my tongue. I shouldn't be begging. I'm a *Princess,* after all. But I can't go back.

Gray shifts slightly, but his grip on me remains firm. His silence stretches between us, thick and suffocating. Then, finally—

"You're just tired. Get some more rest."

I go rigid. That's all he says. Not no, not I can't, just an instruction like my pleas don't even matter. Like this conversation is already over.

I want to scream. I want to rip myself from his arms, throw myself off this damn horse if that's what it takes, but my body betrays me. The after-effects or whatever Gray gave me weigh me down like chains, and as much as I fight it, the darkness drags me under *again*.

I wake to the crackling of fire. The night presses in around me, cold and thick. My body aches as I shift, the rough texture of a cloak against my skin. The firelight flickers, casting long shadows against the trees.

Gray sits on the other side of the fire.

He's sharpening a dagger, slow and methodical, his face half-hidden in the glow. He doesn't look up, but I know he knows I'm awake.

I push myself up, the cloak slipping off my shoulders. "Where are we?"

He doesn't answer immediately. The blade catches the firelight as he slides the whetstone down its edge.

The sound scrapes against my nerves.

"About a day's ride from the palace," he finally says. His voice is quiet, but it carries in the stillness. "You managed to make it further than I thought."

A day. I ignore the admiration in his voice and focus on the panic tightening in my chest. This is real. I'm going back.

I swallow hard, clutching my cloak. "You should've left me."

His jaw tenses. Just slightly. If I weren't watching so closely, I wouldn't have noticed.

But he says nothing.

I hate how calm he looks, always seeming perfectly unbothered. Like this is just another night, just another job. Like taking me back to Tristan is just another order to follow. *It probably is.*

I pull my knees to my chest, staring into the fire. "Do you ever think for yourself?"

The scraping of the whetstone stops.

Slowly, Gray lifts his gaze to mine. His eyes are dark and endless.

"Go back to sleep, Little Flame."

My throat tightens. He's shutting me out. *Again.*

I should stop talking. I should give him the cold shoulder, make him feel as insignificant as he's making me feel. But the words claw their way out before I can stop them.

"What happened to you?" My voice is quieter now, barely a whisper. "To make you like this?"

For a moment, just a moment, something flickers in his eyes. Something raw, something that looks like hurt.

But then it's gone as quickly as it came.

He turns his gaze back to the blade in his hands. "I am the way I am. No need for the whole backstory. Just go back to sleep."

I exhale sharply, forcing back the lump rising in my throat. There's nothing left to say. Nothing he'll listen to, anyway.

The fire crackles between us, warm and steady. But the space between me and Gray has never felt colder.

"No." My voice comes out hoarse, raw from sleep and something deeper, something fractured. Gray stops sharpening his dagger, the one that looks disturbingly familiar. His fingers still around the hilt, but he doesn't look up.

"All I've been doing is sleeping," I snap, my frustration turning into desperation.

He just stares at me, the firelight flickering across his face like a mask.

"Say something!" My voice cracks, the words ripping from my throat, too loud for the quiet of the forest. Somewhere in the distance, birds take flight from the treetops.

He doesn't listen. Typical Gray.

So, I do the next best thing.

I shove myself up on unsteady legs, the world tilting beneath me. My heart slams against my ribs, but I don't think. I just run.

Wild hair. Wild feet. Wild mind.

The cold air whips against my skin as I tear through the trees, my breath coming fast, my heart pounding. My pulse thrums with something electric, not just fear but something sharper—more reckless.

I listen past the blood rushing in my ears, waiting. *Hoping.*

Then I hear it. Heavy boots pounding against the earth.

He's chasing me.

Ha, I knew he would. He always does.

But I don't dare look back. Not yet.

Chapter 50

Keira

The cold wind bites at my skin as I push forward, my breath ragged. My legs burn, my bare feet stinging against the forest floor, but I don't stop. I can't.

Branches whip against my arms, snagging at my disheveled dress, but I barely register the pain. I can still hear him behind me, steady, relentless. He isn't sprinting like I am. He doesn't have to.

Gray is the future Blade of Eclipsar. I'm just a girl running out of breath.

The thought sends a fresh wave of desperation through me, and I veer sharply between two thick trees, hoping to lose him in the dark.

Then—a hand. Fast and unyielding.

Fingers snare around my wrist, yanking me back so hard the ground is ripped from beneath my feet. My back slams against solid warmth, the force knocking the air from my lungs.

I thrash, but his grip tightens, his other arm locking around my waist, pinning me against him.

"Enough," he breathes against my ear, his voice like iron wrapped in silk.

"No," I choke out, my body twisting uselessly in his hold. "Let me go."

His chest rises and falls against my back, his grip unmoving.

"You don't get to run from this," he murmurs.

I don't know if he means Eclipsar, Tristan, *or him.*

"I'll fight you," I whisper, with a burning throat. "Even if I lose, I'll fight you until I can't anymore."

Instead of answering, he shifts. One arm hooks beneath my legs, the other supporting my back.

Before I can protest, I'm weightless. Lifted.

"No!" I thrash against him, but he doesn't falter. "Gray, put me down!"

"You're not strong enough for this," he says quietly as if it's just a fact. No hate. No mockery. Just the truth.

I hate him for thinking so little of me.

But I don't stop fighting.

My elbow jerks back, aiming for his ribs, but he twists just in time. My knee slams against his arm instead, not hard enough to make him drop me, but enough to make him grunt.

"Little Flame," he warns.

I don't listen. I claw at his arms, at his chest, anywhere I can reach. But his grip only tightens.

"Go ahead, keep fighting me" he mutters, voice smooth. "You're only making this harder on yourself."

I grit my teeth, twisting sharply. I get one arm free, shoving my palm against his jaw to push him away—

But in a flash, he has me flipped, my back hitting the cold ground before I can react.

He's over me in an instant, one knee pressing against my thigh, his forearm pinning my wrists. I buck, but it's useless. His weight is solid, unmoving.

For a second, all I can hear is my ragged breathing. The crackling fire nearby. The unspoken words between us.

Gray stares down at me; his eyes find my lips and I don't miss the muscle that twitches in his jaw. His grip is firm but not cruel. I realize, then, that he could hurt me if he wanted to.

But he won't. He never has.

I swallow hard, my breath still coming fast.

"Are you done?" he asks.

I clench my jaw and lift my chin, meeting his eyes with all the fire I have left.

"Not even close."

I twist beneath him, every muscle in my body screaming. But Gray is stronger. His grip on my wrists doesn't falter, even as I lift my hips, trying to throw him off.

"You're wasting your energy," he murmurs, his voice calm, infuriatingly steady.

"Then, let me go" I demand hrough clenched teeth, my breath sharp.

"No." The word is final, unwavering.

But I've never been good at accepting defeat.

I go limp for a beat, letting my body sink into the cold dirt beneath me, my chest rising and falling in sharp breaths. I see it then, uncertainty in his onyx eyes like he's waiting for my next move.

Good.

With every bit of strength I have left, I wrench my knee up, aiming for his ribs. It's not perfect—he shifts just in time to take the blow on his hip instead of his stomach, but it's enough.

His grip on my wrists slackens. That's all I need.

I rip my arm free, curling my fingers into a fist, and strike— Unfortunately, he's faster.

Before my knuckles can connect with his face, he snatches my wrist out of the air and flips me in one swift motion.

Now, I'm on my stomach, my cheek pressed against the dirt, one of his arms wrapped around my waist. The other gripped my wrist behind my back.

A sharp breath escapes me as I struggle, but it's useless.

"You're getting better," he murmurs, his voice maddeningly close to my ear. "Not good enough. But better."

I snarl, twisting beneath him. "I hate you."

Silence. Then—

A low chuckle. Not mocking, not cruel. Just soft. Quiet. Like he finds me amusing.

I shove down the rising heat flooding my face. My heart pounds furiously against my ribs.

He's *laughing* at *me*.

Gray leans in just slightly, just enough that I can feel his breath against my jaw. "No, you don't."

I go rigid beneath him. *I do. I hate him.*

I hate his strength, his onyx eyes, the way he always has the upper hand. I hate that he never lets me win, never lets me run.

But most of all, I hate that a part of me—the part I bury deep—is relieved that he came for me at all.

His grip softens, but he doesn't let me go.

"Are you done fighting yet?" he murmurs.

I press my lips together, my face flushed. I hate that my answer is already written in the way my body sags in his hold, in the way exhaustion finally catches up to me.

For now, at least, I've lost. But I won't always. Not forever.

I swallow hard, shifting slightly against his hold. "I still hate you." He huffs another quiet laugh, but this time, he doesn't argue.

And, for some reason, something blooms in my chest. Something new, something warm. *Something terrifying.*

Chapter 51

Keira

Gray doesn't let me go right away. He lingers like he's waiting for something. Maybe for me to try and fight again. Maybe for me to beg.

I do neither.

Instead, I turn my head just enough to look at him over my shoulder. His face is cast in the dim glow of the morning sky. Faint streaks of gold and pale lavender stretch across the horizon, bleeding into the last remnants of night.

Morning.

I shift beneath him, testing his grip. His arm tenses but doesn't tighten. He's not holding me down anymore, not really.

My throat burns. "What now?"

He hesitates, contemplating something, if only to stall the awkwardness.

"You're going to sleep." His voice is quiet like this is some sort of truce.

I scoff, twisting onto my side. He doesn't stop me, but he doesn't move away, either. "And you expect me to just trust you?"

His lips curve slightly, not quite a smirk, not quite a smile. Nonetheless, it reveals his devastating dimples "No."

Shadows stretch longer now, shifting as the sun climbs higher.

I *should* try again. I *should* use the last of my strength to break away, to disappear into the trees, to do something.

But I don't. Because even if I run, I know he'd catch me.

And a part of me, the one I hate, knows that I'd rather fight with him than be *without* him.

So, I stay—for now.

Gray watches me for another long moment before he finally leans back, putting a bit of distance between us. But not much.

"You should get some rest," he says again, more gently this time.

I don't answer. I just shift onto my back and stare up at the sky. The stars are fading now, swallowed by the creeping light of dawn.

I wonder if the Queen is looking for me. If she knows where I am. If Tristan—

I force the thought away before it can settle.

Gray doesn't move from his spot beside me. He sharpens his dagger once more. *My* dagger, I realize now. The one I left in my room at Eclipsar.

He must feel my stare because he twirls it between his fingers before glancing at me. "Hope you don't mind."

I lift my chin. But don't respond.

His lips twitch, but he doesn't return it. Instead, he flips the blade once more before tucking it into his belt. "Figured if you have something of mine, I could carry something of yours," he says with a shrug.

"Excuse me? I didn't take anything from you." I look down, taking in my ragged state.

He lets out a low chuckle, and I hate the way my chest tightens at the sound of it.

"Oh, Little Flame," he flashes a smile. "That ring you twist around your thumb—who do you think that belongs to?" He nods to the ring.

"I—I got it from someone who attacked me in the woods—" I break off as realization dawns on me.

"It was you!" I yell. "You attacked me that day!? Anything else you care to fill me in on? Perhaps a secret second life?" I cross my arms over my chest. Gray smiles to himself.

"Sorry to disappoint you, but no secret life."

I wear a smile of my own as my mind replays the events of that night. "If I remember correctly," I tap a finger to my chin. "I had you on the ground, breathless."

He huffs out a laugh, the sound spreading warmth throughout my body.

"I let you knock me down. Didn't want to bruise the Princess's ego."

"Oh, how noble of you," I say sweetly, rolling my eyes.

He steps closer, eyes falling down to my lips before meeting my gaze again. "Besides," he adds, "you were sitting on my chest. I was a little… distracted."

My brain short-circuits for a second.

Such a flirt.

I narrow my eyes, trying to ignore the way my cheeks betray me. "You're impossible."

"And yet, here you are," he murmurs, brushing past me like it meant nothing. Like he didn't just casually drop a line that would live in my brain for the rest of my days.

I hate him. I really do. *For now.*

The sound of rain hits my senses before anything else. It's hard at first, a relentless tapping against the leaves, then a rush of wind that cuts through the trees like a blade.

My teeth chatter nonstop, the only warmth coming from the body I'm pressed against. His breathing is steady beside me, but the air has shifted. The scent of the rain is thick, the ground beneath us damp and cold. I blink. The world is blurry from the rain, and my eyes catch on the gray sky above. A storm's rolling in, fast.

The first flash of lightning slices through the sky, immediately followed by a sharp crack of thunder. The earth shudders beneath me.

I don't want to move, I don't want to face the fact that I'm still here... *with him.*

But, the storm is growing, and I can't ignore that.

I shift slightly, my body aching, our fight still lingering in my muscles. I wince as I sit up, not wanting to look at Gray, but I can't help it. He hasn't moved.

For a moment, he's almost peaceful, looking almost boyish.

And then another crack of thunder splits the air, louder this time, closer. I can't ignore the coldness creeping in, the shivers running down my spine.

"We need to go," I say, my voice hoarse but firm. The words taste wrong on my tongue. I don't want to need him.

Don't want to admit it, but I do. The storm is no friend to anyone.

Gray stirs beside me, a slow groan escaping him.

"Just lay back down with me." His dark eyes open, just a sliver at first. He seems disoriented, like he has forgotten where he was and who he was with. Then, the realization hits, and he's up on his feet in an instant.

I brace myself, expecting him to grab me and force me to go wherever he wants. But he doesn't. He stands tall, shoulders taut, watching the storm with unnerving stillness.

"You think we'll find shelter?" I ask, fighting the biting wind that cuts through the trees. The storm is going to get worse, and we're exposed. The thought of being out in this makes my stomach tighten.

"We'll find something," he mutters, glancing toward the thickening woods. His gaze narrows, assessing the landscape as though he knows exactly where to go.

I swallow hard, unsure if I should follow him or make my own way. But then he moves, and I don't think twice. His hand brushes my arm, just enough to steady me, and then we're walking—no, running—through the trees. The rain pelts us, and I can't help but wonder if we're being followed.

But what's worse: the rain or the possibility of Tristan finding me? Then again, he already did. I'm trying not to think about it.

Gray leads the way through the forest, fast, purposeful strides cutting through the rain. I match his pace as best as I can, adrenaline keeping me moving.

The storm seems to build with every step, the thunder growing louder, the wind howling through the tall trees above. I barely notice the way the earth is becoming slick beneath my bare feet. The rain keeps coming harder, soaking my clothes, my hair, my skin.

And then, through the trees ahead, I spot something: a small cottage-like structure, barely visible against the shadows of the woods. Abandoned, but with a roof intact.

Gray doesn't hesitate. He's already moving toward it, forcing me to follow. I try to keep up, but the storm is relentless, and my legs feel like they might give out at any moment.

Inside the cottage, it's dark, save for a few cracks in the wood. Gray pulls the door shut behind us with a grunt, and the sound of the storm outside is muffled. We're safe for now. A false sense of security.

Gray's eyes fall on the closed door, and I notice his stance shift, becoming more rigid. His hand moves instinctively to his—my dagger.

"We can't stay here long," he mutters. "They might be close."

I freeze, and my heart leaps into my throat. *Who's they?*

"I—" I start, but my voice dies in my throat. The rain outside is so loud that I almost don't hear the soft footsteps in the distance.

Gray's gaze meets mine. He doesn't say anything. His hand moves to my dagger at his side again, his fingers brushing over the hilt. He's waiting, his body tense, ready for a fight.

And then, the unmistakable sound of footsteps crunching on wet branches cuts through the air.

Someone's coming.

Chapter 52

Keira

The footsteps grow louder, closing in, too many to be a measly forger. Gray hears them too; his posture shifts, every muscle tensing like a bowstring ready to snap.

I swallow hard, forcing myself to stay still, even as my heartbeat slams against my ribs. A sharp knock against the wooden door makes me flinch.

And then—

"Did you really think we wouldn't find you?"

The voice is smooth, calm, with an edge of amusement. My stomach drops.

Adrian.

Gray moves first, stepping in front of me like a shield, his hand tightening around my dagger. The air between us thickens.

Adrian doesn't wait for an invitation. The door swings open, the storm's howling wind rushing in, whipping rain through the broken gaps in the walls. Silhouetted in the doorway stand four figures, cloaked and armed. Their weapons gleam in the flashes of lightning, and I know without a doubt they didn't come here to talk.

I barely have time to react before the first rebel lunges.

Gray meets him head-on. Their bodies collide, the impact echoing through the tiny space. The rebel swings a knife, but Gray blocks it with his forearm, shoving the man backward. The second rebel rushes in, blade slashing toward me. I stumble back, reaching for anything. My fingers brush against a broken wooden beam, and I grip it like a lifeline.

Adrian watches from the threshold, arms crossed.

"Not even a greeting, Princess?" he muses.

I don't answer. I'm too busy dodging the next strike.

The cottage is too small for this many bodies. The rebels are too many, their movements quick and practiced. I swing the beam at the rebel nearest to me, catching him in the side. He grunts but doesn't go down. I barely register it before Gray slams into him from behind, knocking him off balance.

Another rebel lunges toward Gray, and this time, I see the blade before he does.

"Gray, move!" I shout.

He pivots, but not fast enough. The dagger slices across his abdomen.

Gray hisses through his teeth, staggering back a step. His free hand instinctively flies to the wound, fingers coming away slick with blood.

Panic surges through me.

Adrian hums, tilting his head. "Getting sloppy, Noctis."

Gray forces himself upright, gritting his teeth. His grip tightens around my dagger. I see the pain in the way he holds himself.

I don't think. I act.

Grabbing the fallen rebel's knife, I whirl on Adrian. "Call them off."

He chuckles. "You think you're in control here?"

Gray takes advantage of his distraction, lunging forward. Adrian barely escapes him, but he's forced to step back out of the cottage and into the storm. The rebels hesitate, exchanging glances.

Adrian clicks his tongue. "That's enough."

The command is casual but immediate. The rebels withdraw, slipping into the rain like shadows.

My breath comes fast, uneven. My pulse thunders in my ears. I can still hear the storm raging outside, but inside, it's eerily silent.

Adrian gives us one last look.

"Princess, you should rethink your options." he says smoothly. "I'm telling you, we're your safest option." And then he's gone, vanishing into the storm.

I stare at the empty doorway, my body still filled with adrenaline. The storm swallows them whole, leaving nothing but the sound of the wind and rain. Then, I turn to Gray, and his breathing is heavy, his face pale. Blood drips between his fingers.

I don't hesitate.

"Sit down," I order, already searching the room for anything I can use to treat his wounds.

He doesn't argue, which means he's worse off than he's letting on. I kneel beside him, hands already moving before I can think twice.

Because despite everything, despite wanting to run, to hate him, to pretend he's nothing more than someone sentencing me to a fate akin to death—I can't let *him* die.

Chapter 53

Keira

Rain still hammers against the roof, leaking in from the broken slats, but it's distant now, background noise to the sound of Gray's heavy, labored breathing. I managed to light the dry wood I found resting in the hearth but it provided little warmth.

I kneel beside him, my hands steady even as my heart pounds. His shirt is already soaked with blood, the deep red disappearing into the dark fabric. He watches me through half-lidded eyes as I push the fabric up to assess the wound.

It's bad. Not fatal—but bad.

"Take it off," I say, nodding toward his shirt.

His lips twitch slightly. "At least take me to dinner first."

I glare at him. "If you bleed out, I'll kill you myself."

His eyes smile, but he doesn't argue. With slow, pained movements, he pulls his shirt over his head and tosses it aside.

I pretend not to notice the way his muscles tense beneath my hands or how the firelight casts sharp shadows across his skin. Instead, I focus on the wound. It's a clean cut but deep, bleeding sluggishly. I reach for the bottles, lining a small wooden table next to the fireplace. My fingers fumble through the contents. Dried herbs. Not much, but enough.

Gray watches as I crush the leaves between my palms, mixing them with a bit of water from a canteen to form a paste.

"You've done this before," he observes.

I nod, applying the mixture to his wound. He stiffens but doesn't make a sound.

"The Queen taught me," I say, voice quieter now. "Aetherian Queens don't just sit on thrones, you know."

He raises his hand as if he might run it across my cheek but thought better of it. I drop my gaze, focusing on wrapping the bandage tightly around his torso.

His voice is softer when he speaks again. "You could've let me bleed."

I finish tying the bandage and sit back on my heels, meeting his gaze. "I know."

The silence stretches between us.

Then—

"You're shaking."

I blink. "What?"

Gray nods toward my hands, covered in his blood. I hadn't even noticed, but they were trembling from the cold, from the exhaustion, from everything.

"I just saved your life, and you're worried about me?"

"Someone has to."

I roll my eyes and start to stand, but before I can move, his hand shoots out, catching my wrist. Not rough. Not forceful. Just enough to make me pause.

"Stay," he murmurs.

I freeze. "Excuse me?"

His thumb brushes absently over my wrist. "You're freezing, and I'm not in the mood to chase you through the woods again. Just—stay here. *With me.*"

I stare at him. My argument caught in my throat as my heart pounded wildly in my ears. The only thing that came out of my mouth was, "You want me to sleep next to you?" I try to hide my shock.

He shrugs, wincing slightly at the movement. "Wouldn't be the worst thing, Little Flame."

My heart flutters. I tell myself it's just from the cold, just from exhaustion. I should say no. I should push his hand away and curl up as far from him as possible. But I don't.

Because despite everything, despite the fact that he's taking me back to Eclipsar, despite the fact that I swore I wouldn't fall into whatever game he's playing—I can't bring myself to leave him like this.

"...Fine," I mutter.

He exhales as if he hadn't actually expected me to agree. But he just shifts slightly, making room beside him on the makeshift bed of cloaks and furs.

I hesitate only a moment longer before lying down beside him, keeping a safe distance. Or at least, I try to.

But the cold seeps in fast, the fire is dying, and when I shift slightly closer, Gray doesn't move away. Or protest.

Instead, his voice comes quiet in the darkness. "You're not running?"

I roll my eyes. "I just spent the last hour patching you up. Would be a waste if you bled out chasing me."

The dying firelight cast shadows in the sharp angles of his jaw and cheekbones.

Stars, has he always been this handsome?

"That's the *only* reason?" He looks down at me, flashing his dimples.

I roll onto my side, meeting his gaze. I *should* say yes. I *should* lie.

Instead, my throat tightens as I murmur, "You didn't let me go."

He looks as if he might ask another question. Instead, he simply shakes his head as if he's clearing his mind.

He just exhales, turning his head to stare at the ceiling. "You're impossible." He echoes my earlier words.

I huff a quiet laugh. "So are you."

A beat of silence. Then softer, more tired than anything, he says, "Get some rest, Little Flame."

For once, I don't argue.

Not because he told me to. But because, for the first time in days, I don't feel entirely alone.

And I hate how I don't hate it.

Chapter 54

Keira

The fire has dimmed to embers, casting only the faintest glow. Rain still patters against the roof, softer now, but the storm hasn't fully passed.

I should be asleep but rest is a luxury I haven't been afforded the last couple of nights. My body aches, my thoughts are too loud, and every time I close my eyes, I see Tristan's face, see the palace of Eclipsar, and hear the Queen's voice. And yet, even in the silence, there's something else.

A sound—low, strained.

I turn my head toward Gray. His brows are drawn, his lips slightly parted, his breathing uneven. He's still, but there's a tension in his body like he's bracing for a blow.

Then, a whisper of sound—"No, stop!" It's more of a whisper shout.

I shift onto my elbow, hesitant. I could wake him. I *should* wake him. But some part of me, some foolish, reckless part, reaches out instead.

"Gray," I whisper, barely audible.

His body jerks. His fingers twitch, curling into the furs beneath us. I inch closer, my hand hovering just above his arm.

And then, his breath hitches, his whole body tensing like a bowstring pulled too tight.

"Gray," I say, louder this time, my fingers pressing against his bicep. "Wake up."

His eyes snap open, wild and unfocused, as if he doesn't see me at first. His chest rises and falls rapidly, and for a brief, terrible second, I think he might lash out. But then his gaze locks onto mine. And his body physically settles.

His breathing is still uneven, but his grip on the furs loosens. His fingers flex once before falling still.

"Nightmare?" I ask quietly.

He doesn't answer right away. He looks as if he wants to say something but can't quite find the words.

Finally, he exhales sharply, running a hand through his dark curls. "Go back to sleep."

I should. But I don't. Instead, I tilt my head, studying him. "Do they happen often?"

A muscle in his jaw jumps. "It doesn't matter."

"It does if you're going to wake up like that every night."

His lips press into a thin line. He looks away toward the dying fire. "It's nothing I can't handle."

I watch him for a moment before lying back down, this time closer than before. Close enough that I can still feel the tension in his shoulders, the way his fingers still twitch. I don't know what possessed me to reach for him earlier. Maybe exhaustion. Maybe something else.

But now that I have, I can't shake the feeling that, for all his sharp edges, for all his unreadable stares, he's just as haunted as I am. And maybe, just maybe, I'm not the only one who hates being alone.

I don't say anything else. I just close my eyes, pretending not to notice when, a few minutes later, Gray finally exhales and settles back down beside me.

This time, his breathing stays even. This time, he's the one to inch slightly closer, and I let him. I have no doubt I'll regret all of this in the morning.

But for now, I'll pretend.

Pretend everything is okay. Pretend I hate the Prince lying next to me. Just pretend, most of it.

Chapter 55

Keira

A soft glow filters through the slits of wood that the hut is made from, golden and muted, casting long shadows over the contents of the room. The storm has passed. The air is cool, carrying the scent of wet earth and pine.

I blink, my body sluggish, my mind slow to shake the last remnants of sleep.

And then I realize—I'm warm.

Too warm.

Something solid is pressed against my back, something steady and unmoving. Heat seeps through my clothes, through my skin, and a slow, horrifying realization settles over me like a heavyweight.

Gray. I knew he slept next to me, but I didn't think we would get this close.

I go rigid, suddenly hyper-aware of the way his arm is draped over my waist. The way his fingers rest just above my hip, firm but not tight. His chest rises and falls in a slow, steady rhythm, his breath warm against the back of my neck.

I hold my breath, waiting for him to stir, to realize what he's done, to pull away, but he doesn't. Carefully, I shift, trying to slip free.

His grip tightens. I freeze.

It's a lazy sort of hold like his body knows I'm trying to leave before his mind does. Like he's still lost in whatever dreamless sleep he finally managed to get.

I try again, moving just an inch, but this time, his fingers flex over my stomach, his palm splaying over me as he pulls me back against him.

A quiet gasp slips from my lips.

Gray makes a low, content sound in his throat, his face pressing deeper into the crook of my neck.

My heart slams against my ribs. This *isn't* happening. This *can't* be happening. I twist again, more forcefully this time. "Gray," I whine.

Nothing. I grit my teeth. "Gray."

He lets out a low hum, but he still doesn't wake. Fine.

I shift again, this time pressing my elbow into his side— careful to avoid his cut—not hard enough to hurt, but enough to get a reaction.

It works. Another low groan rumbles in his chest, and slowly, his grip loosens.

I move quickly, slipping out from beneath his arm and scrambling upright. My skin feels too hot, my pulse too unsteady. I don't dare look at him.

Behind me, Gray shifts, exhaling a slow breath.

Then, his voice, low and groggy, thick with sleep.

"Running already?"

I whip around.

He's still lying there, his arm now resting where I'd been only moments ago, his dark eyes barely open. There's something different about him like this—more *boyish*.

I fold my arms over my chest. "I wasn't running."

He sighs. "If you say so."

I scowl. "*You* were *holding* me."

His brows lift, lazy and amused. "Was I?"

"That—" I clamp my mouth shut, heat creeping up my neck. "Whatever."

He lets out a low, quiet chuckle but doesn't argue.

I busy myself with tying my waves up with some string I found, avoiding his gaze. "As enjoyable as that was, if you still plan on dragging me back, we should get going." I try my best to crush the flicker of hope. Maybe he's changed his mind.

Gray stretches, slow and deliberate, with a slight wince, before finally sitting up. His curls are messier than usual, and for once, he looks...*normal.*

I hate that it makes my chest flutter.

"Yeah," he says, voice still laced with sleep. "Let's go."

I turn away first, stepping toward the little door, pretending I don't feel his gaze lingering on me. Pretending I don't still feel the warmth of his touch.

We weave our way through the Hollows silently as we head back toward the first fire Gray had made.

"The horse should still be there." He calls over his shoulder, some of his curls falling in front of his eyes.

I just hum and nod my head. Even if I don't want to go back to Eclipsar, I desperately need to bathe. There's dirt under my nails, dirt in my hair, turning it an awful shade of gray, and I haven't worn shoes in days. No doubt I look as disgusting as I feel.

Gray doesn't seem to care. He must be used to this feeling. I look around praying to the Stars they lead us to a pond. And to my surprise, they do.

I debate asking him to stop, but I risk him saying no. Before I can change my mind, I blurt out—"I need to bathe."

Gray slows, glancing at me over his shoulder. "What?"

"I need to bathe," I repeat, lifting my chin. "Now."

His eyes travel the length of me, my tangled hair, the dirt smeared across my skin, and my bare feet caked in mud.

"We don't have time for that," he says, turning back toward the path.

I huff, planting my hands on my hips. "We do if I say we do."

Gray stops walking. Turns. His dark eyes lock onto mine. "If *you* say we do?"

I fold my arms, refusing to back down. "Yes."

He stares at me for a long moment, then exhales sharply. "Fine," he mutters, already pulling his tunic covered in dry blood over his head as he walks toward the pond.

I blink. "What—what are you doing?"

He tosses his tunic onto a nearby rock. "Keeping an eye on you."

My mouth falls open. "By bathing *with me?*"

Gray gives me a pointed look. "Would you rather I stand here and watch?"

Heat crawls up my neck. "You're insufferable."

"And you're filthy," he replies, stepping into the water with a sharp inhale. "Get in."

I glare at him for a second longer before turning away, stripping down to my shift, and stepping into the pond. The water is cool, stealing the heat from my skin, and I dunk under quickly, scrubbing my hands through my hair.

When I surface, Gray is waist-deep a few feet away, running a hand through his own hair, slicking back his dark curls. He doesn't look at me, but he doesn't have to. His presence alone is enough to put me on edge.

"This isn't necessary, you know," I say, dipping my hands into the water and rubbing the grime from my arms.

He finally glances at me, arching a brow. "I disagree."

"I *could* have just bathed alone."

"Maybe. But you run every chance you get. Thought I'd save myself the trouble."

I splash water at him. He barely flinches, though I catch the slight twitch of amusement at the corner of his mouth.

"Five more minutes," he says.

I roll my eyes and dunk under again, trying to ignore the fact that once this is over, we'll be back on the road.

Back to Eclipsar.

Chapter 56

Keira

Just as Gray said, the horse was still, in fact, there.

"You might want to get comfortable. I need to make sure she's okay to ride." Gray nods in the direction of a tree stump as he starts patting the horse.

"Your horse is a girl?" I settle onto the lifeless stump and cross my legs under me.

"Yes, *she* is." He arches an eyebrow at me. "Little Flame, you didn't think you were the only female in my life, did you?"

Leaning back on my hands; "Oh, please. If there was another woman in your life, she'd have poisoned you by now."

Gray hums, running a hand along her mane. "You say that like I'm unbearable."

"You *are* unbearable." I tilt my head. "What's her name?"

He glances at me, then back at the horse. "Nyx."

I frown. "Nyx?"

"Goddess of the night." He clarifies.

I arch a brow. "How poetic of you."

Gray shrugs. "She's fast, quiet, and doesn't trust easily. Remind you of anyone?"

I narrow my eyes. "Are you comparing me to a horse?"

"I'd say it's a compliment." He pats Nyx's side. "She's got spirit."

I huff, crossing my arms. "You should be grateful I'm too tired to fight you."

"Mm." He checks Nyx's hooves, unbothered. "Yes, so grateful."

I roll my eyes and lean back against the tree stump, watching as he moves around the horse with practiced ease. This discussion is a distraction, one I hate to admit I enjoy. But beneath it, reality lingers.

We're still going back. And I'm still his prisoner.

"Alright," Gray finally says, tightening the saddle. "She's ready."

I glance at him, then at the open road ahead. My heart sinks.

"Do I at least get to ride in front this time?" I ask, trying to keep my voice light.

Gray gives me a look. "Nice try." I sigh, already regretting getting on Nyx.

Gray saddles up first, offering me his hand as I take my place behind him. The last time I rode Nyx, I was unconscious. Hopefully, this time will be a little more enjoyable.

"You might want to hold on." Gray tosses me a look over his shoulder. I glance around and there isn't much to grab onto, *except him.*

"Hold onto what? There's nothing back here." I act clueless just to see how he would react.

Without missing a beat he reaches around to lock his hands around my wrists. My breath catches as he guides my arms around his waist, just above his wound. I can feel every inhale and exhale he takes. His back is fully pressed against my chest, leaving me a little breathless.

I don't have much time to focus on the sudden contact before Gray clacks his tongue, and Nyx starts galloping— faster than any horse I've ever been on. I squeeze a little harder, hoping I'm not hurting him too much. Then again, that wouldn't be so bad. *Just the thought has me wrapping around him a little tighter.*

This isn't so bad. The wind in my hair causes it to flap violently in my face. I *could* have enjoyed this if it weren't for the fact that Gray was practically taking me to my doom.

I try to picture it, me in a black wedding gown. I doubt the King would want me to wear white or sapphire. Walking down the carpeted path to the dashing Tristan, future King of Eclipsar. I probably could be happy in that version of my life.

Unfortunately, that's not going to happen. I had been so lost in the thought of my day dream I hadn't realized we had slowed down to a prance.

That's when I see it—

The field of roses.

"Why did you bring us here?" I don't even mind the shock in my voice. Not when I can feel the steady thrum of heat under my skin. With everything that's happened, I had unknowingly set my magic aside. But being here, being in this field, brought it right back.

Gray hops off Nyx with a loud thud and offers me his hand.

"You didn't answer my question." I hold his gaze as I slide my hand into his. His hands are strong and firm while somehow being soft and gentle at the same time.

"This is the most happiness I could bring you." His voice wavers ever so slightly, his words sounding more like they were meant for him and not me.

I step down from Nyx, my bare feet sinking into the soft earth. The scent of roses is thick in the air, clinging to every breath. I run my fingers along a crimson petal, the familiar warmth of my magic sparking beneath my skin. The fire that has been quiet for too long stirs, stretching, testing.

I don't look at Gray when I say, "You really think flowers are enough to make me forget you're dragging me back to Blackthorn?"

He lets out a small laugh. "No. But it's enough to make you stop looking at me like you want to stab me."

I glance at him over my shoulder. "Oh, I *still* want to stab you. Just... maybe *not right* now."

With pursed lips, he says nothing.

I turn back to the roses, lifting my hand and watching as tiny flames dance along my fingertips. The golden light flickers in the petals, catching in the dewdrops like tiny stars. I tilt my head, feeling the way my magic hums in response to this place. It's different from before. Not just power but something... deeper.

Gray steps beside me, watching carefully. "You've gotten better at controlling it."

I let the flames swirl around my palm before closing my fist and snuffing them out. "Not really. It listens to me sometimes."

"It listens to you now."

I shrug. "The roses seem to help."

Gray eyes look almost sad but he quickly masks it, crossing his arms and nodding toward my hands. "Try something."

I arch a brow. "Try what?"

"I don't know. You're the fire-wielding Princess. *Impress* me."

I narrow my eyes but don't argue. Instead, I turn toward one of the taller bushes, extending my hand and letting the heat rise again. The fire curls from my palm, delicate and somewhat controlled, licking at the petals without consuming them. I furrow my brows, concentrating. The flame flickers, shifting from gold to something softer—almost white.

Gray whistles. "Neat trick."

I grin, pleased with myself—until the fire suddenly jumps, shooting higher than I intended. I yelp, stumbling back just as Gray lunges forward, clamping his hands over mine.

"Steady," he says, voice low and calm.

His hands are warm, but not like mine. His warmth is something different. *Grounding.*

I take a breath, feeling the flame between us ignite, steadying again under his touch. Glancing up to meet his gaze, his onyx eyes are guarded, but he doesn't let go.

"Not bad," he says after a beat of silence.

"Did I impress you?"

He raises both eyebrows. "Almost."

I reply by shoving him lightly, and he actually laughs. It's soft, barely there, but it's real.

And for a moment—just a moment—I forget that he's taking me back. I forget that I should hate him.

Gray still hasn't let go of my hands. His fingers are firm and steady, wrapped around mine as if he could keep my fire from slipping out of control again. And maybe he can.

"I think I've got it," I murmur, but I don't pull away.

His gaze travels to my hands then back to my face. "I know."

Still, he doesn't let go.

The sun is warm in the afternoon sky. This is the warmest it's been in Eclipsar since I've gotten here. The roses sway in the soft breeze, their scent thick in the air. I should step back. I should say something sharp, something to break the moment before it becomes something I can't take back.

But I don't. And he doesn't either.

Gray lifts one hand, carefully brushing his thumb over my knuckles. My breath catches, my heartbeat hammering against my ribs in a way I hope he doesn't notice. He watches the movement, before speaking.

"This suits you," he says after a long moment.

I blink back my confusion. "What does?"

His thumb lingers, tracing slow circles over my skin. "This. The fire. The way it bends to you like it's been waiting all this time for you to claim it." I swallow hard. "I don't think I ever had a choice."

Gray finally meets my eyes, his voice quieter now. "Maybe not. But you're still the one in control."

I don't know what to say to that, so I don't say anything at all. I just let the moment settle between us, fragile and unspoken. Then, to my absolute shock, he lifts my hand to his lips. It's barely a kiss. A brush of warmth against my knuckles, fleeting and uncertain, like he's testing a boundary he isn't sure he's allowed to cross.

And I know how he feels.

He hesitates, his lips still close enough that I can feel the ghost of his touch before finally pulling away. My fingers curl involuntarily as if trying to hold onto the feeling. I don't know why he did it. I don't know why I let him. But the worst part? I don't want him to let go. I take a shaky breath, trying to gather the pieces of my crumbling resolve.

"Gray," I say softly.

His expression shifts, something cautious settling over his features. "Little Flame."

I hesitate, gripping the edge of my dress with my free hand. "If I asked you to let me go... *really* let me go... would you?"

The question hangs in the air, heavy and suffocating.

Gray doesn't answer right away. He looks at me, really looks at me, as if weighing something deep inside himself. The silence stretches, pressing against my ribs, until finally, he exhales.

"I think you already know the answer." He answers, shaking his head slightly.

It's not the answer I want, but it's the one that seals my fate.

Chapter 57

Keira

The sun is now barely lining the edge of the sky. Bold shades of orange and pink line the sky, the clouds a warm shade of gold. I lay my chin on Gray's shoulder as Nyx trots down the path towards the destination I have been dreading.

"Can we maybe just make a quick stop in Shadowmere?" I lean my head further onto his lower neck. His whole upper body tightens.

Gray exhales sharply, his grip on Nyx's reins tightening. "Those aren't my orders, Little Flame."

I sigh dramatically, shifting even closer, my chin still resting against his shoulder. "You're Tristan's little attack dog, aren't you?" Gray stiffens, and I can tell he's trying to ignore me. So I push a little more.

"Just for a little while?" My voice is softer now. "I need to clear my head before we walk into whatever disaster awaits me in Eclipsar."

Gray is silent for a long moment. The only sound is the rhythmic clop of Nyx's hooves against the dirt path and the distant rustling of the trees. I can feel the battle waging inside him. The part of him that wants to remain loyal to his orders, clashing with whatever shred of guilt, or whatever else, he feels for me.

Finally, he mutters a curse under his breath and rolls his shoulders. "We need to be back before sunup."

"I knew you had a rebellious streak in you."

Gray sighs, but I don't miss the way his hands relax slightly on the reins. "Shadowmere isn't far. If we go, we go quickly."

I nod, my heart feeling just a little lighter. A delay, however brief, is still a delay. And maybe, just maybe, I can make the most of it.

Gray hands a small stable boy the reins to Nyx and tosses him a silver coin. He gives Nyx one last pat before he turns back to me.

"What exactly did we come here for?" He asks. I glance around the small, crowded streets of Shadowmere. Then I look down at myself, my shoeless feet, my torn dress.

"Something to wear. I've been in this dirty dress for days."

"I can tell." A look of amusement lights up his face.

"If you're going to make fun of me, you can just stay here with Nyx. I can do this on my own." I place my hands on my hips.

"And give you another chance to run? I don't think so, Little Flame." He starts making his way down the streets, and I roll my eyes as he passes me, reluctantly following behind him.

The town is no different than when I was here the first time—run down in some places, running water in others. For the most part, it's filled with half-fed children and even thinner parents.

"Can I—" I turn to ask Gray a question. But he's gone.

Now's my chance.

Just as my feet finally catch up with my mind.

I notice Gray talking very comfortably with a girl around our age with deep brown hair. Something ugly twists in my stomach, and I do my best to shove it down. Not wanting to think more about it, I turn away and start heading in the opposite direction. I've been distracted long enough by him. Against my better judgement I glance once more over my shoulder, meeting his eyes instantly.

Curse the Stars.

Now, I dart out of the normal path, past carts selling all different kinds of goods. The fig jams and roasted pork smell heavenly, making my mouth water after not having such delicacies for so long. But I contain it and keep my feet moving. I have no clue where I'm going; everything looks the same, to the point I feel like I'm going in circles. Frustrated, I pause outside of a shop named Moonlit Brews.

It's a pub. I take one last look, trying to find a better spot to duck into,when I catch Gray rounding the corner, head whipping back and forth. Again, before I can think better of it, I duck into the awful-smelling pub. It's mostly drunken men and the occasional women. The smell is some kind of wheat rum mixed with sweat. *A terrible combination.*

I walk further into the dimly lit room. This place has less people than I expected, especially since the sun has already gone down. Making my way to the high top tables that surround the back counter with the liquors, I managed a friendly smile when the lady running the counter came over. Somewhat panicking, I decline her service and glance around once more.

Now, noticing a door tucked behind the counters, I lazily make my way over, to not draw attention. Even though I'm pretty sure no one is paying much attention to anything through their drooping eyelids. I slip through the door. This room doesn't have the same dampness in the air that the pub had. The air in this room is stale. There are three tables, filled with men and women playing card games with silvers and other valuables stacked in the middle.

"You're a pretty thing, aren't you?" A scruffy man at the closest table hollers at me.

"What did you just say to me?" Plenty of bite in my tone to send most boys running. Cursing the Stars that I didn't take my dagger from Gray.

"Ignore him. He's been talking to every girl that walks through that door," a woman in an all-green uniform says. She holds a stack of cards in her hand and sits at the head of the table.

"I can see why they don't stay," I mumble, earning a small smile from the woman.

"You play?" She gestures with the cards as she passes them out.

"Actually-"

"Oh, come on, you're not seriously going to deal her in." The same guy huffs.

"What? Scared to lose to a *girl?*" The questions fly out before I can stop them. Unfortunately *I* might be the one losing if I sit at that table.

"By all means, little lady, take a seat." This time, it comes from a fairly handsome young man at the end of the table.

Before I can embarrass myself any further, I take one of the two empty seats and watch carefully as they finish their round of cards. By the time a new round starts, I have an idea how this game is played.

At first it's easy, reading their faces, letting them think I'm just lucky. I play coy, faking hesitation, throwing down a weak hand every now and then to keep them from catching on. The pile of coins in front of me steadily grows. I barely notice how much time has passed or the presence looming behind me until a voice drawls at my ear.

"Didn't take you for a gambler, Little Flame." His breath is warm against my ear, sending shivers down my spine. I freeze for a fraction of a second, my fingers tightening on the cards. I school my features before glancing over my shoulder.

Gray.

He's standing there, arms crossed, gaze falling to the table, then to my winnings. He looks surprised.

"Didn't take you for someone who cared what I did with my time."

One of the men at the table eyes Gray warily, noting his dark cloak and the way he carries himself. "You know him?" he asks.

I shrug, leaning back in my seat. "Not really."

Gray doesn't react. Instead, he reaches over and plucks one of my coins off the table, rolling it between his fingers.

"Funny," he muses, his voice smooth, "That's not what you said last night." Once he noticed how pink my face became, he continued. "And I could've sworn *we* were supposed to be somewhere else right now."

I meet his gaze head-on, shoving away the piled-up emotions in my throat. "And yet, here I am."

The younger man across from me clears his throat, looking at Gray. "You in or out?"

Gray's lips quirk upward slightly, but his eyes don't leave me. "Oh, I'm in." He slides into the seat beside me, lounging back with that effortless confidence that makes me want to punch him.

With Gray sitting beside me, the game changes. He's *watching me closely*. Every time I bluff, every time I hesitate, I can feel his gaze burning into my skin.

And he's *enjoying* this.

The next round is dealt, and I place a coin in the middle. My stack of miscellaneous items is higher than the others now, and the men are growing frustrated.

The scruffy guy slams his hands on the table. "You're cheating."

I raise an eyebrow. "Or you're just bad at cards."

The man growls and lunges forward, but before I can even move, *Gray does.* In one swift motion, he grabs the man's wrist and slams it against the table.

Hard.

The room goes silent.

Gray leans in, his voice quiet but sharp. "You don't want to do that."

The man stares at him, chest rising and falling in quick, angry breaths. Then, slowly, he backs down. Gray releases him and turns back to me, his expression calm and controlled. But when he speaks, his voice is edged with something darker.

"Game's over, Little Flame. We're leaving."

I laugh, picking up another coin and twirling it between my fingers. "You don't get to decide that."

He leans in so close I can feel the warmth of his breath on my face. "I wasn't asking."

I tilt my head, stalling. I *could* push him further—see what his breaking point is. Or I could walk away now before this game turns into something I can't control.

Before I lose.

Unfortunately, I never have been one to cut my losses. I let the moment stretch, feeding off the challenge in his onyx eyes. I know I'm pushing his restraint, but I don't care.

I raise a single eyebrow. "Then maybe you should work on your tone."

Gray doesn't reply. He *moves.*

Fast.

Before I can react, his hand closes around my arm, firm but not painful. He yanks me up from the table. The chair scrapes against the wooden floor, my stack of earnings scatters and the men at the table mutter curses, leaning away like they want no part of this.

"Grayson! You don't get to manhandle me!" I snarl, struggling against his grip, but he's already dragging me through the door and back into the partially crowded pub.

"Enough," he snaps, weaving us between drunken men with sharp precision. "I let you have your little detour. Now we're leaving."

The moment we step outside, Gray whirls on me. His expression is dark with barely contained fury.

"Do you have a death wish?" His voice is sharp, each word cutting through the night air like a blade.

I fold my arms, tilting my chin up. "I was fine."

Gray lets out a bitter laugh, stepping closer. "Fine? You were sitting in a den of criminals, gambling with people who'd slit your throat for a single coin. If I'd shown up five minutes later, who knows what would've happened?"

"Well, you did show up, so no need to throw a fit."

"A fit? Stars, you're impossible."

"And you're suffocating." I throw my arms out. "You act like I can't handle myself. Like I need you to come charging in to save me every time I step out of your sight. News flash Gray, I don't!" I shove down the rage blossoming in my chest.

"No? Then remind me, Little Flame, exactly how many times I've had to drag you out of danger since I met you?"

I glare at him, refusing to answer.

Gray takes another step forward, invading my space. "Do you even think before you act? Or do you just throw yourself into the fire and hope someone else puts it out?"

"Maybe I wouldn't have to if everyone stopped trying to control me!"

His nostrils flare, and his voice drops lower, *colder.* "Control you? Stars, Little Flame, you're reckless. You wouldn't understand being controlled. You play these games, but one day, they're going to get you killed."

His words make something in me snap. "Oh, I'm sorry, I forgot you were the expert on survival—oh wait, you just blindly follow orders like a good little soldier."

Gray's expression turns to ice. "At least I don't put others in danger because I'm too damn stubborn to listen."

My blood boils. He has no idea what he's talking about. So, without thinking, I pull back my fist and punch him square in the jaw. His head snaps to the side, a stunned silence stretching between us. My knuckles throb, but I barely feel it over the rage in my chest—my whole body.

Gray stays still for a moment, exhaling through his nose before slowly turning back to me. His tongue swipes over his bottom lip, and then he *smirks*.

"Feel better?"

I shake out my fist, scowling. "You deserved that."

"Probably," he admits, rolling his jaw. Then, without warning, he grabs my wrist and yanks me forward, closing the space between us. This close, I can just make out the flecks of gold in his eyes, like stars littering the night sky.

I relax in his hold, covering it up with a glare. "Let. Me. Go."

His grip isn't bruising, but it's steady. "Not until you promise to stop running."

I yank my arm back. "You're infuriating."

"And you're predictable."

I should punch him again for that. Instead, I yank my wrist back harder, trying to break free from his grip. "I don't need your protection, Gray!"

He doesn't let go. Instead, he leans in, his breath warm against my face, eyes flashing. "You don't know what you need." His voice is low, a barely contained whisper. "And you never will if you keep pushing people away."

"I don't need anyone." I spit the words out, each one like acid on my tongue. "Least of all you."

Gray's eyes darkened, and his hand tightened around my wrist, just bordering painful.

"Then why the hell are you still here, Little Flame? You want to run, to throw yourself into danger, but you never do it alone. You always have someone there to pick up your pieces. Always have *me* to pick up the pieces."

I feel a mixture of anger and frustration. I want to scream at him, to make him understand, but no matter how much I try to distance myself from him, he's right.

He's *always* there, *always* watching, *always* telling me what to do.

I step forward, my chin almost touching his chest, breathing hard. "You don't get it, do you? You think I need you because I can't do things myself. But every time you open your mouth, you prove how little you actually understand me."

My words hang in the air, heavy. For a split second, his eyes soften, just the smallest hint of a crack in his hardened exterior. But then he masks it, and the wall goes up again.

"Maybe I understand you better than you think," he mutters. "You're just too scared to face it."

I want to shout at him, shout all the things on my mind and in my heart. But I can't. Instead, I glare at him with all the rage I keep inside, letting some of it bubble out. Without thinking, I pull my fist back *again* and punch him *harder* this time.

He doesn't flinch.

Instead, Gray grabs me by the shoulders, shoving me back a step, eyes flashing with dangerous intensity. "Are you done?"

My chest heaves, my heart races in my ears, but I don't look away. "I'll never be done with you." The words are out before I can stop them, and they hang in the air like a challenge. A double meaning to them, like a double-edged sword.

For a long moment, neither of us moves. The distance between us feels impossibly small like we're on the edge of something neither one of us can control. Finally, Gray lets go of my shoulders, but his gaze never wavers. "You're lucky I don't tie you up before dragging you back to Blackthorn." His voice is dangerously low.

My head spins, but I don't back down. "Try it."

His face becomes dark: a smirk, a promise, and a challenge all at once. "You think I won't?"

I step back, lifting my chin high, barely able to keep my voice steady. "I'm not afraid of you, Gray."

He stares at me, and for a moment, the world seems to fade away. Neither of us move. Both of us, locked in a silent standoff.

Then, finally, Gray turns away, shaking his head. "You should be."

Chapter 58

Keira

The silence is almost worse than the shouting. My knuckles still throb where they connected with Gray's jaw. But I refuse to rub them. I refuse to let him see even a speck of regret. Not that I regret it. Not entirely. He deserved it. I should have hit him harder.

He walks ahead of me, his back straight, shoulders tense, his head occasionally shaking as if he's trying to get rid of a thought. The dim lanterns cast long shadows across the worn cobblestone streets of Shadowmere. Most vendors have packed up for the night, their carts abandoned until sunrise. A few linger, their wary eyes following us, but no one dares to speak.

The tension between us is thick, suffocating, wrapping around my throat like an iron chain. I should say something. A sharp remark, another jab to remind him that I'm not done fighting. But the words die in my throat because, for the first time since this all started, I realize—I can't fight my way out of this.

I've lost.

My feet drag as we walk, the weight of inevitability pressing down on me. Every step takes me closer to Blackthorn. Closer to whatever awaits me there.

Closer to Tristan.

Maybe it won't be so bad. Maybe Tristan and I can have a proper conversation about it. Maybe he'll understand what he did was wrong. And maybe, just maybe, he'll let me walk away.

I wrap my arms around myself to lessen the chill running through my body. The streets grow narrower, *quieter.* A dog scurries past, ribs showing. Further down, a woman pulls a thin blanket tighter around her child, tucking him into the crook of her arm as she dozes against a crumbling stone wall.

I slow my steps, watching them.

Shadowmere is a city of ghosts, of forgotten people. People like Cass, people of no rank or status.

Gray exhales sharply, but he doesn't look back at me. "Don't start feeling sorry for them now."

I blink, torn from my thoughts. "Excuse me?"

He finally glances over his shoulder, his onyx eyes catching the lantern light. There's no mockery in them this time. Just something cold. Something I can't quite name. "You look at them like you can save them."

I lift my chin. "Maybe I can."

He turns away. "Little Flame, you can't even save yourself."

The words hit harder than they should. My throat burns, but I swallow it down and keep walking. We don't speak again.

The stables come into view too soon. The young stable boy startles at our approach, rubbing sleep from his eyes before handing Nyx's reins to Gray. He doesn't look at me as he takes them, his grip firm.

I stare at Nyx, at the saddle that will take me back to Blackthorn. My feet won't move. Gray swings up onto Nyx in one fluid motion then looks down at me. Offering me his hand. "Get on."

I can't. Not yet. "What happens when we get back?"

He doesn't answer right away. The lantern's glow flickers across his face, casting sharp shadows along his cheekbones. When he finally speaks, his voice is quiet, almost sad. "I don't know."

The honesty unsettles me more than anything else.

I take a slow breath and step forward, reaching for his hand. I hesitate for only a moment before pulling myself up behind him. Nyx shifts beneath us, restless. Gray keeps his eyes ahead, his body rigid, his hands steady on the reins. He doesn't look back at me as I wrap my arms around his abdomen.

Neither of us says a word as he nudges Nyx forward, carrying us toward the place I no longer have the strength to run from. Instead, I lay my head on his back, content to listen to the beat of his heart.

Exhaustion must have gotten to me because my eyelids droop shut. My mind memorizes the feel of him, deciding I could stay in this moment forever. Just the rhythmic sway of the horse, the quiet hum of his breathing, the warmth of him against me. I swear I only shut my eyes for a few minutes, but when they flutter open again, Nyx is no longer moving.

And we're no longer alone.

The towering gates of Blackthorn loom before us, their iron bars twisted into sharp, menacing points. The torches lining the courtyard flicker against the dark stone walls, casting long, wavering shadows. But I barely notice them. Because waiting for us at the entrance, their figures cut from the darkness itself are Tristan and King Lucian.

A cold dread forms in the pit of my stomach, sinking deeper despite the warmth from Gray's back. Tristan's green eyes are darker than I remember. Fury is all over the King's face, rolling off him in waves as he steps forward.

Gray stiffens in front of me, but he doesn't move, doesn't speak. Neither do I.

King Lucian's gaze locks onto me, looking exactly as I imagined the King of Shadows—lethal. "Tell me, Princess," he says, his voice deceptively calm, "was your little runaway act worth it?"

I don't answer. I don't have to. The answer is written all over my face, in the torn fabric of my dress, the dirt on my bare feet.

His expression darkens. "You are a guest in my Kingdom." His voice hardens. "Yet you behave like a reckless child."

Gray dismounts, helping me off as well. But I keep my eyes on the King. "I'm not a child."

Something flashes in his eyes, something dangerous. "No," he agrees, stepping closer. "You are a foolish, spoiled girl who still hasn't learned her place."

The slap comes faster than I can react.

The sharp crack of his open palm against my cheek echoes through the courtyard. My head snaps to the side, the sting spreading hot across my skin. I taste blood where my teeth catch the inside of my cheek, but I refuse to let my knees buckle, refuse to let him see the pain behind my eyes.

I swallow it down, straightening my spine.

And then, before I can even think to react, Gray moves.

He steps between us, his body rigid, his stance tense, a storm brewing beneath his skin. His onyx eyes lock onto the King's. "That," he says, his voice low and simmering with barely restrained fury, "was unnecessary."

A dangerous silence settles over the courtyard.

Tristan still hasn't moved.

I watch him, searching for something, anything. A spark of defiance, a shadow of anger, some sign that he cares.

But there's *nothing*.

Just that same unchanged expression, his lips pressed into a thin line, his hands clasped tightly behind his back. He does nothing. Says nothing. The realization cuts deeper than the slap.

Lucian exhales sharply, his gaze shifting back to Gray. "Careful, boy," he warns. "You forget who you serve."

Gray doesn't flinch. "I haven't forgotten a damn thing."

The tension is suffocating. The guards watching from the shadows stay still, waiting. My heartbeat pounds in my ears as I watch them—Gray, standing between the King and me, and Tristan, standing there like he's a small boy instead of a future King. Lucian exhales through his nose, his anger still there. But he doesn't strike me again. Instead, he straightens his cloak with a slow, deliberate motion.

"Take her to her chambers," he orders Gray, his voice edged with steel. "She's done enough damage for one night. *Wouldn't want her to end up like Elena.*"

Gray doesn't hesitate. He takes my wrist, his grip firm but not rough—never rough, and starts leading me away.

I don't resist. Not because I've given up. But because, for the first time since I arrived in Eclipsar, I know exactly who my enemies are. And who, despite everything, just might be something else.

Chapter 59

Keira

The walk through the dimly lit halls of the castle is suffocatingly silent. Gray's grip on my wrist doesn't falter, his steps unyielding as he leads me away from the courtyard. The air between us is thick with electrified silence. I should say something. But the sting on my cheek, the weight of Tristan's silence, and the fire burning in my chest—it all keeps me quiet.

Gray doesn't stop until we reach my chambers. He finally releases my wrist, his fingers lingering for just a second longer before he steps back. I lift my chin, pretending I don't feel the absence of his touch.

"Are you going to say something?" I ask, my voice sharp enough to cut through glass.

He exhales, running a hand through his curls. "What do you want me to say, Little Flame?"

I shrug. "I don't know. Maybe something about how your King is a cruel, power-hungry tyrant?"

Gray's jaw tightens. "Careful."

"Or what?" I snap. "You'll drag me back to him yourself?"

His gaze darkens. "You think I'd let that happen?"

Definitely.

I cross my arms over my chest. "I don't know what you'd let happen, Gray. I thought Tristan would do something, but he just stood there." I shake my head, laughing bitterly. "I guess I shouldn't be surprised. The golden Prince wouldn't want to risk tarnishing his perfect image."

The color in Gray's face drains. He doesn't argue.

I step closer, my voice dropping. "You didn't have to step in."

He tilts his head, watching me carefully. "Yes, I did."

I swallow hard. "Why?"

A muscle in his jaw jumps. "For old times sake, Little Flame."

He turns to leave, but before he can take a full step, I grab his wrist. His pulse is steady beneath my fingers, but when he looks back at me, there's something stormy in his expression, something restrained.

"I mean it, Gray," I say softly. "Why did you step in?"

For a moment, I think he won't answer. That he'll just pull away and walk out like he always does.

But then, in a voice so quiet I almost miss it, he says, "Because I already failed one girl I loved."

And then he's gone. Leaving me alone with the sound of my own unsteady breathing and my screaming thoughts. *Who knew love was even in his vocabulary?*

It took me a moment once inside my room to remember I have a real bed and a bath waiting for me. Everything is exactly how I left it, even the tray of food. The only thing that's odd is the dip in the chair by my bed. Deciding not to care right now, I draw myself a boiling hot bath.

I peel the once-pretty dress off and toss it to the side.

It might have to be burned.

I hesitate as I step in. The water is definitely hot. Taking one sharp breath, I sink in, watching as the loose dirt spreads through the water.

Steam rises in curling wisps, the heat seeping into my skin and loosening the knots in my muscles. I exhale slowly, tilting my head back against the edge of the tub. The water is almost scalding, but after days of grime and exhaustion, I welcome the sting.

I run my fingers through my tangled hair, wincing as they catch on knots. The scent of lavender and something faintly sweet drifts from the soap nearby. Vanilla maybe? I reach for it, rubbing it between my palms before smoothing it over my arms, my shoulders, my legs, scrubbing away the filth, the blood, the lingering memories.

The dirt swirls and disappears, but the weight in my chest stays. I squeeze my eyes shut, letting my head slip just beneath the surface. For a moment, the world goes silent. No kings, no orders, no lies disguised as promises. Just warmth and the sound of my own heartbeat, steady but heavy.

But I can't stay under forever.

Breaking the surface, I suck in a deep breath and push my hair back. The dip in the chair catches my eye again, and unease settles in my chest. I should be relieved to be alone, but something about that feels like a lie.

Still, for now, I force myself to focus on one thing at a time.

I sink deeper into the water, eyes fluttering shut, and pretend for just a little while that I am not in Blackthorn at all.

The water has long since cooled by the time I finally move. My fingers are wrinkled, my limbs heavy, but the exhaustion clawing at my bones is deeper than anything a bath can fix.

I stand, letting the water drip from my skin as I step onto the marble floor. The room is still quiet. I reach for a towel, wrapping it around myself as I catch my reflection in the mirror.

A stranger looks back at me.

Pale skin, blue eyes shadowed with fatigue. The bruises on my wrists are faint but still there. My cheek still stings where the King struck me, a reminder of the reality I can't escape.

I tear my gaze away and dress quickly, pulling on the softest nightgown I can find. The silk glides over my skin, a stark contrast to the rough, torn dress I left on the floor. I should feel better, but the unease is still filling my insides.

Just as I turn toward the bed, a sound at the door makes me freeze. A soft knock, barely there but unmistakable. For a brief, ridiculous moment, I wonder if it's Tristan. But I know better. I take a slow breath, steadying myself before walking to the door. My fingers hesitate on the handle before I pull it open.

Gray. And just like that, everything heavy, everything uneasy, leaves my body.

His dark curls are slightly damp like he's just washed up as well, looking like he's been at war with himself. His gaze glides over me, pausing on my face, where the marks from the King are still fresh. His expression tightens, but he doesn't speak right away.

The silence stretches between us, thick with things unsaid.

Then, finally, he exhales sharply, running a hand through his hair. "Are you going to let me in, Little Flame, or are we just going to stand here and stare at each other all night?"

I bite back, the emotions clawing their way up. "You're already halfway through the door."

He doesn't apologize, but there's an unspoken apology in the way his shoulders relax, the tension in his jaw easing just a fraction. I step aside to let him in, but I can't quite shake the feeling that something undeclared hangs in the air between us. He closes the door behind him and leans against it, arms crossed, his gaze never leaving me.

"You alright?" he asks, his voice low, concerned.

It's a question that shouldn't feel so raw. But it does.

I shrug, the motion more tired than dismissive. "What does 'alright' even mean anymore?"

He hesitates, eyes narrowing as if weighing whether to push further. Then he steps forward, closer, his presence steadying something inside me that I didn't realize was shaking.

"Alright enough to sleep, at least." His voice softens. "You need rest."

I meet his eyes, feeling the sharp sting of reality settling in again. "You think I can sleep with all this?" I motion to the door and everything outside this room. "With the King out there?"

Gray doesn't respond right away. Instead, he just stands there. Finally, he speaks. "You don't have to fight him alone."

I swallow, surprised by the quiet sincerity in his voice. It doesn't make the weight on my chest lighter but it does make me feel something I didn't expect: *less alone.*

"I know," I say softly, the words slipping out before I can stop them. "But I'm not sure it matters."

"Little Flame, let me—" He starts, but I cut him off before he can say more.

"Please, Gray," The words are softer than I intended, but I'm too tired to care. "Help me get out of here, and I'll never come back. You, your brother and your father won't need to worry about me ever again."

He steps forward slightly, holding my gaze for one long beat. Then, with a quiet exhale, he gives me a single shake of his head.

"Little Flame, you know I can't do that..." His voice trails off as he walks toward the door.

"Wait!" The word is out before I can stop it.

He spins on his heel a curious look on his face.

"Please, Gray, please." I let the plea creep its way into my voice, not caring how weak I sound.

"Little Flame," His expression is almost painful as he takes a daring step in my direction. "Ask me for anything, anything except that." His hand lifts my chin. His eyes search mine before they fall to my lips. I pull away from him before anything else out of the ordinary can happen.

"If you aren't going to help me, you can leave." My words are a little more than a whisper.

"Little Flame-"

"No, Gray!" My voice is no longer a whisper. Before he can argue again, I turn away and slip into bed. I lay with my back to him, hoping he'll see himself out.

I hear the scuff of his boots, but they sound closer.

Looks like he didn't get the hint.

With my back still to him, I half expect to feel my bed dip with Gray's weight, or a warm arm snake around me. Instead I hear his boots scuff once more, then the click of the door.

And again, I am completely and utterly alone.

Chapter 60

Keira

Morning sun leaks through the thin curtains, pale and weak. It's almost as if the sun is as exhausted as I am. I slowly blink away the small amount of sleep still clinging to me. My limbs feel heavy, and the bed, though very comfortable after days without one, does nothing to ease the ache. I didn't sleep well, not truly. My thoughts kept me awake, tossing and turning with the weight of everything: Tristan, the King, even Gray, though I hate to admit it.

It's only the soft rustle of fabric and the faint scent of mint that gets me to sit up. I blink again, somewhat disoriented, to find a stranger in my room. She's young, younger than me, her dirty blonde hair tied neatly at the nape of her neck. Her maid's uniform is pristine, but she moves with a sort of tentativeness, as if she feels she doesn't belong or is out of place.

She pauses when she notices I'm awake, a soft apology in her eyes.

"Your Highness, I hope I didn't wake you," she says, her voice quiet but not timid. "I've been assigned to help you prepare."

I rub my eyes, trying to shake off the rest of my sleep and sit up slowly. "Prepare for what?"

She glances toward the door, then back to me, lowering her voice. "You are to meet with the King and his new Queen today. They've requested your presence."

I freeze.

The King and his new *Queen*?

The words hit me harder than when the King struck me across the face. Of course, the King would want to parade his new wife around. He probably wants to show off the fact that I'm still here, still a prisoner of his Kingdom.

I push the many blankets off myself and swing my legs over the side of the bed, trying to steady myself. My body protests, but I force myself to stand. The maid is already at my side, hovering like a mother would to a sick child. I give her a weak smile.

"I suppose you've done this before," I say, my voice hoarse. I'm not sure if it's from the lack of sleep or the bitterness in my throat.

She nods quickly. "Yes, Your Highness. It's… part of my job."

I don't know if I believe her, remembering how my last maid turned out. But I don't have the energy to question her right now.

My reflection in the mirror is not much better than the one I saw last night. The circles under my eyes have just barely faded, a few bruises still linger, and my hair falls in a heap over one shoulder. This poor maid somehow needs to figure out a way to make me look presentable.

She lays out a fresh gown at the edge of the bed. It's a deep lavender with puff sleeves. She's quick and efficient, helping me into it with practiced hands. Her touch is soft but professional, and I can't help but feel a strange sense of detachment as I let her lead me through the motions.

When she finishes, she steps back and sweeps over me with adoring eyes.

"Shall I arrange your hair?"

I nod mechanically, and she quickly gets to work, brushing through my hair with gentle strokes. The silence stretches between us, but it was better than her asking question after question.

After a few minutes, she steps back, "You look… beautiful, Your Highness." I glance at myself in the mirror, taking in the paint covering tired eyes and dry lips, as well as my hair, now in white coils hanging loosely.

I force a smile, though it's a weak attempt. "Thank you."

She hesitates before speaking again, her voice softer this time. "If… if you ever need anything, Your Highness, I will be here. I may be new, but I've heard the whispers. I know what you've been through."

I meet her gaze, surprised by her candor. "You don't have to say *your Highness*—just Keira."

Her lips press together and she doesn't respond right away. There's something in her eyes connecting us—sympathy? I don't know if I can trust her, but at this moment, she's offering me a safe place.

I take a deep breath. "Is there anything else I should know?"

She glances at the door again. "Only that you must be ready soon. The King and new Queen are waiting."

The last words hang in the air, ringing in my head. But I nod, grateful for the brief comfort. I don't know what today will bring, but I do know I can't run from it again.

I just hope I'm ready.

My maid leads me through the halls at a steady pace, her posture straight and focused. I trail slightly behind, still not entirely awake, my limbs heavy with exhaustion. I can feel the weight of the dress pulling at my shoulders, the stiffness of the corset keeping me upright.

The palace is quiet as usual, save for the distant echo of footsteps and murmured voices. My body tingles with anticipation.

"Do you know why I'm meeting with the King?" I ask, my voice still hoarse.

My maid doesn't slow her pace. "I was only told to bring you."

Of course, she was. Yet another person blindly following orders.

The massive double doors of the throne room come into view as we turn the corner. My stomach tightens. I'm not sure if it's from the lack of breakfast or fear. Two guards stand at attention with their gazes fixed straight. She stops in front of them, dipping into a quick, practiced stiff curtsy before stepping aside.

One of the guards pushes open the door.

I step inside.

The room is filled with Lords, Ladies, and Nobles, their voices hushed as they stand clustered together. Sunlight filters through high windows, providing a small amount of light to this shadowy palace. My eyes scan the room quickly, searching for anything out of place.

And then I see him.

Tristan.

He stands near the base of the dais, one hand resting on the hilt of his sword. His usual confidence is present in the way he holds himself. Not a lazy bone in his body. There's something in his gaze that catches me off guard. Something sharp, expectant maybe? He's watching me closely like he's waiting for me to do something.

My steps falter for just a moment before I force myself forward, ignoring the sudden prickle at the back of my neck. Then, my gaze shifts slightly, catching a small glimpse of dark curls near the edge of the room.

Gray.

He's standing further back, partially covered in shadows. I can feel the weight of his stare. *That explains the chills.*

A strange awareness settles over me, my stomach twisting uncomfortably. I tear my eyes from him, my pulse quickening as I step closer to the dais.

And then I see her.

The world narrows and my vision blurs.

The throne beside King Lucian is not empty.

A woman sits there, poised and regal, dressed in black. A color I've never seen her wear before. Her white blonde hair is swept into a delicate crown, her blue eyes piercing as they meet mine.

Familiar eyes. *My mother's eyes.*

I can't move.

Everything feels distant, muffled. The murmurs in the room seem to fade into nothing, drowned out by the sound of my own heartbeat pounding in my ears.

This *isn't* real. It *can't* be real.

And yet—

She *smiles*.

Not a warm, motherly smile. Not the kind one would see in their childhood. It's something else entirely. Measured. Calculated. Like she knows exactly what she's doing.

Like she was expecting this reaction.

Lucian speaks, but I barely hear him. My body is frozen, my mind still trying to process what I'm seeing.

She's here. And she's sitting *beside* the King of Eclipsar.

Tristan shifts slightly, and for the first time, I realize just how much my shock is showing. The way my fingers tremble slightly at my sides. The way my breath is uneven. I force a blank expression. But I know the damage is already done.

Lucian is watching me now, his gaze sharp and assessing.

I swallow hard.

The world starts to spin once more. I'm not sure it ever stopped. I do the second thing I think of. *The first was running, and I'll be damned if I let the Queen see me run scared.*

I slip on a mask of cool, calm, collected grace and continue my way to the dais.

Chapter 61

Keira

Tristan waits expectantly, his emerald eyes sweeping over me as I step closer toward my doom.

The room is suffocating, too many eyes and too many whispers. I step next to Tristan and feel him shift beside me. His presence is solid, like an anchor in the sea. His hand brushes against mine. *Subtle.* I force myself to ignore the undeniable flicker in my chest. This is *not* the moment.

"Keira," Tristan's voice is low, almost gentle. "You don't have to do this."

I glance at him, my eyes narrowing. "Do what? Face the inevitable?"

Tristan's brows furrow, but he doesn't break eye contact. "You don't have to be so defiant. You don't have to make this harder than it already is."

"You think this is hard for me?" My voice cuts through the air, sharp and brittle. I take a step back, needing the distance to feel steady. "Or is it just that *I* make it harder for you?"

He doesn't answer right away, and I don't wait for him to.

"You've been playing this game since the day I stepped foot into this palace," I say, my voice steady despite the fire burning inside. "Don't pretend like you're on my side, Tristan. You've probably been a part of this from the beginning."

There's a fleeting moment of hurt on his face but it disappears a moment later. He takes a step toward me, his gaze softening, but only for a second. "I'm not playing a game, Keira. I'm trying to help you, but you're making this impossible."

I laugh bitterly, cutting through the air like a blade. "Impossible? I'm the one trapped here. I'm the one who has to play by their rules while you sit there with your crown-to-be and your father's favor."

Tristan's stiffens, and for a moment, I think he's going to snap. But he doesn't. Instead, his tone drops, becoming quieter and more measured.

"I'm *not* my father, Keira."

I want to argue, but there's something in his voice, something I can't quite place. I swallow hard, trying to keep my composure.

"Then *prove* it."

He takes another step closer, scandalously closer. We stand there in silence, the world around us vanishing for just a heartbeat.

His voice is barely above a whisper. "You don't have to make this harder for *yourself.*"

"I'm not making it hard. I'm simply choosing."

Tristan's eyes narrow, confusion flickering in his gaze. "Choosing what?"

I look him dead in his eyes. "I'm choosing not to be *manipulated.*"

He opens his mouth to speak, but the words don't come. Something between us grows thick, but I can feel something shifting, something deep. I don't know if it's for the better or for worse. I don't have much time to dwell before the King's voice rings through the room.

"High court of Eclipsar, I hope you have found the festivities pleasant. I have gathered you here today to make everyone aware we no longer are on ill terms with the Kingdom of Aetheris." He pauses for a moment as everyone leans in to hear his words. "As this beautiful woman sits beside me, we now mark a new era—one that includes the people of Eclipsar and Aetheris conjoined." The King stares, eyes scanning over the crowd.

Everyone seemed to have steam rolling off of them. Not one pleasant expression in sight. When no one cheers or makes any movement, for that matter, the King continues.

His first few sentences are a blur as I scan the room for a certain onyx-eyed boy with curly black hair. Something akin to disappointment snakes through me when I don't catch a glimpse of messy curls but only pristine straightened, combed over, or pulled back hair, none of which belong to him.

I force my attention back to the King. "I can see I am boring you, so I will have you all direct your attention to my eldest son," He's practically beaming as he says those words. Well, as much as the King of Darkness can beam. "Tristan, would you please join me?" As soon as Tristan leaves my side, I can feel his absence. I didn't realize how soothing his presence was until he removed himself from my space. *Maybe it wouldn't be so bad to care for him.* Maybe I could grow to love this life. If I try hard enough, maybe I could be Tristan's perfect little Queen. A chill runs through me, though I can't tell if it's from that sudden thought which I quickly dismiss or something else.

Either way, I know I can't settle for this life. I *won't* settle for this life. Not being able to run wild, do as I please, whenever I please sounds miserable. People assume being a Princess means all the freedoms a woman could want, when actually it's more like being locked in a prison your entire life, with fancy dresses and self-absorbed men— much like the one who isn't here. Just the thought of him fills me with unexpected warmth.

"I have much to prepare for my upcoming coronation," Tristan carries himself as if he is already King. "My studies are pleasant, training is a breeze and…" He glances at me but decides to look away when we make eye contact. *No, please, not again.* "I have some disappointing news for the eligible girls of Eclipsar…and now Aetheris, I suppose." He pauses once more to glance in my direction, almost urging me to acknowledge him. The lords and ladies in the room hold their breath. "I have sent all the ladies who attended the Midnight Masquerade back to their families except for one. I have picked my future Queen…" He seems unsure of himself. "If she chooses to accept," he finishes, eyes finding mine yet again. This time, everyone else's eyes do, too.

I suck in a shaky breath, looking between Tristan and the crowd I was once hiding among. Technically, it wasn't a proper proposal. It wasn't even a question. With that realization, I tip my chin up and square my shoulders, deciding once again that I don't owe any of these people anything. I catch the icy gaze that belongs to the new Queen of Eclipsar. Resisting the urge to crumble, I spin on my heel and make my way out of the throne room, head held high.

Chapter 62

Keira

I let my new maid get me out of my dress before I send her away for the night. I manage to figure out her name is Lilith before I lock myself in my room. Drawing myself a boiling bath, I soak until I'm wrinkled.

I can't get Tristan's words out of my head or the fact that I barely saw Gray. The thought of him brings a rush of memories from our last encounter. I *could* seek him out, but that seems a little unbecoming. *That's never stopped me in the past.*

Before I can come to my senses, I grab a robe to throw over my slip and head to the door. Waiting until I hear minimal movement on the other side, I slip out into the dimly lit hall. It probably would've been smart to bring a gas lamp with me, but I can't be bothered to go back now.

It would have been most definitely wise to know where Gray's sleeping quarters are before taking off to find him. Fortunately, Tristan decided to relocate me closer to *his* quarters, so Gray should be in the same wing.

I walk past so many doors, not being able to tell which is which. They all look the same. It isn't until I pass one particular door that the ring on my thumb starts to warm. I slow my steps, feeling as if only my thumb was being dunked in warm water. *Weird.* Yes, the ring has felt warm before, but never like this. I look up to find a simple, worn door to my right. I knock, deciding barging in wouldn't look good on my part.

When no response comes, I try the handle, to find it won't twist. Upon further inspection there's a circle in the middle, where a key should be. I glance around the empty hall, trying to find a place where one might hide a key. Nothing but matching doors and gas lamps line the hall. I feel around the gas lamps on either side of the door. Coming up with nothing, I debated just going back to my room. Under the cover of night, no one has seen me. I could just walk away and pretend this embarrassing event didn't happen, until I notice the ring on my finger hasn't cooled. In fact, it feels like it's getting even warmer.

Suddenly, the nights Gray and I spent in the Hollows come rushing back. *This is his ring.*

I take a closer look at the door, examining the worn wood. This one seems more used than the others I've passed. I slide my fingers along the panels, not sure what I expect to happen. When nothing out of the ordinary occurs, I move on to the handle. The unusual circle-shaped keyhole is strange. I brush my thumb over it. The tip of my thumb fits perfectly in the center of the circle.

The ring.

The keyhole is about the size of the ring. Deciding to chance it, I slip the ring off my thumb and press it into the knob. With a click, the ring slides into place before popping back out. Sliding the ring back on, I wipe my palm down my robe. Twisting the knob, I try my best not to let the door creek as I slip into the room of shadows. I fumble around in the darkness, tripping over everything. I throw my hands out, trying to find something to grab onto.

I silently curse the Stars for not bringing that gas lamp.

I decide to take the chance that this is Gray's room. I fumble around in the dark until my stomach connects with a wooden table. With a quick swipe of my fingers over the smooth surface, I find a match box.

Perfect. Now all I have to find is a candle.

Retracing my steps, I make my way to the bed—matches in hand. With my hands out in front of me, I reach for the empty space until they brush soft covers. I run my free hand along the length of the bed until I bang my knee against the bedside table. *Ouch!*

Again, I slowly run my hands over the table top, stopping when my finger tips touch metal. My hands dance up the candle holder, meeting the wax candle at the top. I pull it to what I assume is the edge of the bedside table before opening the match box and grabbing a match. It took three strikes against the box before the match lit. Dropping the box on the table I light the candle, shielding the flame as I pick up the holder.

Now that I can see a few inches in front of me, I roam around the room. Everything is hazy with the candlelight. *Or maybe it's my drooping eyelids?* I shake that thought from my head as I set the candle on the opposite bedside table. With the dim light I look around the room. The only intriguing thing I see is a bookshelf, tucked in the corner with a worn leather chair. Scanning the shelf, I try to find any familiar books. I nearly give up until my eyes snag on "The Secrets of the Missing Moon". Memories flood my mind of the first time I met Tristan—in the library with a stack of books—this was the first one I grabbed.

Without a second thought, I pluck the book from its spot on the shelf and slowly make my way back to the bed. I hesitate at the foot of the bed. *If this* is *Gray's room, would he even want me to touch his bed?* I almost laugh out loud at that silly thought.

Of course. It's Gray. He would want me in *his bed.* This time I do laugh at such a lunacy thought. Deciding it didn't matter what Gray wanted, I sink into the bed. *I want to see him, whether the feelings are mutual or not.* When that thought settles in the back of my mind, I turn my attention back onto the book. It's clearly a different copy than the one from the library. This one is well loved, the pages are thin and wrinkled, while the cover is frayed. I handle it with care as I skim through, letting my body relax.

My eyes close every so often, all the sentences blur together, and suddenly my head feels so heavy. I curl myself under the covers trying to fight back against the sleep I so desperately need.

Deciding I'm not strong enough to fight whatever monsters are coming for me tonight, I let my eyes close fully, with no intention of opening them.

Gray can wake me up when he gets here.

Chapter 63

Keira

Cracking my eyes open, I find the warm glow of candlelight littered around the room. Noticing the sun still isn't up, I decided to close my eyes and sink into the warmth behind me.

I freeze, my entire body going rigid. I feel warm hands brush over my stomach. Turning my chin over my shoulder, I find Gray asleep behind me. I gently turn to face him, taking in his messy black curls, long eyelashes, and the shadow of stubble lining his jaw. In his sleep, he always looks so boyish, with sharp, rough cut edges turning softer from a nightmare to a daydream. I let my eyes roam over his face, letting them linger longer than necessary, until I notice his eyebrows crease together.

He stirs, his fingers splayed on my lower back, digging gently into my skin. With his eyes still closed, a panicked expression appears. I reach my hand to the rounded part of his ear. I run my thumb over and over until he stills.

"Elena..." He whispers, stirring one last time before falling back asleep.

My thumb freezes at his words. *The second time I've heard that name..* Something ugly twists inside my stomach. I push it down. That's a problem for the morning. I roll back over, distancing myself as much as possible from his chest but still leaving his arm draped over me. It's not like I care for him anyway. With that lie in mind, I let my eyes drift shut again.

The next time I open my eyes, the warm sun is leaking in through the all-black curtains. I sit up, letting my eyes adjust to the light.

Then I remember the body that was supposed to be next to me. Instead, there's just an empty sunken pillow.

Had I dreamed it?

There's no way that's possible. The spot next to me definitely looks slept in. I scan the room, looking for any signs of Gray. Instead of him, I find piles of books and stationery on a desk. In the daylight I can see the leather chair faces a window, with a few scattered knives on it. *Good thing I decided to sit on the bed last night.*

I flop back on the bed, debating whether or not to close my eyes *again.*

"Your room was so terrible you had to steal mine?"

I shoot off the bed to see Gray.

"I…" The rest of my words trail off as my eyes roam over Gray. Standing in the door with a black cotton towel hanging low on his waist and his chest bare. Catching my fluster, I quickly look away, trying to shove down the heat spreading up my neck. This is nothing like all those days ago in Tristan's room.

"You're staring, Little Flame."

"I'm—" I snap my gaze up to his smirking face. "I was not."

Gray crosses his arms, looking entirely too smug for someone still dripping water onto the floor. "No? Because it looked like you were admiring the view."

"I was not." I huff.

He leans against the doorframe, "Were too."

"Are we really going to argue about this?"

"That depends, are you going to tell me why you're in my bed?"

I glare at him as I try to cultivate a believable reason. "Maybe I just got lost?"

"Did you now?" He pauses, thinking. "So what, you just left your room and tripped into *mine*?"

I open my mouth, then shut it. He has a point, but I refuse to let him win. "Well, maybe if you labeled things properly, I wouldn't have made the mistake." Even though

I was the one who tried seeking him out first. *It's irrelevant now.*

Gray chuckles, pushing off the door. "I'll be sure to have a sign made. Little Flame's stolen quarters."

I suppress a laugh. "I'll be leaving now."

He taunts, stepping closer. "No rush. Unless, of course, you're running away."

"From you? Hardly." I lift my chin. "I just prefer rooms that don't come with arrogant, half-dressed princes."

Gray tilts his head, a teasing glint in his eyes. "Shame. I was just starting to enjoy your company."

I roll my eyes. "Enjoying my company? You've barely been here a minute."

Gray steps closer. "Exactly. Imagine how much fun we'd have if you stayed longer."

I roll my eyes and move to the door, but he shifts just in time to block the doorway. I stop short, barely a breath between us. His skin is still damp, the scent of soap and something distinctly him lingering in the air.

He tilts his head. "Are you actually leaving?"

"Unless you have better plans, yes."

Gray hums as if considering it. "You could say please."

I arch a brow. "You could put on clothes, yet here we are."

He chuckles. "Fair point." He leans in slightly, his voice lowering. "But you still haven't said please." I give him my sweetest smile before shoving my palm against his bare chest and pushing him aside. He lets me, though the glint in his eye says he's enjoying this far too much.

"If you're not tired of *my* company, meet me at the training field after lunch," he calls after me, amusement dripping from his voice.

I don't look back. I refuse to give him the satisfaction of seeing the flush creeping up my neck. Instead I simply shut the door behind me and smile to myself.

"Keira?" I freeze, dreading to look at the person belonging to that voice. Deciding to rip the bandaid off quickly, I paste on a shaky smile. Something like deja vu takes hold.

"Tristan...good morning." I keep my tone even.

"Wh-" He looks from me to the door. "What were you doing in Gray's room?" He runs a hand down his face as if he knows what I'm going to say. I force a light chuckle, folding my arms to keep from fidgeting.

"Apparently, picking the wrong room for the night."

Tristan doesn't return my smile. His gaze lingers on the door behind me. "So you stayed the night?"

His tone is careful, restrained. I resist the urge to bolt. "Not like that. I got lost," *A lie.* "It was late. No scandalous intentions, I promise." I'm not sure why I feel the need to explain myself. Scandalous intentions or not, I don't owe Tristan anything.

His lips press into a thin line. "And Gray? What were *his* intentions?"

I blink. "What?"

He exhales sharply, shaking his head. "Nothing. Forget it."

I should. I should just walk away, pretend I didn't notice the way his expression darkened or the way his shoulders tensed when I confirmed I had stayed the night. But something about his reaction unsettles me.

"Tristan…" I start, but he cuts me off with a strained smile.

"Enjoy the rest of your day, Princess." His voice is smooth, but the edge beneath it is unmistakable. And before I can say another word, he turns on his heel and walks away. I exhale, dragging a hand through my hair. *Great.* Tristan had all but proposed to me yesterday. *For the second time.* And, of course, I ran right to Gray, who I'm supposed to hate. He's a liar and a rule follower, doing everything he's told to do.

First, I woke up in Gray's room. *Which I remind myself is what I wanted.* Now, I've managed to irritate Tristan, all before breakfast.

Today is off to a *fantastic* start.

I decided to have Lilith bring breakfast to my room. I figured it was the smarter idea, not having to face Gray *and* Tristan again. I shouldn't have made it so easy for Gray to

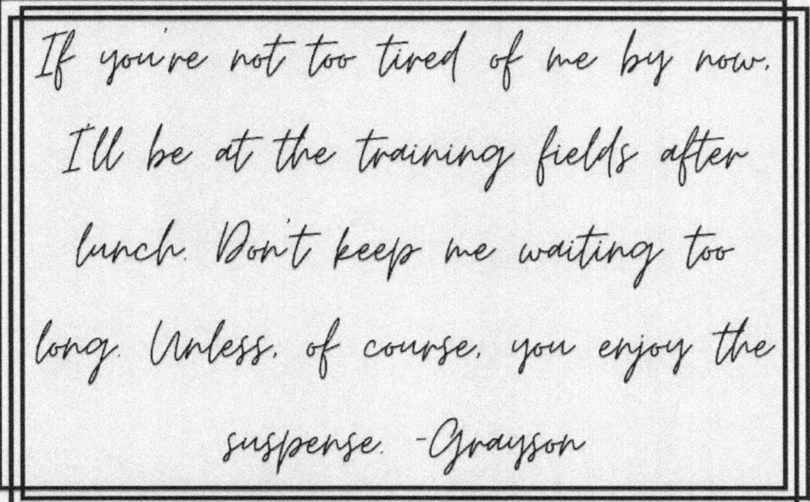

drag me back here. Should have fought harder. Yet, I'm not sure I regret it. Gray has a way of not just dragging me back but dragging me to *him.* I shake the sweet thought from my head as I pick up a flakey moon puff, and pop it in my mouth. Reaching for my steaming hot tea, I notice a slip of paper that looks as if someone slid it under the door. Abandoning the tea, I pick up the note and nearly toss it into the fire.

Pushy much?

I shouldn't go. No doubt as I stand here, arrangements are being made for me to marry Tristan. But at the moment, I can't will myself to care, or to convince myself Gray is so wrong for me. The itching curiosity in me isn't helping either. Deciding to blame the curiosity and not the somersaults in my stomach, I scarf down my now room-temperature tea and lukewarm breakfast before I throw open my wardrobe to find my training leathers.

Chapter 64

Keira

I was gone before Lilith came to collect the breakfast tray. It took me several tries to find the training grounds; this place is either a maze or a prison.

I suppose time will tell.

Once I stumble upon the training yard, I sweep my eyes over sweaty bodies and flashes of shiny silver. The sun is higher in the sky now. *Gray should be here already.* I make my way to the wall of weapons with mostly varying sizes of knives, swords, and sparring sticks.

If Gray doesn't want to train with me, I'll find someone who will.

I stand directly in front of my options; I did sheath an extra dagger to my thigh, so a bigger one would be best.

"What's a Princess like you doing out here?" I turn to find a tallish boy with dirt eyes and sand hair.

"Excuse me. Who are you?" I turn my attention back to the knives. Noticing out of the corner of my eye, he's taking small steps toward me.

"I train with Prince Grayson. Shouldn't you be at some luncheon? You don't look like the kind of girl to be caught dead in a place like this." His eyes have a spiteful glint to them. I try to remember he's just trying to get under my skin. *Even if it is working, he* doesn't need to know that.

"Actually—"

"Back off Theo." I feel my chest warm at the sound of his voice. Feeling stupid, I push it down and whirl around. There he is. I remind myself he's a lying, *murdering* prince. *The future Blade.* A fresh wave of awareness clears my head.

"He wasn't doing anything wrong." I cringe at my own lie. Gray tears his eyes from Theo to look at me, a silent fire burning behind his eyes.

Gray doesn't respond right away but I can see his urge to reach for a weapon. Theo, however, isn't as hesitant. He tilts his head, a slow smirk stretching across his face.

"See? The little lady doesn't mind." His voice is thick with amusement, and I know he's trying to get a reaction.

Gray steps forward, closing the space between us in an instant. "I said back off." His voice is low and controlled but there's something dangerous beneath it. Theo might be an idiot, but apparently, he knows when to listen. With a shrug, he raises his hands in mock surrender.

"Fine, fine. Just having a bit of fun." He casts one last look in my direction before sauntering off toward the other trainees.

I exhale slowly, my fingers tightening around the hilt of a dagger I hadn't realized I was holding. Gray shifts his dark eyes back to me.

"You shouldn't be out here alone. I wanted to meet with you *before* you got to the training fields."

I bristle, turning my focus back to the weapons laid out before me. "I can handle myself."

"I know you can, but you shouldn't have to."

That catches me off guard. My fingers falter over a blade as I glance at him. He's watching me carefully, but there's something different about the way he's looking at me.

Shaking my head as I counter, "I don't need a knight in shining armor." Gray huffs a quiet, humorless laugh. "Good. I'm not one."

I roll my eyes and turn my attention back to the weapons, choosing a longer dagger and testing the weight in my palm. "Are we training or not?"

Gray watches me for a moment longer, then nods. "Fine. But don't complain when you can't lift your arms tomorrow."

I shrug, gripping the dagger tighter as I follow him toward the open space of the training grounds. "I think I'll survive."

Gray doesn't say anything as he leads me toward a quieter corner of the training yard, away from the others. The sun is hot overhead, making the air thick, but the ground beneath my boots is firm. Steady.

He turns to face me, rolling his shoulders back, his dark eyes scanning me from head to toe. "Let me see how you hold it." I grip the dagger in my right hand, keeping my stance firm. Gray tilts his head slightly before stepping closer.

"Too stiff." He reaches out, wrapping his fingers around my wrist before I can flinch away. His touch is firm but not rough, guiding my hand into a looser grip. "You need control, not rigidity."

I swallow hard, forcing myself to focus. "I know how to hold a dagger."

"Clearly." He releases my wrist and steps back. "Show me, then."

I shift into position, lifting the blade and taking a testing swipe through the air. It feels good—solid, powerful. The weight is balanced just right, and I already know this will be my weapon of choice.

Gray watches, arms crossed. "Not bad."

"Not bad?" I arch a brow. "That sounded dangerously close to a compliment."

"Don't get used to it." He steps forward again, motioning for me to strike at him. "Come on, Little Flame. Let's see if you can actually fight or if you're just good at picking out weapons."

I roll my eyes but adjust my grip. "Don't cry when I beat you."

He lets out a breath of laughter, low and amused. "I'll take my chances."

Without giving him a warning, I lunge forward. Gray dodges easily, his movements fluid as he sidesteps my attack. Before I can regain my footing, he twists, sweeping his leg beneath mine. I barely manage to leap back in time, my heart pounding.

I glare at him. "You're holding back."

"Obviously," he says, like it's the most natural thing in the world. "You're not ready."

I tighten my grip on the dagger. "Then stop treating me like I'm fragile and fight me."

His expression shifts—just slightly, but I see it. Then, in the blink of an eye, he moves.

This time, he doesn't hold back.

I barely have time to react as he swings toward me, forcing me to block his strike with the dagger. The impact vibrates up my arm, but I don't falter. I twist, ducking under his next move and aiming a swipe toward his ribs.

He catches my wrist before the blade can make contact, yanking me forward until I nearly crash into him. He leans in just enough for me to hear him.

"You're so predictable," he murmurs.

I refuse to let him rattle me. Instead, I do the one thing I know will take him off guard—I drop my weight, twisting out of his hold and spin behind him. Before he can react, I press the cool edge of the dagger to the back of his neck.

Silence stretches between us.

Gray exhales a slow breath. Then, without warning, he moves. Faster than I can process, he grabs my wrist, twists out of my hold, and within seconds, I'm the one with a blade at my throat. His other hand grips my arm, steady but firm. His onyx eyes lock onto mine with intensity.

"You hesitated." His voice is quiet, but there's something sharper beneath it.

The heat between us is unbearable. My heart pounds against my ribs, but I refuse to look away.

I lift my chin. "I won't next time."

His grip lingers for a second longer before, finally, he steps back.

"Good," he says, sheathing his own dagger. "Because in a real fight, hesitation gets you killed."

I roll my shoulders back, forcing my pulse to steady. I won't give him the satisfaction of knowing how much he just affected me. Gray steps back, rolling his shoulders like that was nothing to him. Maybe it was nothing. Maybe he's used to having a blade against his throat. I hate how steady he looks. How completely unaffected.

I toss my dagger to the side, letting it land in the dirt with a dull thud. "Let's go again."

His gaze flicks to the weapon, then back to me. "Barehanded?"

"You scared?" I challenge, lifting my chin.

Gray exhales through his nose; amusement flashes in his dark eyes. Then, in one smooth motion, he unbuckles the sheath at his waist and tosses his own dagger aside. It lands next to mine.

"Alright, Little Flame," he says, stepping closer. "Show me what you've got."

This time, I don't hesitate.

I move fast, aiming a sharp jab toward his ribs, but he catches my wrist *again,* twisting me off balance. I recover quickly, stepping into his space and using my momentum to drive my elbow toward his stomach.

He blocks that, too.

His reflexes are unfairly fast, each movement calculated but I don't let it stop me. I fake left, then spin right, aiming for his legs. This time, I manage to sweep them out from under him, but just as he falls, he grips my arm and pulls me down with him. We hit the ground hard, but before I can react, Gray moves. In a breath, he flips me beneath him, pinning my wrists against the dirt. His weight presses against me, solid and unyielding, and I realize—too late—how close we are.

His dark curls fall into his eyes, his breathing slightly uneven. I'm sure mine is worse. My pulse pounds, my skin burning where his fingers wrap around my wrists. I should be thinking about how to escape, how to throw him off, but all I can focus on is the way his eyes find my lips—just for a second—before snapping back to my eyes.

His grip tightens. I swallow hard. "You hesitated."

"I don't hesitate."

"Then why am I still breathing?"

The space between us is nonexistent, the air too thick. I can see the exact moment he realizes it too. His grip flexes like he's torn between letting go and holding tighter. For a second, I think he might move closer. But then, just as fast as he pinned me, he released me. He pushes off me, standing in one fluid motion. I stay on the ground a second longer, catching my breath. When I finally push myself up, I meet his gaze.

"Next time, I win."

Gray holds back a smile. He bends down, grabs his dagger, and secures it back in place.

"Looking forward to it, Little Flame."

Chapter 65

Keira

I stumble my way to my room in a swirl of flush, dizziness, and warmth. Lilith was waiting patiently in the same chair I ate my breakfast in. She snaps up once I enter the room.

"Please, you can sit." I take in the bags under her eyes.

"This is urgent, Princess. The Queen has summoned you to the throne room. She has made it clear to get there as soon as possible." She takes one look at my sweaty form and hurries to draw a bath. As I notice a deep blue gown with off-the-shoulder tool sleeves and gold leaves going down the bodice, sitting on my bed.

"Do you have any idea why she needs to speak with me?" Stars know she's the last person I want to speak with.

"I was given no other information other than to make haste." She motions to the steaming tub.

"Fine," I grumble in response.

Lilith did exceptionally well. In no time I'm washed, dressed, and approaching the throne room doors. We decided to keep my waves down to make up some time. Lilith also thought it complemented the off-the-shoulder sleeves.

I take a steadying breath and nod for the guards to open the doors. The moment I step into the throne room, I know something is wrong.

The doors close behind me with a heavy click, sealing me in. The grand chamber stretches out before me, the cold stone walls adorned with tapestries of battles long past, golden light filtering through the tall windows. At the center, seated on the onyx stone throne, is King Lucian. His gaze is sharp, his posture unnervingly composed.

Beside him stands Tristan, his usual calm demeanor on display, but there's an undercurrent of tension in his posture. His gaze meets mine. There's a storm building within his, just below the surface.

And then, there's my—the Queen.

Her hair is braided meticulously, her robes an elaborate display of gold and blue, but her eyes—my eyes—are colder than I remember. She studies me with the calculating gaze of a stranger. *Looks like she hasn't grown immense love for me in our time apart.*

"Keira," she says, her voice smooth, sickeningly sweet. "Come in. We've been waiting."

I walk toward them, my heart pounding, an instinctive unease spreading through me. I don't trust the air in this room, thick with expectations I can't escape. But it's the person standing at the side that makes my stomach churn.

Gray stands there, leaning against the wall in his usual relaxed stance. His onyx eyes watch me intensely, but his presence is like a weight pressing against my chest while also easing it at the same time. He knows something is coming. He knows what they're about to do.

He doesn't look surprised.

"Keira," King Lucian says, his voice like a whip. "There are things we need to discuss. Matters concerning your future."

I stiffen. The words hit me like a stone, heavy and permanent.

Tristan steps forward. "We've come to a decision," he says smoothly. "You and I are to be married."

I freeze, the words crashing into me like a tidal wave. I suppose I should've expected it, since he has asked me multiple times. But he at least gave me a choice last time. I look at Tristan, trying to piece together his motives. This isn't how things are supposed to go.

A bitter laugh bubbles up from my throat. "Is that so?"

"Yes," he responds, as if it's the most obvious thing in the world.

My mother's smile is calculated. "We believe it's in the best interest of the Kingdom, Keira. For all of us."

"And what about me?" I snap. "What about my choice?"

Gray's gaze spreads to me, cool yet warm at the same time. He doesn't intervene, but I can feel his presence, the tension thick between us. Lucian leans forward, his expression hardening. "You don't have a choice, Keira. This marriage secures peace and strengthens our Kingdoms. And, most importantly, it ensures that we have control over you and your *abilities*."

"Control?" I choose to ignore that last part, steadying my voice even though I can feel the fury rising in me. "I'm not some prize to be claimed, your *Majesty*."

Gray shifts slightly, but he doesn't speak.

The Queen steps forward, looking directly into my eyes. "You've felt it, haven't you? The power inside you, Keira? The magic running through your veins, waiting to be unleashed?"

I freeze at the mention of my magic.

I catch the look in Gray's eyes. Concern? It disappears almost immediately, replaced by that impenetrable guard of his.

Lucian leans back on his throne, his piercing eyes more dangerous than before. "You are the key to everything, Keira. Your magic will shape the future. And your marriage to Tristan will bind it all together."

My heart pounds in my ears. "What are you saying?"

The Queen's gaze darkens, with no hint of warmth left. "We need you, Keira. Not just as a Princess but as something more. You're the key to securing our future—and the future of both Kingdoms. The magic in you must be harnessed and controlled. The sooner you accept your place, the better it will be for everyone."

Her words hang in the air like a suffocating fog.

I take a step back, a pit of dread forming in my stomach. "I won't do this. You can't force me."

Again, Gray studies me, and I can't help but wonder what is going through his mind.

"You think you have a choice?" Lucian's voice is like ice, biting and final.

I glare at him. "I do have a choice."

My mind knows I don't, but that stupid part of my heart wants to think otherwise.

"You don't, Keira." The King's voice is low now, deadly calm. "The marriage will take place. You will obey. And if you don't…"

His words hang in the air. The threat is real.

Tristan, silent until now, takes a step forward, his gaze steady. "This is the way things must be. It's for the good of all of us. For your own good, Keira."

I shake my head, my hands trembling at my sides. I can't breathe. I can't think straight. They've told him lies. The Tristan I know wouldn't do this. Or maybe I don't know the *real* him.

"I won't be your pawn."

Gray shifts, standing straighter now, his eyes still locked on me, though I can't read what's behind them. He clears his throat, breaking the silence.

"Keira," he says quietly. "You don't have to do this alone. There are ways to make this work. We can—"

"Enough," Lucian snaps. "Grayson, step aside."

I glance at Gray, trying to plead with my eyes, but he only gives me a brief look before stepping back into the room's shadows. I want to scream. I want to fight. But the room is suffocating. I feel the weight of their expectations closing in on me.

I look back at the Queen. "You don't know what you're asking." Her gaze hardens, but she doesn't answer.

The King's voice cuts through the silence like a blade. "You will marry Tristan. And we will make it happen, whether you want to or not."

The tension in the air thickens as the Queen's voice rings out with finality, her words like chains wrapped around my throat.

"You will marry Tristan," she says, her tone unwavering. "For the Kingdom. For the future. There is no other choice."

I feel the walls closing in around me, the weight of their words pressing harder with every word. My breath quickens, my pulse hammering in my ears. I try to swallow, but it feels as though my throat is too tight to breathe.

"You can't control me," I manage to force out, my voice trembling with anger. "None of you can."

Lucian's cold eyes narrow. "You forget yourself. You are a Princess. You will do your duty, Keira, for the good of the Kingdom."

"*Your* Kingdom," I mutter bitterly, but the words seem to slip away into the suffocating air.

The fire is starting to rise inside me, low and simmering, like an ember threatening to consume everything. I feel it in my chest, a heat that I can't ignore. *My magic.* It's clawing its way to the surface, demanding release, and I don't know how to stop it.

Tristan steps forward. "Keira," he says gently, but I hear the edge in his voice. "This is for all of us. You can't keep fighting this. We need you."

"I don't need you," I spit out, taking a step back. "I don't need any of you."

The flames respond to my anger, sparking to life inside my veins. I can feel them, flickering, teasing the edges of my control. My hands tremble at my sides; my fists clenched so tightly that my nails dig into my palms.

"You don't understand," I growl, feeling the fire crawl up my arms, swirling around my wrists like it's alive. "I'm not your puppet to control."

Before I even realize what's happening, the heat builds. The air grows heavy and thick with the power surging within me. I hear the crackling of fire in my ears and see the tendrils of flame flicker at my fingertips, eager to burn.

"Keira, stop!" Tristan's voice breaks through the haze, but it only drives me further. The flames roar to life, igniting in my hands, burning in waves of heat that surge across the room.

I lift my hands, and the fire obeys. It floods the air, curling around me like an inferno, spreading out in every direction. The tapestries on the walls catch fire first, then the furniture, and within seconds, the room is consumed by the blaze. The heat is unbearable, and I can feel the flames licking at my skin, but it feels right, almost liberating.

I'm not trapped anymore. Not by them. Not by the fate they've written for me.

"Keira!" the Queen shouts, but her voice is swallowed by the roaring fire. I turn away from them, from the chaos I've created. The heat is everywhere now, enveloping me, the world flickering orange and red as the flames rise higher.

The door to the throne room bursts open, and guards rush in, but I don't wait to see their faces. I don't wait for anyone to stop me. With one last look at the chaos I'm leaving behind and also *at Gray,* I push through the door, the fire chasing me out into the hallway. I run, my heart pounding in my chest, my feet moving faster than they ever have before.

Behind me, the flames lick at the walls, crackling with power, but I don't look back.

I can hear shouting and the sound of my name being called, but I push it all away. The fire is *mine* now. And I won't let anyone control it or *me*. I round a corner, breathless, my hands shaking as the flames still burn hot inside me, though I can feel them receding. But the anger... the fire... it's still there, lingering beneath the surface, waiting.

I keep running, my footsteps echoing off the stone walls, until I find an open window and leap through it into the cool afternoon air. The wind is sharp against my skin, but it feels like freedom, like I can finally breathe again. I don't know where I'm going, but for the first time in a long time, it doesn't matter.

Chapter 66

Keira

I manage to swipe a horse from the stables before setting off into Shadowmere. It wasn't my best idea but it's the best I've got for right now—especially if I want somewhere to sleep as the sun is already slipping away in streaks of bright gold.

The city is alive, even at this hour; figures move in the alleys, shadows stretching long under the lantern's light. The stinging scent of smoke clings to my skin, a reminder of what I left behind. *What I did.*

I don't let myself dwell on it. I press forward, guiding the stolen horse through winding streets, trying to ignore the gnawing uncertainty. I have no plan. No destination. Just the desperate need to be anywhere but there.

The further I ride, the more I feel the weight of my decision settle over me. I've burned every bridge behind me. There's no going back now. Then, just as I steer the horse toward a new street, a figure steps into my path.

"Going somewhere, Princess?"

I yank on the reins, forcing the horse to halt. My pulse spikes, but I recognize the voice before I see the face.

Adrian.

He stands in the street like he was waiting for me, his dark coat blending into the night.

"You must be desperate if you're running into Shadowmere alone," he says, tilting his head. "Not the safest place for someone like you."

My only response is to grip the reins tighter.

"Relax," he says, stepping closer. "I'm not here to drag you back. I'm here to offer you something no one else has." His gaze locks onto mine. "A choice."

I stiffen. "I don't trust you."

"You don't have to." He shrugs. "But tell me, Keira— where exactly are you planning to go? Because from where I'm standing, you're running blind."

I hate that he's right and that he *knows* he's right.

"Come with us," Adrian continues. "No Kings. No cages. No one deciding your fate but *you.*"

The words sink in, circling around the part of me that has always craved freedom. The part that has never belonged anywhere.

I exhale sharply, my resolve wavering—

"Keira!"

The sound of my name slices through the night, a name he's rarely used. I whip around to see another figure approaching, his pace urgent and uneven.

Gray. I can't escape him, can I?

His dark curls are tousled, his clothes dusted with dirt, like he's been riding hard to catch up. His eyes—black as night—lock onto mine, and for a moment, I forget to breathe.

"Thank the Stars," he mutters, stopping just a few feet away. He looks like he wants to strangle me. Or pull me into his arms. Maybe both.

I force myself to keep my voice steady. "Let me guess. Tristan sent you to drag me back?"

Gray shakes his head, frustration crosses his face. "I came because I knew you'd do something reckless," he pauses. "And clearly, I was right." He eyes Adrian, sharp with distrust.

"She's not a prisoner, *Blade*," Adrian says smoothly. "She's making a choice."

Gray stiffens. "And you think running with the rebels is a better option?" He turns back to me, his voice lower now, more desperate. "Little Flame, don't do this."

Hearing him plead is almost enough to make me stay. *Almost.*

"You think they're giving you freedom, but they're just using you differently." His voice is raw, searching. "You don't have to run. Not from me."

He kills innocents. I remind myself.

Adrian watches us, saying nothing—letting *me* decide.

Gray takes a step closer. "Come back with me." His voice is quieter now, almost pleading. "If you go with them, there's no turning back. And I—" He stops, forcing back words he doesn't want to say. Finally, he exhales sharply. "I don't want to have to hunt you down again."

That sends a chill through me. Not because it's a threat—because it isn't. It's the truth. I swallow, my fingers going bone white around the reins.

"That sounds a lot like a threat," I murmur.

"It's not." His voice is barely above a whisper. "It's a promise."

For a moment, neither of us move.

Then, I inhale sharply and steer the horse back—toward Adrian.

Gray's expression hardens, but I see something vulnerable before it slips behind his mask of indifference and disappears.

"I think I'll take my chances," I say, voice steadier than I feel.

He doesn't stop me.

He just watches as I disappear into the night, his figure swallowed by darkness as I ride away with Adrian. And for the first time in my life, I feel like I'm the one in control.

Chapter 67

Grayson

She chose *them. The rebels.*

The words echo in my head over and over, but I can't make sense of them. I stand frozen, my hands clenched into fists at my sides, listening as the sound of hooves fades into the night. The forest swallows her whole, and I'm left here, rooted in place, unable to move.

I should have stopped her. I should have said something more.

But what was there to say? She made her choice.

Little Flame—sharp-tongued, reckless—looked me in the eyes and walked away. And not just from me. From all of it. From the life she swore she never wanted. From the people who had caged her. From everything I could have offered her, but didn't. And I don't blame her; if anything, I admire her.

The night air is cold against my skin, but my blood is burning.

Tristan sent me after her, trusted me to bring her back. I was supposed to be the one person who could reason with her, the one who could get through to her. I don't even want to think about why.

I failed. And maybe part of me is happy she didn't choose to stay—didn't choose him.

My fingers tighten around the reins of Nyx. It takes everything in me not to mount this horse and ride after her. Not to drag her back, kicking and screaming if I have to.

But I won't. Not because I don't want to.

Because I saw it in her eyes—she never planned on coming back. Not to rule this Kingdom at least.

A sharp exhale leaves me as I run a hand down my face. The truth is, this was inevitable. Little Flame was never meant to be tamed. I knew that the moment I met her, when she stood in the firelight with defiance in her gaze, daring the world to burn around her.

I foolishly thought I could keep her. That part of me is an idiot. She isn't even *mine*.

Not mine to keep. *No.* Just mine to lose.

With a slow, shaky breath, I swing myself onto my horse. My body moves on instinct, but my mind is elsewhere, still lingering in the space she left behind.

She thinks she's free now—that she has control over her own fate. She doesn't understand. She's only stepped from one battlefield onto another. And the war is far from over.

I glance once more into the darkness where she disappeared, before spurring my horse forward. Tristan is waiting. And when he hears what I have to tell him, hell will follow.

But that's a problem for tomorrow.

Tonight, all I can think about is how Little Flame slipped through my fingers. And how I'm not sure I'll ever forgive her for it. Or myself.

This isn't over.

Not even close.

She may have walked away, but the fire *we* lit won't burn out so easily.

Acknowledgment

First and foremost, I want to thank my incredible team for their constant support, attentiveness, and open communication throughout this journey. Your belief in this story helped bring it to life.

To my Nana, thank you for nurturing my passions and encouraging my creativity. I owe so much of who I am to you; the spark of imagination that drives my writing began with your love, generosity, and creativity.

To my Pop pop, you have so many cool random facts about life, adding to my love for stories. You inspire me too, always having your nose in a book. I love you, my Pop pop man.

To my Mama Karen, thank you for always showing up for me and being one of my biggest cheerleaders. You've supported me in more ways than I can count, and I wouldn't be where I am today without you. Thank you for always making me feel special.

To my Popsy, thank you for keeping life fun and for always finding a way to make me laugh, even in the middle of my chaos. You've been my reminder to breathe, enjoy the little things, and not take myself too seriously.

To my Mother, thank you for supporting me on this dream from the very beginning. You are quick to take note of my passions, even before I am and guide me from beginning to end. You continue to provide unwavering belief in my ability to thrive. I would pick you to be my mom in every lifetime.

To my Papi, much to your surprise, this book has your influence, too. You taught me to find what I love and run with it. You show me what follow-through looks like and I'm most proud of this execution. Thank you for all you have done for me.

To my Aunt Britt, who read even the messiest drafts with a smile. Your encouragement, your kind eyes, and your honest, nonjudgmental advice mean more to me than I can express. You are one of my biggest supporters, and I'm endlessly grateful.

To my Uncle Tommy, the original gangster, you showed me perseverance. I learned how to get through hard things from you. All those years watching you run your own business, seeing you go through the good and the bad, makes you my role model. (P.S. One of these days I will beat you on the golf course.)

To my Leighna, your excitement around this book is contagious. You always manage to spike my creativity—from playing with dolls to watching movies together. We really are inseparable, you are my other half!

To my Aunt Sarah, who first ignited my love for writing, you would be so proud of what that spark became. I still read your poetry whenever I experience writer's block and find comfort in looking at all your unique photos. I just want you to know this book carries your spirit, always.

To my Readers, thank you for taking the time to read this book and following Keira's journey. Don't hold your breath but expect more of her story to come!

And finally, thank you to the many authors whose stories lit the path for mine. Your words inspired me to find my own.

About the Author

Victoria Bailey is a YA fantasy author and was born in Margate, Florida. She currently lives in Milford, Connecticut with her parents, two siblings and her cat. Victoria grew up with her nose in a book and started writing to bring all the ideas in her head to life. Reckless Hate is her debut novel, blending fantasy and romance with the kind of characters that stay with you long after the last page. When she's not writing she's either baking a sweet treat or working on her golf swing.